The Orb

Dr. John Mauldin

The Orb

by
Dr. John Mauldin
ISBN 978-0-9987958-1-2
Copyright © 2022 John T. Mauldin, Jr.
All Rights Reserved
No part of the book may be reproduced, scanned, or distributed in any printed or electronic form without written permission.

This is a work of fiction. Names, characters, places, and incidents are either the product of the author's imagination or are used fictitiously, and any resemblance to persons, living or dead, businesses, companies, events, or locations, is purely coincidental.

Cover Design
by
John Randall Mauldin
Copyright © John. T. Mauldin, Jr.

DEDICATION

To Jeannie, my partner in all things, and love of my life.

CHAPTER 1

Sand pierced Jake MacCorkle's exposed face and hands like needles. Metal shards ripped his clothes and body. Weightless, his body rose from the ground. As if manipulated by puppet strings, he became an unwitting marionette, spacewalking until an unseen blade slashed the strings. Gravity snatched his body, froze the upward motion, and flung it down. Time slowed until the ground slammed into his back.

Breathe. Dazed, blood and dirt shot up and away.

Muffled sounds registered without recognition. Arms and legs flailed in a crawl that took him nowhere. People flitted in and out of focus. A face leaned toward him—beautiful auburn hair, odd eyes, the smile—*Vivian?*

The face changed.

His eyes closed, and he disappeared.

****

The double kitchen window over the sink framed the backyard where he had grown up. A white and green swing set that once rocketed him into the stratosphere stood in the corner—now rusted and unused. On the back edge was the sandbox where G.I. Joe won the war. By the gate was the concrete picnic table, where peanut butter and jelly sandwiches materialized, now weathered a lichen-mottled gray.

A wire fence enclosed his realm. Woven in and out of its holes were thin vines of honeysuckle where single drops extracted by careful work were a reward for the taking. It had been his private sanctuary.

Jake covered the scrambled eggs with a paper plate. When his father, John, came down at six o'clock, the cozy kitchen smelled of coffee and bacon.

"The Braves won again," Jake said. "Amazing catch at first."

"I know. Did you see the double play in the eighth?" John asked.

"Yeah." Jake hesitated before he added, "I had a weird dream. It was so vivid. I felt like I was living it."

"Was it about the war?" John asked.

"No. Ancient time. I was in an odd little boat putting out fishing nets. I heard this guy yelling down the river. I paddled down to him, and three guys were beating him up. That's what I remember of it." Jake grinned, knowing how silly it sounded.

His father didn't return the smile. Jake squirmed. *What's going on? I feel like he's looking right through me.*

Keeping his eyes on Jake, John set down his coffee cup. His hand shook, and black coffee splashed onto the honey-yellow oak table.

"What is it?" Jake asked as he snatched a paper towel from the holder and passed it to his father. His father wiped the table. No response. Jake hadn't seen that look since he told him he was going into the Army.

His father's eyes never strayed from Jake's. "I'm going out of town. When I get back, we need to talk. It's important."

"What about?"

"There are some things about our family, about your mother, that you need to know."

They hadn't mentioned Jake's mother in years. Jake pulled out a chair; it scraped across the linoleum. He sat down next to his father. "Like what?"

"It needs to wait. It's a long story, but it's time you heard it all."

Weird. "When do you leave?"

"Right after breakfast." His father stood and touched Jake's shoulder.

"Be safe." Jake reached across to his father's hand and returned his touch. "I'll do my best."

Again, his father gave him that look.

CHAPTER 2

Karland Drive was empty, no traffic. The small houses stood close together. Each had a tiny yard with enough space to offer a semblance of privacy. Simion's target was the white house with green shutters. His routine hadn't deviated in three months. It was maddening. Watch the house. Get the note. Report to Isobel. Repeat. *I'm sick of her.*

The notes were useless. One or two words like "No" or "Prepare." Nothing of value. Every day he traveled to get them, dropped them off and *… And that witch has the gall …*

A memory of Isobel sparked simmering rage, and he fumed. The thought of her rolled over and over in his mind stoking his ire. The sawed-off witch had belittled him again. He loathed her. The misshapen spikey haircut. The ample breast she flaunted in his face. The stench of her perfume. Even the tone of her voice grated his nerves. The angrier he got, the slower he walked.

"Watch and report. Watch and report. Be careful. As if I couldn't handle a stupid human Wyzard." He spit the words out as he mimicked her twangy voice.

Behind a thick bush, he transformed and slunk into his outpost across from the white house, crawling into a shallow indentation in the earth.

"I've done this so long this hole fits my body," Simion thought with disgust. A car backed out of the drive, headed right, and turned left onto Roswell Road. Should he report it? He closed his eyes and slept.

****

Jake's car's rearview mirror reflected nothing suspicious. He took another long look.

"Just because you're paranoid doesn't mean they're not out to get you," Jake said out loud. The saying was from a poster he had kept on the back of his college dorm room door. But humor didn't change the prickly feeling that made him double-check every place he went.

The mid-morning drive to the Atlanta VA had taken Jake an hour. He veered off North Druid onto Clairmont Road. The VA's multistoried, cream-colored box rose on his right. He cruised the lower and upper parking decks. *Not my day.* Twenty minutes passed before he found a space and joined the growing herd of vets drifting into the hospital. VA time was hard time, like molasses in winter, like waiting for a root canal, like—

A voice called.

"Lieutenant? Lieutenant MacCorkle!"

Jake turned to the familiar voice and grinned. "Not anymore."

For the moment, Jake's joy at seeing him alive overrode the memory of their time together. He forced the lurking memory back into its box. To share and survive war made them brothers. Neither wanted the war memory but seeing each other conjured it. Like a wave against a beach, persistent and measured, it heaved against Jake. He hammered it behind another thought, mixed them, and buried both as deep as he could. There it lurked, waiting, postponed, until the next surge. They hugged, exchanged what-are-you-doings, and carried the same burden to different parts of the hospital.

****

The Council adjourned. John MacCorkle didn't linger to chat. Transporting to his car, he rushed to get home as early shadows lengthened. His attention had wandered throughout the meeting, struggling to devise a strategy to educate Jake. On the drive home, he contacted Prince Lothian. As they spoke, The Prince's words sounded as if he was standing next to him, even though miles separated them.

"The dreams have started," John said. "Jake doesn't understand what's coming. I plan to talk with him as soon as I get back."

Prince Lothian replied, "His training has begun."

"I hope to bring him to you soon." John MacCorkle braked to negotiate a sharp curve.

CHAPTER 3

The psychiatric clinic was in the basement. The elevator opened to gray walls, florescent lights, white ceiling tiles, and the overpowering smell of bleach. Jake turned left. Bright polished floors danced with multicolored sparkles in the corridor.

Maybe they care more about the floors than the people. He found his hall and went to the glass window.

"Last four," a monotone voice spoke. They didn't ask for his name, never his name.

Four numbers. For the VA, the last four digits of his social security number defined his identity.

"It's 3524."

The monotone voice handed him a number.

In a gray room, crammed with hard, black, plastic chairs, massed with thirty other vets, Jake waited. Since he had come home, Jake marked time, like standing in formation moving his legs up and down, pretending to march, going nowhere. The VA's sterile architecture, bland decor, and impersonal management deepened his stagnation.

Scratched into the plastic back of the chair in front of Jake were the words *Kilroy was here*. He ran his fingers along the outline, smiling at the tiny act of defiant autonomy.

The loudspeaker cited the last four of his social security number. Jake rose. He dissolved into an unbending system that scrubbed off another layer of his identity.

Kilroy didn't miss him.

Jake waited in a different black plastic chair outside the pharmacy. He couldn't imagine what his dad wanted to talk about. He had been so serious after Jake told him about the dream.

Killing time, his mind wandered. He daydreamed, a pleasant memory from his undergrad days at college. The library had been his favorite place to study. Days before finals, he and two buddies occupied a table near the librarian's desk. His friend's hand blocked Jake's page. When Jake looked up, his friend nodded toward the librarian's desk. A pretty—no, beautiful—girl leaned against it. Like a siren's call, Jake went to her. *How do I do this? Play it straight.*

"What is your name?" Jake asked. Her eyes were fantastic.

"Vivian. You're staring."

"I've never seen anyone with two different colored eyes before."

Vivian had smiled but walked away.

Jake's mind savored the memory like a fine wine. He let it go before it soured. *Strong, independent ... beautiful. I blew it.*

A new daydream materialized. *River Gress? Why that name? I don't know it. Do I?*

Long green weeds waved in the current of dark grayish-green water. The first rays of daylight sparkled on tiny wave tops. Coarse heather, cattails, and grass grew in and around the water's edge. He floated in the same boat as before, feeling sun and wind touch exposed skin. It was the same, and yet it wasn't, more like a continuation of last night's dream. Jake let it come, piloting his small craft down the river. In this vision, Jake was not a distant witness seeing the man in the boat, he was the man in the boat. A storyteller spoke. Each word deepened his experience, like falling deeper and deeper into a hypnotic trance, as the storyteller's words carried him into the story.

****

Cold water splashed against my leg. I sat on a thin board in the middle of a small, round, tippy boat filled with rough-woven fishing nets. Using a short, stout, hand-carved paddle, I guided my boat as it bobbed along the edge of the current.

Shouts rose downstream. A river bend blocked my view. I eased the wobbly boat into tall cattails along the bank. Knee-deep water chilled my legs as I eased through the reeds dragging my little boat. From my hidden place upstream, I saw three men dressed in tunics with thick leather belts around their waists. Three long swords lay on the bank. They were laughing, punching, and kicking a tall man dressed in a yellow shirt, leather vest, and silk leggings.

The brigands dragged the nobleman to shallow water, pushed his head under, and held him there. Before he drowned, they pulled him up by his hair. Despite his gasping and sputtering, within seconds, they forced him under again.

I slid the boat through the reeds and moored it against the bank. My paddle in both hands, I—

****

"Number 3524 for the third and final time, or I'm moving on." A loud monotone voice dissolved Jake's dream, and the storyteller's voice vanished.

"Here, 3524." Like a passenger coasting through a dream, he went where directed, did what he was told, and signed for his medicine.

Done with the VA, he drove home. The dull, anonymous feeling faded in slow waves. The turn to his father's house signaled safety. He relaxed and exhaled the VA stranglehold. His mind wandered to dinner. Steaks on the grill. Steamed vegetables. Dad will love it.

CHAPTER 4

Thomas Augustus Weir sat in his study, his overstuffed office chair situated behind his carved mahogany partner desk with inlaid leather. On one wall hung an ornate tapestry depicting a hunting scene. He unfolded the stiff parchment and read; *All is prepared.*

Across from the tapestry hung a framed floor plan of the castle, his ancestral home salvaged from decay in Scotland and restored stone by stone on West Paces Ferry Road in Atlanta, within spitting distance of the Governor's mansion.

The grounds, twelve acres surrounded by a thirteen-foot stone wall, held back the world. Forty-foot magnolias and eighty-foot oaks guarded overhead. The gardens were beautiful but unseen. Curious looked-loos passed outside but never got a second peek through the massive iron gates. Few had seen the house or grounds. Few would.

According to Atlanta gossip, his family was Laird in Carluke, Scotland for centuries. Though he never mentioned it, people knew he liked the title.

He reclined in the beige-yellow chair, as if relaxed, but his soul twitched like the tail of a tiger stalking prey—one moment, deeply calm and confident; the next moment, edgy and raw. Not a patient person by nature, Weir commanded, people obeyed. Tonight was different. Tonight, he waited.

Hours ago, light had faded outside. He hadn't moved other than to run his fingers across the chair's rich leather. He rolled the plan over and over in his mind. As an afterthought, he pulled the chain to light the green-shaded banker's lamp. The single bulb spread light three feet left and right, half-cutting the darkness, half-lighting the heavy man mulling the consequences of failure.

Again, he considered his decision to send Isobel. She was good, but her anger made her impulsive, unpredictable, and often savage. When aroused, she lost her wits and ran into battle like a driven banshee. It amused him when the stakes were low, but tonight her foible might cost him everything. Weir shifted in his chair. His nerves twitched. The trap was well designed, but its success hinged on her execution. *What if—*

Speculation was useless. Midnight. He waited.

The clock chimed once. He heard it three times more before the click of her heels on the hardwood floor roused him. Isobel opened the door to his library without knocking and strutted in. He pulled his head out of the lamplight and into shadow. His rotund body remained lit by the dull yellow light.

He knew by her arrogant stance, the nonchalant, unconcerned, matter-of-fact look of her, that she had it. He relaxed. He had the combination, he needed only dial the numbers. Nothing stood in his way. Nothing.

"I require a full report tomorrow." Weir rose and went to bed.

CHAPTER 5

A Sheriff's cruiser sat at the curb in front of the house. Jake worked to dull the tiny panic sprouting in his chest. His breath caught. A small wheezing sound escaped. He inhaled and exhaled deeply to collect himself.

The steering wheel felt solid, and he clung to it. He parked in front of MacCorkle's folly, his father's garage, measured to the exact width and length of a car and built to spec. But Dad forgot to leave space for car doors to open, a running family joke.

Jake watched in the mirror. The officer's expression was amiable but non-committal. Walking up the drive, he reached the tail of the car and stood behind the driver's side like he would in a traffic stop. Something was wrong. Panic rose again. Every muscle in Jake's body screamed *run*, but he kept his body rigid, tightly controlled, while his mind shrieked.

Jake checked the mirror again. The officer's demeanor disclosed nothing. But in combat, he had seen the look before. Something bad had happened. This guy was the messenger. He won't push, but his message was going to be bad. *Can't stay here. Man up.*

Jake's hand trembled. The door creaked. He twisted in the seat, sat on its edge, and tested his legs. Moving to the officer, he leaned on the car like a crutch, its door left open.

The officer smiled and put out his hand. Jake met his grip and looked him in the eye. "Jake MacCorkle."

"Are you related to John Terhune MacCorkle?"

"Yes, sir."

"Can we go inside and sit down?" The officer asked.

"Tell me now."

"I'm Sergeant … bad news … accident … father's dead."

Jake heard the important bits. The rest didn't matter. "You'd better come in," Jake said.

Dirty clothes were piled on the washer in the mud room. Dishes stacked in the sink. By way of apology, Jake said, "I was going to do those after the VA."

The officer nodded.

Jake placed his father's chair between him and the officer and leaned against it. His hand stroked the rough oak. The kitchen seemed smaller, dingier, needing fresh paint, or maybe he needed to tear everything out and start over.

The officer pulled out a notepad. "From evidence at the accident scene, your father lost control on a curve, headed North on Highway 19. He left the roadway and hit a tree. There were no witnesses. I am sorry for your loss. Can I have a chaplain come by?"

No.

"Is there anybody I can call?"

No.

"Do you have a friend who can stay with you?"

The last question hit Jake like a nine iron in the face. *No one. Dad's gone. Vivian! She'd want to know. She'd care, but she's gone. Could I call? No. She said never call again.*

The officer handed Jake his card. Without purpose, Jake turned it over and over in his hand. Standing on the small, red brick porch with the wrought iron railings, Jake thought he remembered the deputy leaving. He wasn't sure. After he opened the front door, time vaporized. He came to himself while leaning against the front porch rail, staring after the long-departed deputy and not knowing how long he'd been standing there.

The drive to do something, anything, pushed him. But nothing needed doing. The frustration welled with no outlet.

I need a drink.

The search began. Jake looked in the regular places, back of the closet, under the sink. When he cleaned it all out, he did a good job. But he left one. A forgotten plastic half-pint bottle was wedged behind garden pots in the garage. His promise to Dad was null and void. The heft of the bottle, the rough feel of the cap, the slosh of the liquid, the sour smell, the first burning sip would ease him through this—for now.

CHAPTER 6

A distant sound. One that required—some action. Louder. *Da dum, ditty, dum, ditty, dum, dum, dum.* Jake grabbed at it before his head exploded with 1812 cannons. Pushing every button on the phone, he dropped the thing, and it landed somewhere on the bed. A distant squeaky voice sought him. *Be still. Don't move.*

"Hello? Hello? Is this Mr. MacCorkle?"

Jake slapped the bed, searching for the little person in the phone. *Make her shut up.*

Jake drew the phone to his chin.

"Yeah," he slurred. Mossy teeth, tongue thick—thirsty.

"A few questions … VA experience … Two minutes …" A pleasant voice mocked him.

"No." The phone hit the bed again. Within seconds, it rang. Eyes closed, he slapped around until he found it.

"Yeah."

"Jake?"

I know that voice. "Yeah, waddayouwant?"

"This is Nathan Greenfield. I heard about your father's death. I wanted to see how you're doing."

"Sorry, Nathan, rough night." He sat up in bed. A mirror above the dresser reflected an unshaven man, hair sticking out at odd angles, clothes disarrayed with raccoon circles under his eyes. The reflection didn't look like him, and he touched his head to be sure it was.

I'm a train wreck. The thought bounced through his diminished wits before the voice jerked him back to the conversation.

"I know how close you were to your father. If it's a bad time, I can call back."

"It's okay," Jake mumbled.

"I called to let you know that your father requested cremation and had several specific instructions for his ashes. I prefer to give you the details when we meet."

Jake listened, but his mind was on the memory of another call, an H.M.

Patterson Funeral Home call. His father's body arrived. They needed arrangements. He'd put them off, too hung over to think about it.

"John wanted his will read three days following his death. That would make it this Sunday. Further, he wanted it done at 12:00 p.m. I know that's an unusual time and day. I have made arrangements on my schedule. Is any of this a problem for you?"

"No, I got nowhere to be."

"Thank you. I am very sorry about your father. He was a good man. I enjoyed his friendship. I will see you Sunday."

A good man. The best. God, I miss him.

Jake's head throbbed. Sadness swelled. He itched to move. The deputy's card lay on the night table.

****

The day was cloudy. Rain threatened but hadn't materialized.

Jake pulled in behind the cruiser at the accident site, a curvy mountain blacktop north of Atlanta. On the outside of the curve, double yellow chevrons foreshadowed danger. Halfway into the curve, dark-black rubber skid marks caked the road's surface. They twisted into an oval as if the car scorched its tires trying to escape the crash. *Odd.* Not a straight line, not a simple loss of control, no direct slide off the road.

No, it was Jake wanting something to be wrong, like that stupid paranoid feeling he got when he left the house.

When the marks left the pavement, the vehicle plowed a swath of dirt, small trees, and mangled plants until a huge oak tree ended the uncontrolled slide. The collision wounded the tree, but from the colored plastic, glass, metal, and other debris littering the site, it obliterated the car. *Weird.* It looked like the car tried to climb the tree. It would've had to have been airborne to hit that high. *Stupid. You can't make it something it's not.* But the tire marks. How could a car, out of control, go backward?

The marks on the roadway goaded him. Back on the blacktop, he squatted and peeled up a thin piece of rubber from the oval. The acrid smell nauseated him. It didn't make sense. *No. I don't get it because I don't want to get it.*

Jake shook the officer's hand and thanked him.

Driving home, a nagging feeling arose. *What's left? Vivian?*

In his mind, he saw her gliding across the quad at college to their last meeting.

When he told her about the Army, she hesitated before she said, "I respect your choice. It's clear it doesn't include me. From this time forward, don't contact me."

Jake's gut wrenched when he thought about his final words to her, "Wait a minute. Who's leaving who? I told you, I love you. What do you want? Forget it. Screw you. I'm done."

Smooth, Jackass.

After Vivian had left, calls went unanswered, no Facebook, no Internet. She disappeared.

****

The towering magnolias filtered the pale afternoon light and allowed random shafts through Weir's library window. Dark oak wainscot completed the room's image of solid respectability. Isobel was seated across from him at the partner desk. Weir listened to her report.

"Satisfactory," Weir said. "Will you be suspected?"

"No, John MacCorkle is dead. An automobile accident. He was a mortal, trained in the old style. He never saw it coming. I took the key from his body."

Isobel was haughty and arrogant as she pronounced the words. Weir knew it was an overstatement, a personality flaw he tolerated in her. His thoughts moved to the next step.

She held out a silver chain with a key on it. The large key was plain and ordinary, the chain magnificent and handcrafted. He raised his hand to refuse her gift. He knew better than to touch it. He knew its significance, felt its power. It would open everything for him. She ignored the key and chain, treated it causally. He knew she sensed its power but chose ignorance. She swung it around her finger like a trinket, pocketed her bauble, and turned to go.

"What of the son?" Weir asked.

"After Simion secures the message, he will watch. The son is isolated, a waste. If the house enchantment ends with the old man's death and I can get at the son, I will turn him. Untrained, he is no threat."

Another understatement.

"Watch closely. With the father dead, they will contact the son as heir. He may rouse. Turn him or kill him, either will suffice, but do it quickly."

CHAPTER 7

Today is the day, 12:00 p.m., Sunday, Dad's will. He knew he would get everything, so there was no reason to make a big deal about it. Jake wrestled with the idea—and with the sick feeling in his stomach. He called Nathan Greenfield, his father's attorney, to postpone.

"No, it has to be today."

"Why this day, this time?"

"It must be today. No mistake. At 12:00 p.m. or you forfeit the inheritance."

Nathan was firm. *Damn it.*

Jake wandered through a shower and grabbed Tylenol. He had trouble lining up the little arrows on the childproof cap. Slurping tap water from his hand, four maximum strength tablets went down.

Clothes lay in haphazard piles across his room. He put on the first pair of jeans he touched. He sniffed a green plaid flannel shirt and turned his face away. The best he had. His deodorant stick was empty. *I can't go through Dad's stuff, not yet.*

Under the sink was a bottle of Old Spice left over from adolescence. Pouring the distinctive scent into his hands, he slapped it under his armpits. The over-strong reek made his stomach lurch.

The instant coffee spilled, and he brushed the brown-black grains into the sink. The pungent smell nauseated him. Too hot, it burned his tongue, but his head cleared, a little.

He threw on his jacket. He backed out of the drive, turned left on Roswell Road and right on Piedmont, which brought him to a six-story glass office-box on the left. Nathan waited out front to guide him in.

"Park here. No one will be in the building today," Nathan said.

Jake killed the engine and got out.

"How are you?" Nathan asked. Nathan was an old family friend, probably his father's best friend.

Jake didn't answer. Before Jake protested, Nathan opened his arms and folded him in a bear hug.

"Okay," Jake mumbled into Nathan's jacket.

They rode the elevator to the top floor. Stepping off, *NATHAN GREENFIELD, LLC,* greeted Jake in large, silver, block letters. A polished mahogany reception desk with a marble top shouted respectability. The carpet was gray, flecked with shards of red. A Chippendale sofa emblazoned with flame stitch offered comfort to clients. Nathan led him behind the reception area, down a hall, and into a conference room. A bank of windows looked out over Piedmont Road. *Nice view.*

"Do you have the whole floor?" Jake asked.

"Yes."

Apart from the view, it was like a thousand other conference rooms in a thousand other lawyers' offices. It had the standard hunting print hung over the perennial mahogany sideboard, the long conference table with high-backed, black leather chairs flanking both sides, and light- gray walls with glossy white trim. Everything screamed stability. *Except ...*

At the end of the room, one painting graced the wall. Bright colors flashed in reds and greens that caught Jake's eye. The image was an abstract-looking forest, refreshing yet bizarre. It matched the decor well enough, but its presence was odd. He never expected Nathan to own anything like it.

"Wait here for me. I need to get your father's file from my desk."

The forest scene was oddly familiar. Jake merged with it. He could smell the earth and feel the sunlight. He swore he saw small beings scurry deep in the shadows of the painting. The stillness soothed him.

When Nathan returned, Jake jumped like a kid caught with his hand in a cookie jar. *I lost it again. Did Nathan see that?* It felt like his dreams, like he was pulled into the picture.

Nathan put a folder on the table, opened it, and handed Jake a copy. His tall, gaunt frame was covered by a button-down blue shirt, gray slacks, and a raucous red sweater. It suited him. His curly gray hair grew thick and wild around his ears. It looked as if he never touched it with a comb. His hair was the only non-conventional aspect about him. In all other ways, he looked like a lawyer. His face was thin and intelligent. His quick, observant eyes complemented a prominent, sharp nose. His eyes sparkled in a way that made his mouth ready to smile, like Nathan believed life held some secret joke. He started the meeting promptly at 12:00 p.m.

"I, John Terhune MacCorkle, Sr., leave all my worldly possessions and property to John Terhune MacCorkle, Jr., hereafter referred to as Jake."

A lump grew in Jake's throat.

The first part was standard and expected. His father wanted to be cremated—done. He wanted Jake to spread his ashes in the mountains—no real problem.

At the mention of mountains, Jake's mind wandered to a large, open field near the confluence of three streams where he camped with his father when he was a boy. The next sentence brought him back to the office.

"The ashes must be spread within three days of the reading of the will," Nathan said.

"Three days? Why three days? What's the rush?"

"I am relaying your father's wishes." Nathan waited patiently.

"That's crazy. Where would I do it in the middle of winter?"

Nathan moved on. He skipped the legalese until they reached the last page. He paused. "This last section is critical. Your father gives to you for protection, and in perpetuity, a tract of land in the mountains that must be left exactly as it is. It can never be sold. The timber can never be cut. It can never be developed. No buildings, roads, or improvements can be made to it. It is to be left exactly as it is, forever." As he said this last sentence, he looked Jake in the eye.

"Property? What property?"

"Let me finish and I will answer what questions I can. As I said, the land can never be sold or improved. It must be left exactly as it is. It is held in a blind legal trust. No one knows you are the owner. I understand it is the same property you and your father visited many times when you were younger. You may recall there are a series of locks on a gate that are locked onto each other. By opening any one lock, you can remove the chain and enter. You will have one of several keys to the gate. I cannot tell you who has the other keys. This is the way your father designed it."

"Wait a minute, I didn't know he owned any property."

Nathan took a plat map from the folder and laid it on the table.

Jake said, "I know this property. Dad took me there as a child. I thought it was a National Park or something."

"The plot is surrounded by national forest. It covers three thousand acres—"

"What?"

"Let me finish. It covers three thousand acres. It is surrounded by national forest on all sides, making the usable land area about 1.3 million acres."

Thousands of acres? A million acres?

"Regarding the property, there is nothing for you to do legally. According to the State records, I am the agent for the corporation that owns the land. Any person seeking information must go through me to get to you. They will never get to you. Just as they never got to your father. You are an absentee landlord. I handle all the legal and tax matters. I make all financial decisions. I field all requests for information and deny them. I am the face of the land. No one will ever know you are involved. One critical issue."

Nathan's blue eyes pierced Jake.

"This system was designed by your father to protect you and the land. It works as long as you tell no one about the land. I cannot stress this enough. Tell no one. No one can know that you own the land." Nathan waited.

"Why not?"

"It was important to your father that the land remain a protected sanctuary. Had he lived, your father would be having this conversation with you. He had many details that I don't have."

The talk. He had wanted to talk. "I don't understand any of this."

"The conditions only require one thing: that you spread your father's ashes on this property. Once that is done, you may continue your life as before. From your time there, you may remember a large stream that is the union of three creeks."

The one I just thought about.

"Where they join is a boulder that juts into the center of the river. From that rock, you are to scatter the ashes. The ashes are to be dispersed in a certain way. Start at the lower left to upper right around in a circle and back down to the lower left. Here is a map to its location. By the terms of the will, the ashes must be spread within three days of the reading."

"I remember the place. I don't know if I could find it." Jake rocked back in his chair. "How long has Dad owned this land?"

"I don't know. As long as I have been his lawyer."

"What's the big deal about keeping it secret?"

"It was your father's wish."

"All these years, Dad never told me. Why?" Questions flew at Nathan. No answers.

Jake slammed his fist on the table. "You can't tell me anything? All these demands, waste my time going to stand on a rock in some river waving ashes around, for what? Oh, I forgot. You don't know. Because it's in the will. Does it affect my inheritance, the house, car, money?"

"Since you attended the reading within three days, no, it has no effect on the other parts of the will. It is a request from your father."

Nathan's calm voice didn't slow Jake down. "Dad's dead. No trip to the mountains is going to change that. What if I don't want to do it? What if I just go and dump the ashes in the Chattahoochee?" *Go to a place I loved without Dad? I can't …*

The rant felt good, but it wasn't changing anything. As Jake became more agitated and demanding, Nathan grew calmer and more compliant. Jake felt Nathan was measuring him, watching him. *Why?*

"How are you spending your time these days?" Nathan asked. It came out of the blue, not spiteful, but it stung.

Jake's thoughts went to the last few days. *What does he know?* Jake felt exposed. Within moments, the reading of a simple document had become an emotional wake where Jake was using anger to express his grief. Nathan waited and watched.

His father's last words: *I have something very important to talk with you about.*

"One last thing." Nathan pushed an envelope across to Jake. "I will leave you to read it on your own."

CHAPTER 8

Jake gazed at his name. Grief fought curiosity. His father dead; his mother gone years before. Jake leaned his chair away from the envelope but couldn't remove his eyes. Resolved, he picked it up. He turned the envelope in his hand, and something slid back and forth inside. He felt the weight and caressed the paper. With a finger, he traced his name. He broke the seal and opened it. Old struggles banged in his head like bumper cars … the Army … Dad and I fought … Vivian hated it … Dad didn't push me … he wanted something … expected something from me … never asked but I sensed it … but what? Why did I have to be so hard-headed? Ruined everything. Like Afghanistan.

He took out two pages and a silver chain with a key on it. He spread the papers, sighed, shuddered, and read.

My dear Son,

If you are reading this letter, something has happened to me that I would not have chosen for myself. I regret leaving you.

In addition, you have met with Nathan and begun to see the treasures of our family. I know you are reeling from the sheer magnitude of the information, so I will do my best to anticipate your questions.

First, the property, I did not buy it. It was purchased by your great, great, great grandfather for a specific purpose. It is the same property we used to visit when you were younger. I know it has been a while, but I believe you will remember how to get there. To refresh your memory, I included a map on the second page.

The land protects something sacred to our family. Because I want you to experience it for yourself, I will not tell you what it is. To have the experience, you must go to the land and camp in the spot I designated on the map. Do not take the map with you. Please memorize it and leave it with Nathan. It is safer that way.

Jake paused. Safer?

The chain and key are for you. If you would, please wear it around your neck at all times, never taking it off for any reason. The key opens a lock on the gate at the entrance to the property. You probably remember opening the gate when we went there. Ask Nathan to put it on for you.

I want my ashes dispersed on our property. Nathan will explain how to do it. This is important to me. You are the only one I trust to do it. It would be a great favor to me.

I love you. I enjoyed our talks and am pleased to pass the family treasure to you. I am confident you will do an excellent job. I am proud of you.

Love, Dad.

Jake reread the letter several times. Images of the property rose and fell in his mind. The visits to the property with his father were highlights of his summers. They'd camped near the river in a small cave, the same river where his dad wanted his ashes spread, the same cave where his father asked him to camp now.

A tear trickled down his cheek. He flicked it away like it was an irritating insect. The full impact of his father's death clobbered him. Loneliness welled in his chest until it suffocated him. He caught a breath, controlled a sob, took a deeper breath, blew it out, and knew he had to move. He paced the conference room like a caged lion.

"Nathan."

To Jake, his voice sounded like a coarse whisper, but Nathan appeared at once. Jake handed him the chain. Nathan stepped behind him, opened the clasp and placed it around his neck. The weight of the key met his chest and offered a small comfort. The chain felt light as a feather.

"Beannachd Dia dhuit." Nathan touched Jake's shoulders with both hands.

"What's that?"

"A prayer for God to bless and keep you safe."

On the ride home, a quarrel broke out between Jake's head and his heart. Go to the property? His stomach churned. Go home and drink? It churned until he felt nauseated. He couldn't ignore Dad's last request. He had to go.

What could happen?

CHAPTER 9

Jake packed for the mountains. Rather than go stinky, he decided to wash clothes. While the machine whirred and shifted gears, he put together the essentials for a six-hour trip, up and back, one stop for gas. A search in the attic produced a water bottle and small backpack. The compass and pocket knife were in his junk drawer. For food, he gathered MREs from the garage and crackers from the kitchen. A sleeping bag was thrown onto the passenger seat.

Leaving Atlanta, the F-150 purred up the highway. *Get to the property, do my duty, and get home.* Two hours into the trip, a shift came.

Outside Jasper, the mountains came into view. Jake's heart soared. He felt the tug of childhood tangled in white pines and flowing rivers. He loved these trips. New energy, almost excitement, flooded him. *I'll do it to honor him.*

The four-lane changed to windy, narrow mountain roads. Landmarks came easy until the final turn. Three rocks he and Dad had stacked to mark the turn had fallen over in the weeds. He stopped the truck where he thought they should be, and after walking back and forth, he located them. With careful pride, he restacked them like he and his father did years before. *For Dad.*

Picking up the final rock, an odd piece of thick, folded paper was stuck to it. Jake opened it. On the paper was a single handwritten word in black ink: *No.*

Jake turned the paper over. Nothing. *Kids sneaking out?*

Puzzled, Jake stacked the top rock and left the note under it. A sneaking paranoid feeling made him shudder. He scanned the brush and trees, half expecting to see a face spying from the forest.

Nothing.

He turned the truck onto a single, overgrown, dirt lane.

****

Simion stepped out of the forest, kicked over the stones, snatched up the note, and stuffed it into the pocket of his jeans. Glancing after the truck, he strode back into the forest and disappeared.

CHAPTER 10

Bouncing down the rutted road, hopping potholes, the truck came to a four-foot-wide gurgling brook intersecting the road. Jake knew where he was.

Beyond the brook, the road flattened and narrowed, forming two tire ruts filled with tall brown grass. Tree limbs laced overhead into a light-filtering arbor. Bushes encroached on the road space, pinching the truck in an ever-shrinking embrace, as their branches shrieked against the metal.

Captive on the narrow track, Jake eased forward until an aluminum cattle gate blocked the road. As a boy, his job was to open and close the gate while his father drove the car through. The road. The gate. The land. *Good memories.*

Jake forced his door open. Springy branches jumped back into the door space. Gingerly, he pulled them away and closed the door. Laying his chest over the warm hood, he sidestepped to the front of the truck. Brush plucked at his legs and ankles.

Four padlocks, as large as his fist, were locked onto each other through a heavy linked chain. The chain looped through the gate and around a telephone-pole-sized fence post buried in the ground. At the hinged end of the twelve-foot gate was a similar post. *Odd, no rust or wear on the chain or locks.*

Past the gate to the left and right were woods, no fence. The gate was the only indication that the property started here. It was its only protection. Anyone could walk around it. *Protecting the property from what?*

He pulled the key from his shirt and tried it in the first lock. No good. The second, nothing. As if it was well-oiled, the third lock flipped open with ease. He unhooked his lock from the others and dropped the chain through a slat in the gate. It bounced off the metal gate twice, making a clang-clang sound that rekindled memories of Dad. Jake's chest swelled with bittersweet joy.

Jake drove the truck through, closed the gate, reached between the aluminum slats, replaced his lock, and as his father taught him, tugged on it to ensure it was secure.

After another hundred feet, the road ended in a small, overgrown clearing surrounded by tall oaks and white pines. Jake placed his father's ashes, a water bottle, and food in the backpack. He tied the sleeping bag underneath, slung it over his shoulder, and checked his compass. A remembered trail, northeast, toward an old railroad bed would take him into the heart of the property.

****

Lothian watched the people's excited preparations from a small meeting room window that overlooked the town. They prepared as if Jake's arrival was a royal visit. His earlier conversation with John MacCorkle gave him hope—and pause. His friend and adviser, John, was dead. Jake was ignorant. *How will he respond when he learns of us?*

Minister Thish entered to report. "He is in the Gleane."

"Are the enchantments removed from the forest?" Prince Lothian asked. "Is all prepared for the ceremony?"

Of the two questions, Minister Thish answered only the second. "The ceremony is arranged."

CHAPTER 11

Jake loved the military. Ranger training taught him self-reliance. The Army taught him to be effective and efficient. Every question had an answer. Every skill had a manual. Every objective had a plan. Jake's forte was execution. No messy emotions. No tangled relationships. Do the job. Move on. This wilderness offered no challenge he couldn't handle.

Fifteen minutes later, he wasn't so sure.

Trails appeared, only to disappear within twenty feet. Trees grew thicker the farther he went. Drooping limbs caught at his arms and legs. Unseen roots tripped him. He stopped to rest against a large tree. *I should have reached the old railroad bed by now.*

An ugly memory broke into consciousness and besieged his confidence. When he saw his buddy at the VA, he'd stuffed it as deep as he could, but since his father's death, disorientation and confusion sucked at him like a leach. *I can't …*

Even though the temperature was cool, sweat rolled down his face and seeped through his clothes. *I need to go back to the truck and get the hell out of here. I can't …* The compass pointed a direction to the right, but thick cover meant he'd make little progress that way. Rushing water indicated a stream to his left. He gave up on finding the railroad bed and shifted toward the stream.

The forest did not relent. Mountain laurel, twisted, crooked, and nasty to walk through, weighed on his legs like a child sitting on her father's feet and begging him not to go. He picked his way between the limbs and twisted his body through teeny passages. Frustration gnawed in his belly. *A forest can't attack me. Can it?* The stream's rush told him he was close, yet he saw nothing. Twenty feet, fifteen, ten, he followed the sound.

The stream's bank was guarded by more perverse plants. He slid on his belly; dirt, moss, and leaves ground into his jacket, sneaked into his shirt, and stuck to his sweaty face. He spit the mucky mess out of his mouth. The backpack caught on a limb. Jake jerked hard but couldn't shift it. He wriggled out of the strap, rolled over, and struggled to turn in the tight underbrush. As soon as he made the turn, it dropped to the ground as if released by a giant hand. *Damn it.*

Jake pushed the backpack ahead of him through the leaves. A twenty-foot canopy of rhododendron branches offered only a twelve-inch opening near its trunk. He squirmed like a snake under the lowest branch. With nothing to hold up the front half of his body, he slid four feet into the shallow streambed. Two inches of cold water splashed into his face and doused his right side.

In the creek bed, the banks rose and created a secret tunnel shaped by the intertwined branches overhead. In and out of the water, he splashed, but he made progress. He stopped to rest against the bank. The burbling of water over rocks was the only sound. No squirrels scrambling in the leaves, no birds, nothing. He calmed his breathing and listened again. Still nothing. The creek bed should pass an open field. *I'm all screwed up.*

Hours later, Jake scrambled up the bank into the field he recognized. Mountains drew down along the edges, forming a circular hidden cove the size of a football field. The field was overgrown by tall, withered, brown grass. He knew where he was. The stream junction lay across the field to the left. The grass swished against his legs and seeds stuck to his clothes as he crossed it. Guided by the roar of fast water, he found the stream's intersection that formed a beautiful shallow river forty feet across. A thin cool breeze stirred. Downriver, sunlight danced in diamond sparkles. The large rock, the one he remembered, jutted into the center of the river.

Tired and sweating, Jake sat next to the river's edge. Swift, shallow water surged along, hit the upper side of the rocks, slapped obstructing stones, channeled through a narrow sluice, and rejoined the main channel. The sloshing sound soothed Jake's soul. He became mesmerized by the tumbling water and drifted into another spontaneous vision. The storyteller spoke: "I took the paddle in both my hands and slipped in behind them."

Jake had heard the storyteller's voice like someone was sitting next to him. The rough wood of the paddle felt so real as if he held it in his own hands. It wasn't like any dream.

Weird.

Jake roused. Time had slipped away. The grueling trek pushing through the forest, the mesmerizing sound of the river, and his mixed feelings about the trip had stolen hours. The last glimmers of sunshine offered a magical twilight. The gray, leafless trees stood barren, waiting. The earthy-brown leaf litter sprinkled along the bank glinted red and gold. The shimmering river, broken by variants of gray, brown, and black rocks, was fired purple, blue, and red by the setting sun.

I'll do it now.

On the rock, he unscrewed the top, faced downstream, and held the canister high toward the waning sun. A lump grew in his throat.

"I love you, Dad."

As instructed, Jake started at the lower left, swung the canister in a large circle, and jiggled the ashes out. Ashes emerged and dispersed in a thick cloud. A gust of wind swirled. Jake caught a full dose of ash in the face. He clutched the canister to his chest and closed his eyes.

A noise, a shuffling in the leaves, not far, something large, was on his right. He shifted the canister to his left arm and bent to reach the water. He flailed with his right hand until he found frigid water and splashed it into his eyes. Vision blurred, he shook his head and struggled to see.

Both sides of the river were lined with hundreds of somber, oddly dressed, respectful people. Jake's heart leaped to hyper drive. The canister fell and clanged off the rocks. He swiped his eyes and slapped gritty water out of his face.

This is crazy. He blinked over and over, eyes stinging, wanting to look up but afraid of what he might see. His eyes cleared. The riverbanks were empty. No people.

Jake backed off the rock and slipped into the river. Cold water splashed up his leg and into his boot. He jumped to the bank. *Wipe and look. Wipe and look. Don't cover up both eyes. I have to see what's coming.*

He drew his sleeve across the side of his face. He stared up and down the riverbank. He jumped away from the river, sweeping around like someone might sneak up on him. Nothing. Jake's heart pounded like a timpano drum. He grabbed his stuff. *Gotta get outta here now.*

The lost railroad bed lay across the field, or did it? Jake was twisted around. Which way was out? The sun was below the mountain rim. Deep shadows filled the cove. A chill grew in the air. Everything was colored pre-black. The compass face was dark. Hands shaking, he couldn't keep it level. He cursed himself for not bringing a flashlight. He slapped his back pocket where he kept his cell phone but remembered he had left it charging in the truck. He felt trapped. *Find the cave.*

Jake ran from the river junction, turned right, and sought the cave before it got pitch dark. Ahead, a dim outline of a rock overhang materialized, twenty-feet long, heavy boulders guarding either end.

Jake threw his stuff into the opening and backed against the interior wall. He froze like a victim in a slasher movie. Nothing came. He organized his meager possessions to keep his mind off what happened at the river. *Am I crazy?*

Hugging the back of the cave, he crawled into his sleeping bag. For hours, the rocks stuck in his back and his mind wouldn't shut off. *The riverside people … Dad's death … this land … What's next?* Repeating thoughts faded, but one image returned over and over like a persistent puppy wanting to play.

CHAPTER 12

Simion materialized behind his empty lookout post on Karland Drive. It frustrated him that he couldn't transport directly to Weir's house. But Isobel told him over and over it was too public. And unlike his betters, he couldn't transport into Weir's property because it was enchanted. He had to walk up Karland to Habersham and down West Paces Ferry to Weir's Mansion. It wasn't fair.

While he walked, he saw people in passing cars stare. He didn't know why. Simion was tall and thin as a rail. Pale as a ghost with a thick black mane of unruly beard and hair. His long Ichabod arms and legs pistoned up and down covering six feet at a stride. Watching for the teenagers that taunted and threw cups of soda at him, he tramped on at a good pace.

As he approached, Weir's gate pulled back for him. He liked that part. It made him feel important. Now came the part he despised, reporting to Isobel. As if he were an idiot, she made his life miserable with her incessant questions, embarrassing him in front of Weir. This time was no different. She started on him before he sat down.

"What are you doing here? Go back to the house and watch," Isobel told him.

"What for?" It was a job for a simpleton. Simion felt he was capable of much more.

"To ensure my visit tonight won't be wasted."

"What visit?"

"None of your business. Do as I tell you."

"Why do I …?"

"Quiet," Isobel said. Her voice commanded him as if he were a simpleton.

Vexed, Simion pushed his tall frame up to tower over her. He knew the moment he challenged her it was a mistake. Before he reached his full height, Isobel slapped him hard.

"Do what I say."

A head taller than her and a hundred pounds heavier, Simion barely flinched. "It's useless. I'm not gonna waste my time sitting under some house waiting for something that's not gonna happen."

"Do as you're told." She raised her hand again.

"But MacCorkle's not there," he whined.

"What are you saying?"

"His truck is gone." He didn't add that he knew where it was.

"Idiot," Isobel said through clenched teeth. Her eyes changed to coal black, her face went deadpan, and her fingers twitched. This wasn't going to be a slap in the face. Simion slunk away from her and headed for the door.

"Simion," Weir said. His deep baritone voice commanded. Both Isobel and Simion stopped and turned to him.

"Do you have something for me?" Weir asked.

"I forgot." Simion dropped a note on Weir's desk.

"Go back and stay until he returns."

****

In an early morning half-awake state, Jake's dream pestered him. He drifted into it. *The man in the boat is Corcle. How did I know that?* In twilight sleep, the question rippled through his consciousness but didn't hold his attention. He pursued the dream. The same voice narrated the story. As Jake entered it, he became, not a witness, but a participant who saw, heard, and felt every happening in present time. He became Corcle, the story's narrator.

****

My small boat scratched against stones and landed on the low side of the tiny island. I stepped into ankle deep water, carrying my paddle.

The three men dragged their victim to a small channel between the island and bank. In two feet of water, they kept dunking and pulling him up, laughing at his gasping and choking.

Three against one was unfair, but I hesitated. Soldiers? Their tunics meant they were part of some army. The price for interfering might mean death. The bullied man sputtered and coughed. Three bullying one was more than I could stand.

To even the odds for the poor victim, I held my paddle with both hands and came into range. Preoccupied with their man, they never saw me. I swung. The first man went down in the shallow water like a sack of potatoes.

A second man circled me to the river side. The man skidded on the slick stones. Before he regained his footing, I thrust the oar square in his chest, knocking him backward into the current.

"Damn you, meddling fool." The current swept his curse away.

Seeming near to death a moment before, the victim regained strength and thrashed the third man. Their would-be victim grinned at me like the two of us just had the most sport a person could have. "This is my fortunate day," he said, "and you are my salvation. What is your name?"

"They call me Corcle."

****

Jake stirred. The storyteller's voice flowed away into the rush of the river.

Nice dream. I love it when the underdog wins. The thought morphed and bumped against a hidden fear. He pushed it away.

For the first time in a year, Jake felt rested. Eyes closed, he floated on the morning's stream sounds—flowing, bubbling, rushing, swirling water that reached into his soul and generated a quiet serenity. Sore muscles, worked in yesterday's trek across the property, complained. But the soreness reminded him of life lived. He'd sat in his dad's house for over a year waiting on something to change. He hadn't used his muscles to do anything he enjoyed. It felt good to move, to act.

The sleeping bag cradled him. A bird sang. Wind rustled. New sounds blended with the shushing water. Sunlight slanted through the trees and highlighted his cave. In this small mountain alcove, an exceptional thought came to Jake. *I own this. This land belongs to me.* Savoring the thought like a fine wine, he shifted in the sleeping bag, sat up, and reached for his jacket that he'd used as a pillow. A layer of fresh dirt lay sprinkled over his sleeping bag.

To his left, not a foot away from his sleeping bag, a dark opening had appeared in the mountain wall overnight. He jumped to his right, trying to run. The sleeping bag grabbed his legs. He fell, squirmed out of the bag, and stared at the hole. *Where did that come from?*

Tall and wide enough for a man to enter, the opening wasn't there when he went to sleep. *Was it?* Jake looked left and right. Old feelings of being watched wormed in his mind. Present since he was a child, the paranoia had been twenty-four/seven in the last few months.

Jake reached for his sleeping bag and jerked it out of the cave like it had a rattlesnake under it. *I'm outta here.* Possessions recovered from the cave, he gathered them in his arms and started for the field.

Ten feet from the entrance, his father's voice spoke: "The land protects something sacred to our family. Go to the land and camp in the spot I designated on the map."

Jake's body twitched as if he'd grabbed a hot electric wire. He spun in a circle, looking up, down, left, and right for his father. The quiet sunlit morning, crisp and cool, replied with nothing. *I'm going schizo.* The words were clear; they were a quote from his father's letter. His heart chugged like a fawn hiding from a mountain lion. He stood still, looking back at the opening. *I can't—*

CHAPTER 13

Minister Thish stood with Prince Lothian in a small, round, gray stone room, watching a projected image of everything Jake did.

"He lacks courage," Minister Thish said with disgust.

"He knows us not. Curb your eagerness to pass judgment. Your Prince requires your assistance with him. Be patient in your covetousness of Bard John's position, my Minister. His family has been Bard for over six hundred years. He must have the opportunity."

Thish bowed his silver head. He held his tongue—for now—but his mind whirled. No untrained, uninitiated human would keep him from his desired destiny. This human, who had done nothing and, based on his last year's behavior, would do nothing, would not walk into a role Thish saw for himself. These thoughts flew through his mind as anger grew in his chest. *How can I twist this human to my advantage?*

****

His father's words came to Jake again: "Experience it for yourself." Experience what? Jake checked the situation. Nothing chased him. No voices. No footsteps. No movement in the bushes. The sun shone. The river flowed. Nothing was … wrong. Except the weird crap.

Staring into the cave from fifteen feet away, it looked as if a giant gently pulled the rocks apart. No sign of tool marks or digging. *Don't overthink. Experience it.*

Getting closer, Jake peeked into the opening. A foot of dirt and leaves overlay a section of rock easily twelve feet thick. An opening into the mountain, a tunnel.

Inside, the stone was smooth and dry to the touch. A jolt of excitement rushed through his body like an ecstatic four-year-old ripping the wrapping paper off a Christmas present. Jake slipped inside.

****

"His choice is made," Prince Lothian said. Minister Thish said nothing.

"Prepare the Orb for his arrival," Lothian said. "Place it at the lower end of the town. I must speak to Erceldoune. If you represent me, can you be civil until I arrive?"

"As my Prince commands." Minister Thish bowed and waited for the Prince to leave. He waved his hand, and the image of Jake in the tunnel disappeared. A glowing softball-sized object rose from the table to his hand.

****

Minister Thish stopped by his home before doing his Prince's bidding. His house was the finest in town, the only house with a small white fence and gate. His wife Grezil required it.

Grezil sat in her comfortable upholstered chair in the living room. She was a tall woman, taller than Thish. Her raven black hair was woven into thin braids tucked into a whitish cap. Gray-green eyes that changed color with her mood and company complemented a pretty, oval face. Her beauty and body were a good match, and where Thish would have taken time to appreciate both, today he did not.

"He has come," Thish fumed to his wife. "Sleeping in the entrance like a vagrant without knowing what he does or where he is."

"Don't fret. He may lack the courage to enter," Grezil said.

"No, he is in the tunnel as we speak." Thish's tone was disheartened.

"If he does manage the tunnel, you are not diminished. You are Chief Minister of the Clan. You have the ear of the Prince. No untrained human dissuades you. Why not assist rather than detract?"

"What do you mean?" Thish knew Grezil possessed more cunning and political acumen than he.

"The human is trifling. He may be untrainable. He may be unsuited to the job. If you appear helpful, when he fails, your new station as sole voice in the Prince's ear is assured."

"How would you do it?" Thish asked.

"If I had the chance, I would offer something cheap. A view from the mountain, a gallop in the forest, or a tour of the town. The human is a visitor. Offer a simple sideshow. Distract him and watch. Appear helpful but gather his deficiencies and limitations as they arise. Challenge him and show him inept. That would be my way."

Thish smiled. This he could do.

****

After her husband left on Prince Lothian's errand. Grezil called Afton, their son, to come downstairs. "Go at once," she said. "Place this note under the rock and return."

Afton was tall and handsome, not in a rock-and-roll, popstar way, but like a Greek Adonis, and he knew it. Pampered since birth, an only child, he never extended his hand without enhancing himself in some way, except when his mother spoke. Her rule was absolute. Afton rolled his eyes like a teen being told to clean up his room. "But I want to be in the town with my friends when he comes."

"Do it now. The human can wait."

"But mother"—Afton whined—"putting notes under stones makes no sense."

Grezil said nothing as she held out a small, folded parchment. She knew he would do it. He always did. She also knew he would not remember doing it. He submitted his head, and she kissed it.

CHAPTER 14

With no idea what "experience it" meant, Jake eased down the tunnel as though he was lowering himself into a scalding bath. His left hand held to the smooth surface of the tunnel wall. His right reached out like a blind man seeking a light switch.

The flat dry tunnel floor maintained a gradual decline arrowing straight into the mountain's heart. The entrance's light dimmed to a soft glow. The gray stone walls took on a shadowed hue, but the dim light was enough to guide him. He kept moving. Fear rose. He fought it back and traveled deeper.

"Experience it myself. Experience it myself." Jake repeated it over and over like some daft mantra, but it steeled his nerves as he blundered along. Nothing cataclysmic happened, his step gained confidence.

From Army orienteering courses, Jake knew his stride was two and a half feet. He counted his steps and stopped every fifty paces to listen. Air whooshed past and ruffled his clothes. "One hundred one … two hundred." At two hundred and fifty paces, worry crept back to him. He took several deep breaths to quiet it. I can follow the tunnel out anytime.

At one thousand paces, the tunnel ended. The distance from the entrance was maybe a mile. Jake sensed he was in a massive subterranean room, but the dull light from the tunnel penetrated only a few feet. How can light from the entrance still be with me?

And then it wasn't. Like a candle snuffed, the light disappeared. The black was thick, blinding like standing in an endless puddle of black ink. Fear overtook excitement. What if I'm lost in here forever? What if …?

Jake froze. Talking out loud calmed his nerves. "Don't move. Get oriented. I'll feel my way down the tunnel, get supplies, and come back. I've got this. Just follow the passage out." He shifted his left hand from the stone wall, replaced it with his right, and reached for the tunnel opening.

He groped across the rock.

"Don't panic. You just came up it," he said to himself.

Both hands contacted solid rock.

"What the hell?"

Jake stretched further, reaching to the end of his fingertips. Nothing but rock. He went back to the right. Nothing.

"Impossible. I just walked through it." Jake slid to his knees in a black so gripping he couldn't see his hands, groping for a tunnel opening he couldn't find. Panic froze his ability to move or think. His head swam. Confused and disoriented in the subterranean blackness, he flailed his arms against the rock. His fingernails dug for any loose stone.

He was trapped.

CHAPTER 15

Simion hated orders. Stupid orders were the worst. He waited up the street, partly hidden under the house, pouting and whining to himself. "Wait on MacCorkle. Wait on MacCorkle. I tried to tell her, but she won't listen. She never listens."

In the early afternoon, a white panel truck with lettering, words Simion never bothered to learn, pulled up across the street. A man and woman got out with a long pole, a noose on the end. He didn't like the look of them and wiggled deeper into his hidey-hole. The pair walked past once, twice, before they headed straight for him. Not good. The woman leaned over, looking under the shrubbery. The man with the noose waited behind her.

"There he is," she said.

Trapped.

Simion charged from his hiding place, growling and barking. His would-be captors stepped back. He stole the opening between them and ran. Within seconds, the two were after him. The woman ran for the truck. The man chased on foot. Simion raced up the street. Brakes screeched as he crossed in front of an oncoming car and ran up an alley.

The panel truck pulled up to the curb ahead of him. He skidded to a stop and squeezed under a wooden fence, tearing fur off his back. He panted hard. Fear drove him. He cut back down a driveway. Stopping behind a wooden gate, he morphed. In man form, he clothed himself. He stood up, breathing hard, sweating, heart pounding, lungs grabbing. He tried to act natural.

The man ran past him but then stopped and turned around. "Have you seen a large black dog?"

"No," Simion said, heaving breaths. His back ached where the fence skinned it.

"He's not on Karlan," the man spoke into a radio and ran on.

Simion loved it when his tricks worked. Making a fool of humans was his greatest joy. The truck passed him two more times as he walked out of the neighborhood, feeling smug. A wooded lot suited his purpose. Stepping behind the first tree, he vanished.

****

Simion dropped the note on Weir's desk and stepped back. He preferred to be in a corner with his aching back against the wall.

"Was MacCorkle at the house?" Isobel asked.

"No. He is in the Gleane."

"What did you say?"

Now she wants to hear me. Simion glanced at Weir. "I saw his truck drive down the road to the Gleane when I picked up the note." He left out that it was yesterday's note. "I didn't see the driver, but it was the same truck."

Weir looked up. "Say that again."

Simion shrank back. Isobel hits hard, but Weir's strike would be far worse. "I watched the house for months. I know his truck with the stupid *RANGER* sticker on the back window. When I picked up the note, I saw his truck turn into the Gleane."

Weir looked at Isobel with disgust.

Gotcha, bitch! Simion watched Weir. Simion had seen Weir crush people for less. Weir glanced at Simion, then reread the note, *Tonight.*

"Contact Lucius. It happens tonight," Weir said to Isobel.

****

At a small table away from the partner's desk, Isobel sat with Weir, Simion, and a new face, Lucius. The midmorning sun was well up. Pushing through drapes behind the table, it lay in streaks, heating wide floor planks of yellowish yew wood and highlighting the designs in the Persian carpet. A small square of cream parchment lay folded on the table.

Isobel took charge. She knew that she should go rather than send this miscreant, Simion, but Weir's instructions were clear. Since she had killed John MacCorkle, she was hunted by the Clan. If she entered the Gleane, she would be captured, and his entire gambit would be exposed.

"Tonight. Lucius does the killing," Isobel said. "Simion, find the Orb, and bring it to me."

Lucius stood and left the room.

"Why him? I could do it."

Simion whined when he wanted a job she knew he could not handle. "Killing is nothing," Isobel said, her soft words were to placate him. "Let Lucius do the killing. The important job is the Orb. You must get it. I want you free to find it and fetch it here."

"I don't believe you. You think I can't do it."

Simion's whining grated Isobel's nerves. She reached across the walnut table, grabbed Simion's jaw, and squeezed. Bright red talon fingernails dug into his flesh. He pulled back to escape, but she held him.

"Do what I tell you." Her hard voice silenced him. She shoved his face away.

Lucius was her attack dog, straightforward and vicious. Simion was dangerous, but in a different way, like a cur that bit you when you turned your back.

****

Isobel walked with Weir in the wooded grounds behind the castle. The day was cool. No wind. Bare trees stood stark in the afternoon air.

"How did you miss MacCorkle?" Weir asked.

"I don't know."

"That answer is unacceptable. I tasked you to end their Bard." Weir frowned, not a simple look of disapproval. His mouth curved down, further and further until it reached the bottom of his jawline, replicating an upside-down horseshoe. Isobel knew the horseshoe symbol. Turn the open end up to hold good luck. Turn it down and luck ran out.

Isobel faltered. Her eyes widened. "It was Simion. I—" Isobel stuttered. "I sent that fool to do a simple job. You know how he is, sloppy and lazy. When he went to watch yesterday morning, MacCorkle must have been already gone and he lied about it. I can't abide incompetence."

"Neither can I."

Weir's quiet words mortified her soul. Shame coursed through her. Weir could shatter her like a mirror hit with a hammer. His point made; he changed the subject.

"Can Simion handle the job?" Weir asked.

"Simion can fail, and we will still succeed. If the opportunity presents, Lucius will kill both."

37

CHAPTER 16

Jake stopped to listen. Nothing, not even wind. Sweat beads trickled under his shirt. The absent wind was worse than the dark. Panic rose into his chest and shrank his breathing to short gasps. Fear overtook his entire being as his legs buckled. He slumped to the stone floor.

A sudden sharp beam of light cut the black like a tactical flashlight. Jake's head and shoulders were outlined against the rock like a giant shadow puppet. Spinning to face the light, his eyes burned, but he wouldn't close them for fear it would go away. He twisted to the tunnel. Solid rock, no tunnel. The light brightened, shifted away from his eyes, and illuminated a path across open rock. Pushing himself up, Jake wobbled seventy-three paces to the light source.

Curious suspended light flowed off a carved stalagmite stand as if it were water swirling in a fountain. The stand appeared to be a gnarled, gray stone tree growing from the solid rock floor. Four feet up, it coiled into an oval bowl. Sitting in the bowl was a dazzling softball-sized pearl. Light streamed off the stand and flowed to the floor like dry ice melting. It was— magnificent.

The pearl flickered in pulsing, undulating, and shifting colors. Soothed by it, attracted to it, Jake felt obliged to hold it. Reaching a hand, he neared it, hesitated, but couldn't stop. Lifting with both hands, he picked it up. It was like holding a solid ball of glowing air. *A huge pearl? No. What is this?* Light flowed around and off his hands.

The soft light sharpened over Jake until it formed a four-foot circle around him as if he were an actor under a single spotlight. Beyond the circle, the subterranean room was as black as a crypt.

"Are you a thief?" A booming voice questioned from the darkness.

Jake jumped.

"Who's there?" He saw nothing.

"Are you a thief?" The voice came again, louder, demeaning, demanding.

Surprise quashed his ability to speak. The inquisitor's tone couched it, not as a question, but as an accusation. Jake's body tensed for a fight.

"No." Jake's suppressed voice sounded annulled.

A tall man, equal to Jake's six-foot-two frame, stepped into the glow of the sphere, his head seemingly too small for his body. The man's bulk lay hidden under a huge blue robe. His hands were small with thick sausage fingers, each wearing a gold ring. A gray beard, meticulously trimmed, grew around his thin mouth.

Around his neck and down to his waist was a thick gold chain with small square blocks of gold covered in odd symbols. White streaks ran down his beard from the corners of his mouth as if he had eaten white paint and, in his gluttony, it gushed out either side. Golden hair sprinkled with gray flecks capped his head. He stood ramrod straight. His face remained impassive as if he was accustomed to passing judgment on others. His brusque attitude insinuated he wanted to end this meeting as soon as possible.

"You do not speak as if you believe your words."

"I'm no thief." Defensive anger crept into Jake's voice.

"We allowed you into our sanctuary. You hold our sacred treasure. And yet, you claim to be no thief. Explain yourself."

"You want me to explain? I don't know why I'm here. I feel like you trapped me. Who are you? How did you get in here?"

The man smeared a thin, patronizing smile on his weasel face. Jake tightened his grip on the pearl.

"You are here, Son of Corkle, for the same reason that your father, your father's father, and your ancestors, for six hundred years, came to our People. You are here to serve."

The word *serve* stuck in Jake's craw. He replaced the pearl on its pedestal, feeling an odd regret when he released it. The face gloated. Jake's spine stiffened, and his anger bristled. He stepped aggressively toward the pompous weasel-faced man, and the weasel raised his hands like a maestro calling an orchestra to attention.

"Enough!" A second voice commanded, and a younger man walked into the light. The younger man fixed the weasel-faced man with a withering glare until he bowed and backed away to stand half in and half out of the light.

"Hello there," the younger man said in a warm voice. He raised his hands, palms out, to show he was no threat. His smile exuded kindness, unlike the sarcasm of weasel face. A small silver crown sat on his head. "I am Lothian, Prince of the People of Peace. I requested your first meeting be pleasant. Minister Thish failed me."

The weasel-faced Thish kept his head down.

"Well come, Jake MacCorkle. I apologize for your poor reception." Prince Lothian bowed to Jake.

"What is this place?" Jake asked.

"First, I offer my deepest sympathy on the death of your father. He was a great man and my close, personal friend."

Lothian's sincere look touched Jake, and he relaxed, a little.

"Second, though you are unaware, you are a longtime friend. My guest. Please forgive the mismanaged entrance."

Prince Lothian extended his hand. For a long second, Jake considered his circumstances. Here he was standing in a pitch-black cave, in light generated by some pearl, and about to shake hands with a king or prince of something. If he wanted out of there, he would have to play along. Lothian smiled and pushed his hand closer. Jake took it.

"I'd like to go home," Jake said.

"I understand. I will arrange it. Before you leave, I must speak to you. A short walk?"

Jake nodded. *Play along.* "How did you know my name?"

"We played together as children," Lothian said as if it was obvious.

"We ... what?"

Lothian stepped to the pearl, waved his right hand over it, and said an odd word. The cave flooded with light as if someone twisted up a dimmer switch.

In a voice like a circus ringmaster, Lothian announced: "Jake MacCorkle. Son of Bard John MacCorkle."

"Bard?"

"Hail! Bard! Jake!" Hundreds of voices shouted in unison.

Jake ducked as if someone had thrown a fastball at his head. More, many more, people were in the cave, watching. They must have seen what happened with Minister Thish. Blood rushed into Jake's face.

CHAPTER 17

"You are among friends. No harm will come to you while you are in my kingdom." Prince Lothian's voice was calm and firm.

Jake's eyes adjusted to the light. For the first time, he saw the vast expanse of where he was. *It's … It's a town carved inside a mountain.* He stood on a smooth road twenty feet wide. It wound in serpentine curves uphill and out of sight. Byways and alleys snaked off it.

Along the roadside, houses were sculpted from the gray granite. They looked like condominiums, rising three stories with porticos and balconies overlooking the road. The houses were painted in pastels of red, blue, green, yellow, and purple. Nothing was dull. No space wasted. Wildflowers grew in window boxes. Plants wound up columns.

The ceiling, at least eighty feet above, was sky blue. Clouds floated across it as if there was no ceiling. The entire town was festive, warm, and welcoming. It looked like a miniature French Quarter in New Orleans. In his astonishment, Jake forgot his embarrassment.

People stood on the road above him. People stood in doorways. People stood on balconies. Everywhere he looked, people waited to see what the Prince would do. Thish pulled back, not far, and watched.

As if he was introducing Jake to the town, the Prince raised his arm and waved toward the people. "Greetings, Jake MacCorkle. I give you the Daoine Sìthe."

Every person smiled—except one—in a welcoming and comforting way.

"Walk with me. Your possessions are enroute to your room."

The tunnel was open. *How can they open and close solid rock?* Questions flooded Jake. He chose the greatest wonder first. "Do all these people live in here?"

"No. Some of the merchants live above their shops. Most live in the surrounding forest. We call it the Gleane. But today, everyone is here to greet you."

"Greet me? Why do—"

Before Jake could ask, people thronged them. A heavyset man wearing a leather apron smiled and shook Jake's hand. "I am Angus—blacksmith. If you need weapons, I'm your man."

A lady curtsied and said, "I am Mistress Blackburne. My shop has the finest clothes in the Gleane."

Faces and voices blurred one into the next and mixed with unremembered names. People cheered him, smiled, bowed, shook his hand, and offered him gifts. It was like being a rock star. Unused emotions arose, a feeling he couldn't name. He wanted to be their friend. *I want—this.*

Moving up the road, the throng parted before them. Shops opened. Men bowed and offered their hand. Women curtsied. The town came alive. The baker, butcher, bladesmith, and cobbler stopped work and stepped out to greet them. The gray stone sidewalk filled with people, bowing to their Prince, and welcoming Jake.

A brass band, and it would be a parade.

The people dressed in utilitarian clothes. Everything looked homemade but the finest quality. The men wore colored shirts and pants in muted green, gray, or brown. Women wore the same but with the added red, bright green, or yellow to make beautiful plaids.

Shop keepers offered samples. The Prince picked and chose among the offerings, praising the person who offered it. Jake was hungry. He ate everything.

The food was delicious, seasoned to perfection, and the people who offered it to him were delighted by his enjoyment. The Prince was in no hurry and ambled through the shops and byways. When the novelty wore off, Jake became impatient.

"Why am I here?"

"In due time. First, please enjoy."

The people, even though they witnessed the altercation between Jake and Thish, seemed to ignore what happened. Jake met no one holding ill will. Over his shoulder, Jake noticed Thish following within earshot.

Why was this so easy to accept? In the middle of a mountain, greeting a group of people who live here as if he was meeting long lost cousins. *Am I still asleep? Hallucinating? What?* He couldn't wait.

"Where are we? Why am I here?"

"If you would allow it," Lothian said, "let me anticipate your questions. At first, I know my words will be strange to you for we are not people of your world. We are a Clan of faeries."

Jake choked on a delicious piece of cooked meat from a plump woman who had offered him the entire platter. "Faeries?"

"We are an ancient people living in the world of man since the beginning. We are the Daoine Sithe, in English, People of Peace. Legends tell we descended from angels who left heaven and became entrapped on Earth between heaven and hell, but no one knows for sure. For eons, we lived in the islands of Scotland. For centuries, your family was *anam cara* to us. In your language, it means having the soul of a friend."

A thin man pressed next to Jake and offered him a vest.

"Centuries?" Jake said and shot Lothian a look.

"Yes, our relationship began when your ancestor did a great service to our People. He saved countless lives by returning the Orb to us after it was stolen."

"The Orb?"

"The object you held earlier. It is the creation of a great Wyzard, Sir Michael Scot. When he was dying, he gave it to our Clan for safekeeping."

A six-year-old grabbed his shirt and offered her hand. Jake took it without thinking and held it as she skipped next to him.

"What does an Orb do?"

"Would you like to experience it for yourself?"

CHAPTER 18

Lothian raised his hand. The Orb appeared.

"How'd you do that?" Jake asked. Wonder replaced worry.

"Let us begin at the time the Orb was given to our People," Lothian said.

Like vapor off dry ice, a mist swirled and surrounded them. A white sheet of it wound from the ground to three feet overhead. The sides were close enough for Jake to touch. Reaching a hand out, he put a finger against the mist.

It's solid.

The sheet flexed and gave when he pushed it, like a plastic bag. Inside, Jake was warm, as if being wrapped in a favorite cozy blanket. Through a translucent fog wall, he saw the street, people going about their business, behaving as if a fog, ten feet high, five feet around, wasn't floating in the middle of the street. The scene shifted.

"Whoa." Jake reeled. He reached for something to hold onto. Lothian put his hand under Jake's arm to steady him. "What just happened?"

"The first time you experience the Orb," Lothian said, "it tends to disorient. Be calm and know this is just another experience, new and different, but nothing beyond your ability."

The room stopped spinning, the white fog became transparent, and Jake witnessed the scene as if he were standing in an out-of-the-way corner.

The stone room had a vaulted ceiling of oak beams that met in an arch overhead. A large four-poster bed sat across from a glowing hearth. The room was airy and warm. An odd smell, like liniment, hung in the air. Rich damask covers, matching curtains, and inviting wool blankets and books covered the bed. A desk near the bed held more books, charts, and writing parchment. Servants came and went. Two men entered and approached the bed where a bony, aged man lay almost hidden in the covers.

"The dying man," Lothian pointed, "is Sir Michael Scott. My great grandfather, Torrinn, on the right, and my great uncle, Corraidhín on the left."

The uncle was short, round, and heavily muscled with the look of a warrior. He wore a red tunic over finely woven chain mail that ended below his knees. A sword and dagger in a thick leather belt were tied at his waist. Leather leggings flowed to his boots. His face was curled in a look of disgust.

Prince Lothian's great grandfather, Torrinn, was tall and fair. The resemblance was clear. He wore a brown silk shirt and forest green pants with a leather vest over top. His face showed a gentle kindness for the older man.

"Listen and watch," Lothian said.

****

"I have asked you here because I am dying," Sir Michael said. "I have created a talisman that will ensure balance." He reached beneath his blanket and retrieved a glowing ball of white light. He handed it to Torrinn. As if the effort depleted him, he fell back on the bed, his breathing shallow. His voice rasped. "I entrust this Orb to your Clan for safekeeping. Its power is immense, beyond even your understanding. Guard it with care. It maintains a balance between your world and man's world."

Without examination, King Torrinn accepted the gift and passed it to Corraidhín, keeping his eyes on the old man. Corraidhín glanced at the bedridden man, turned without comment, and left with the Orb. King Torrinn sat down on the bed to say a prayer for the dying man. As he rose, a bony arm grabbed his sleeve.

"Beware your brother," Sir Michael warned the King.

The scene changed. The two men stood deep in a thick forest. Corraidhín hunched over the Orb. Greed, like a miser coveting gold, etched his face. His hands shook as he stared into the Orb's shifting colors. King Torrinn joined him.

"Brother," Corraidhín said, "that old Wyzard has given us the means to dominate man's world."

"No," King Torrinn said. "He gave us the means to live in harmony with that world, to balance evil, so that we can live in peace with man."

"What matters good or evil? We hold the power to control both."

"Brother, you ignore the truth. Sir Michael gave us a task with the Orb. We are responsible for keeping a balance between our world and man's world. A balance that maintains peace, a transitory luxury, at best."

"Who cares what the old fool said. This gift will end war. When we conquer man, there will be no war ever after." Corraidhín was agitated.

"Brother, again, you are misguided. Peace is not the absence of war through the dominance of one people over another, nor is it the absence of disagreement, nor the constant unerring boredom of agreement. It is a personal sense of wellbeing and safety in the absence of danger that exists by agreement between peoples. If this Orb has power to create and keep peace, I will use it as it was given."

King Torrinn outstretched his hand for the Orb. Corraidhín withheld it.

"There would be no real war," Corraidhín said. "A simple conquest. We could—"

"We could not. Your way breaks trust and denies change caused by time and circumstance." King Torrinn took a step toward his brother and held out his hand. "Man is no longer a spurious pet to be caged."

Corraidhín pulled the Orb closer. "Don't be a fool, brother. Think of the wealth in man's world. We can take it and make man our servant. With man's toil, we shall leave Middle Earth and live as kings."

"Lest you forget, I am King. The judgment is mine." The King took the Orb and put it in a leather pouch. He mounted his white charger and cantered into the forest. His brother stared after him with his lip curled.

The scene dissolved in the mist of the Orb.

****

"What happened between the brothers?" Jake asked.

"Corraidhín became obsessed with the Orb," Lothian said. "To gain it, he chose the path of evil. He led a group within the Clan that desired to dominate and domesticate man like a farmer domesticates cattle. When Corraidhín stole the Orb, we fought. Years later, your ancestor intervened to save King Torrinn and helped our Clan regain the Orb. Even so, our cousins found ways to induce human submission."

"How?"

"Magic."

Lothian didn't elaborate. Jake didn't understand enough to ask a question.

"Can I see the part where my ancestor helped?" Jake wanted to confirm his suspicion.

"Of course."

The mist swirled, and another scene appeared. This scene was familiar to Jake. He and Lothian watched a man in a small boat paddle to shore, enter a fight, and rescue a man attacked by three others.

It's my dream.

The mist dissipated. They stood in the street. People went about their routine as if nothing happened.

"How does the Orb know my dreams?" Jake asked.

"The Orb commences your training."

CHAPTER 19

The road ended at a large building colored a pristine white and carved into the wide back of the mountain. Broad curving steps forty feet across swept up to a twenty-foot-wide portico. Along it, offset columns supported a stone patio twenty feet above. Double doors three times Jake's height were centered in the wall. No handles. Four windows, equally tall, flanked the doors on each side. Prince Lothian waved a hand. The great doors swung back without a sound.

"This building is my residence and the Ministry offices. A room is prepared for you."

Past the doors, the foyer was twice as wide as the portico. Gleaming polished floors of inlaid marble boasted intricate Celtic designs. Across the foyer, two flowing white marble staircases arched up to a second-floor landing. Other steps led higher left and right to different wings on the second floor. In the foyer to the right and left were closed doors. Tapestries, flags, and large prints of hunting scenes hung from the ceiling and along the walls. To Jake, these seemed to shimmer and move.

Portraits adorned the second-floor landing. The ceiling was pale gray with wisps of clouds floating through it. Lothian took the right-hand stairs up to the second floor and turned right into a hall. At the last room on the left, he motioned Jake in.

The room was a large oval shape, four times the size of his room at home. No windows. The bed was a large four-poster with a canopy over top. Made of cherry, it matched a five-drawer dresser, nightstand, and dressing table. Comfortable-looking overstuffed chairs sat around a small inlaid table. A beautiful oriental carpet graced the floor.

Jake's meager belongings were on the bed. He pressed the mattress. *Beats sleeping on the ground.*

Prince Lothian sat down and motioned for Jake to take the other chair. "I am confident you have questions. I requested a guide to meet and orient you to the Gleane. He will answer all questions you have. There is water," Lothian pointed to a bowl and pitcher on the dressing table, "in the basin. A facility is down the hall. Your guide will show you. I must leave for a few moments. We have a small feast in your honor this evening." Prince Lothian bowed and turned to leave, but Jake stopped him.

"You haven't answered my question. Why am I here?"

"Your father was my Bard for many years. I desire for you to take his place." Lothian seemed in no great hurry. Jake pressed him.

"Bard?"

"An important role to the Clan. A Bard advises the Clan Leader and maintains a record of the Clan activities. The Orb keeps an archive."

"My father was your Bard?"

"Yes. He advised my father and myself. We sought his murderer, but in vain."

"Murdered?" Jake asked. "Are you saying my father was murdered because he was your Bard?"

"Would you like to judge for yourself?"

"How?"

"The Orb has the ability to follow anyone who touches it. It followed your father, and we have his memory of what happened. You will see through your father's eyes."

"I want to see it," Jake said. Jake's pulse quickened.

"You will see him die. Do you wish to continue?"

Without hesitation, Jake said, "Yes."

Lothian raised his hand. The Orb appeared and floated between them.

"State what you wish."

"Show me my father's death."

Fog swirled. It flowed down the pedestal, across the floor, and around the room. A thin, white, smooth sheet covered the walls from top to bottom. A scene projected onto the sheet.

Jake's chest tightened. Sadness tinged with fear grew. The scene focused. He rode inside his father's car and saw through his father's eyes. He glanced at the speedometer. The car blew through small curves and crossed the centerline to shortcut big ones.

"What's his hurry?"

"He was returning to meet with you."

Five road signs with sideways V's signaled a steep curve was coming. Jake recognized the accident site. He felt the car brake as it entered the curve. Above the curve stood a hooded figure. Brakes punched, hard. The car skidded sideways to a stop in the middle of the road. Jake stared out the passenger window.

A dust devil rose and moved toward the car. It grew larger. It overtook the car with the force of a tornado. The gearshift slammed into reverse. Tires spun. Fighting the wind, the car eked back. It rocked, struggling to break away.

The malevolent figure, hands raised, head tipped toward heaven, gave the impression of a person praying. The wind quickened. Branches and leaves whipped past the windows. Panic stormed Jake. The tachometer spun, tires whined, black smoke billowed.

The car froze in place, unable to escape. By degrees it moved, not backward but forward, driven by the tornadic wind.

Like a giant's hand, the wind plucked the car off the road as if it were a toy and careened it toward the woods. One of the V-signs showed for a second before the car wrenched it flat.

Velocity increased. A huge oak tree loomed on the driver's side. Jake's hands became useless lumps, steering nothing. His father's foot jammed hard against the brake. Jake's muscles tensed for impact. The car blasted into the tree like a piece of pine straw hitting a rock.

Everything became airborne. His body left the seat, fighting the seatbelt to fly. He was aloft until the door frame smacked him. He hit glass. The car crushed around him.

Curious thoughts followed—a person laughing, Jake playing in the sandbox, someone grabbing at his neck. A face, rooster-cropped and dyed-blonde hair, drew close to his own.

Blackness. Nothing.

Jake shook. He felt weak, and his stomach lurched. He was quiet for a long time. Lothian did not intrude.

"Who was that person?"

"Her name is Isobel. She works with the Droch Sìthe, the group led by Corraidhín.

"Why would she kill my father?"

"We know not. We pursued all leads to find her but she has disappeared."

****

Lothian left Jake. He crossed the landing and went straight to his quarters. As he approached, the double doors opened as if they knew his footsteps on the stone.

Lothian's room was larger than Jake's. On the right wall, away from the doors, was a large, centuries-old four-poster bed made from heavily carved oak. On either side of the bed was an antique nightstand of dark cherry. A fireplace was cut into the stone. Dark oak wainscot rounded the room. On the far wall was a large mahogany writing desk with a glass-doored bookcase above. Centered in the room was a small table on a red, black, white, and purple oriental carpet. Comfortable overstuffed chairs called from the fireplace. Lothian went to the chairs and projected his thoughts through the Orb.

"Contact Erceldoune."

"Yes?" Erceldoune's voice answered.

"Jake is here."

"Is he adjusting?"

"I don't know yet. He is intrigued. Perhaps interested, but overwhelmed. I will meet with him again after the feast."

"And Thish?" Erceldoune inquired.

Lothian smiled at the question. "Thish is Thish."

CHAPTER 20

Within the hour, a knock came at Jake's door. A man clad in brown pants, a robin-egg blue shirt, and a light brown leather vest stood outside. His face was an odd shape, long and drawn, horse-like. Dark brown eyes were close set, and ears prominent. His sandy brown hair and plain features were different from the startling blue, green, and gray eyes and handsome faces of the other faeries he's seen. He was an average guy, but Jake felt there was something—

"I am Clackmannan. Please call me Clacks. Prince Lothian asked me to orient you to the Gleane." Clacks smiled, not a dazzling smile but a calm and friendly one that was welcoming as if nothing was wrong or could ever be as long as you were with him.

Jake returned the smile. He liked him. "Sounds good."

Clacks turned left, and Jake followed. Five feet from Jake's room, turret stairs wound up and down around a central gray stone column.

Clacks pointed down. "Those stairs lead to the kitchen. So, if you get hungry later …" The smile again.

They went up. The steps were narrow and close set, edges worn smooth by a thousand feet. Jake placed both hands on the close rough stone for balance as he went up tight, dizzying circles. No windows, no reference point. "How high are we?"

"A few steps below the peak of the mountain."

Jake's head rose level with a smooth granite floor. The stairs emptied into a small domed room. The walls were solid granite. No exit.

"Where do we go from here?"

At the far wall, Clacks spoke several odd-sounding words and waved his hands up and down. Granite evaporated. Beginning as a dime-sized opening, the hole expanded to the size of a small rectangle and continued widening until a door formed. Cool air he could almost taste licked Jake's face. He heard birds. Forest smells sailed in.

Clacks stepped aside. Jake eased through the door. Rock changed to earth covered by three feet of mulch and leaves. He rolled dirt between his fingers. He missed the outside.

The mountaintop view was unimpeded. To the north and east, other tree-topped mountains rose. To the south and west was the field, creeks, and streams junction. Beyond lay unending forest.

Clacks picked up a small stone. He tossed it away. And another until he found the one he wanted. He cupped his hands around his final choice, and said, "Use the stone. To clear the eye. Make it bright. Magnify."

"What are you doing?" Jake asked.

The stone rose off Clacks's palm and spun. It widened into a prism about two feet square. He removed his hand. It hovered at eye level. Clacks motioned for Jake to step behind it.

"What is it?"

"A child's toy."

The prism was like looking through a powerful telescope. Vista detail became larger, clearer, and more intense. Snatches of his truck, hidden under trees, came into focus. The door handle, mirror, and tops of the seats looked as if he was standing next to them. Sighting between the trees, Jake followed the road and saw links of chain looped through the gate.

Jake turned. The prism anticipated him like the advanced weapons system in a jetfighter. The river and stone, where he distributed his father's ashes, came into view. He looked over the prism, and the view turned into an indistinct blob.

"Can I ask a question?" Jake said.

"Anything."

When I was spreading my dad's ashes, were people on both banks of the river?"

"Yes, our entire Clan attended to honor your father."

"Clacks, what did my father do for the Clan?"

"Bard John continued a six-hundred-year-old relationship to keep our Clan safe. He kept Clan history and protected the Orb. He was a valued adviser to the Prince and his father. And, he was an excellent Wyzard."

"Wyzard?" Jake laughed.

Clacks smiled. "I know the idea is unfamiliar to you. When he was murdered, the Clan lost a calming voice."

"But why was he murdered?" Jake's voice cracked.

"We know not. Our world seeks the murderer, but she has vanished." There was nothing more to say.

Jake asked, "Why is Lothian a Prince and not a King?"

Clacks gathered his thoughts before he answered as if the subject was painful. "When the Prince and Princess were children. The King and Queen traveled to Ireland. They never arrived. The Orb tracked their journey but cannot show people in transit. To this day, the Journal shows them traveling. We know not if they are imprisoned, are dead, or alive. The Prince and Princess were grief stricken. As Prince, Lothian could have claimed the throne, but he loved his parents so much that he and the Princess slipped into a shared leadership role without taking the title."

"Where is the princess?" Jake asked.

"The Princess studies in Scotland."

Jake chatted away the afternoon with Clacks as if they were two old friends catching up. Afternoon shadows gathered in the valleys.

The prism reverted to a stone. Clacks set the stone on a larger rock like a totem. Back into the oval room, Clacks turned. He said the words to close the door. Nothing happened. The cool breeze drifted in. He tried it again. Nothing. A sheepish look crept across his face.

"Until you master magic, it can be as fickle as a willful puppy."

"Can we just leave it open like this?"

Clacks smiled his reassuring smile. "I will come back and close it later, but first, would you like to go to the Swan?"

"What's that?"

"Our pub. Faeries love a good pint, hunting, and dancing. The dancing is tonight at the feast. But can't hurt to get a start on the pint." Clacks smiled.

"Hunting?"

"Great sport. We ride to the hunt. In past years, a real fox or stag was hunted. Now, we create one using enchantment. The challenge is greater because the enchanted creature has the will of its creator. Finding it and racing to touch it is great fun. I will arrange it for you."

"I can't ride a horse."

"Easily remedied." Clacks smiled.

CHAPTER 21

To Simion, the landscape around Weir's house was sacred ground. Garden spaces converged with woody areas in a seamless tapestry. But Simion knew more. He knew the secret places—places he hid in plain sight while he watched people scurry, searching for him, finding him only when he chose. He sensed the building, knew its past, and reveled in the dark underbelly of its evil history.

Simion was no fool. He blundered, but he knew things. Some things his uppity superiors didn't know he knew. Information, sensitive information was free and he knew how to get it. Some at keyholes, but most by sitting nearby like a sleeping pet, always listening while others talked. If it bored him, he went to explore other people's secrets while they were occupied. When he listened, his portfolio of information expanded.

Simion revered the building and grounds, but he feared Weir. Around him, he struggled like a bug under a microscope, wiggling and squirming to escape. He never did. There was no way to anticipate what Weir knew or how he used the information.

Isobel was different. Her magic was strong, but her bitchy treatment and her temperamental swings were predictable. Take the first punch, grovel, and she let it pass. Out loud, he practiced his excuse.

Simion figured he'd had a good day. He'd escaped from the noose people and made Isobel look like a buffoon in front of Weir. He slowed his pace. He meandered among mammoth magnolias. If he was late enough, she'd have to let him go without punishment. He ambled toward the back corner of the property. As he reached the meeting place, he overheard Isobel quizzing Lucius.

"Tell me how you get in? Which room? How do you get the knife?"

Simion was glad he missed this crap.

"Where have you been?" Isobel's voice rose. She raised her hand but held back. "I'll deal with you later."

"I did what you told me. I watched the MacCorkle house. I did everything I could to be on time. You won't let me transport onto the property. It wasn't my fault." Simion blew the words out in one breath and ducked away before she could hit him. He could tell her anything, and she'd buy it tonight. She needed him.

"Come on, I want you in place when everything quiets for the night. The opening is secure. Lucius, you kill him. A prick from the knife will do, but cut him. Simion, get the Orb. Do you hear me? Get the Orb. Don't fail me."

The trio walked to the back corner of Weir's property. Three slender ash trees grew in a perfect triangle. The lower branches were pruned up ten feet above ground level. The upper branches intertwined, forming a gazebo-type roof. A small mound rose at the exact center of the trees.

"Stand there," Isobel ordered. In place, Lucius and Simion looked like the odd couple: Simion tall, dark, and rangy; Lucius short, muscular, and compact. Isobel held out the silver chain and key. Simion reached for it. Lucius snatched it away. Simion complained. Lucius smiled and ignored him.

She spoke the enchantment. "Travel with the wind. Travel to the Gleane."

Air whisked dirt around Simion like a dust storm. He held his breath to stop from breathing it. The trees glowed as if they had tiny white Christmas lights on the branches. The light shifted from white to gold. The roots glowed. The pair floated off the ground.

CHAPTER 22

From the turret steps to the foyer and down the wide front steps, Jake followed Clacks into the street and off the main road. They entered a series of narrow, shop-lined lanes that ended in a wide mall area. The granite ceiling shrank from eighty feet to eighteen. Steps led up between the buildings, curving to the right and up again like a switchback on a mountain road. Voices and laughing came from above. Red oak doors swung open. Noise escalated in random rhythms. The clink of glasses mingled with garbled words.

A large stone room splashed with bright rainbow colors welcomed them. The rounded ceiling arched down into stone nooks separated by narrow windows looking out over the city. Tables and chairs, booths and barstools stood sentry around a circular serving bar made from dark wood. Overhead, racks of wine glasses, mugs, and bottles awaited filling.

Clacks found a booth along the outside wall. The open window formed a triangle, wide at the booth, narrow where the arch met above it. Over the din, Clacks motioned for Jake to sit while he went to the bar.

Left alone, Jake watched the crowd. Each time he caught someone's eye, they smiled at him, welcomed him, or raised a tankard as an offer to buy him a drink. He hadn't felt support like this since the Army. A good happy feeling grew in him, as if he were accepted, as if he were one of them.

Thish entered the pub. A chill snuffed Jake's good mood.

****

Clacks turned, carrying two topped-off tankards. Thish was in his face before he took a full step. He grasped Clacks's shoulder and maneuvered him away from the bar. Fresh ale spilled down Clacks's hands.

"Yes, Minister?" Clacks voice showed his irritation. Thish missed the hint.

"What have you learned?" Thish asked, as if he was owed an account.

"I like him."

"He is no Bard. He lacks ability," Thish said.

Clacks changed the subject. "I'm glad you're here. There was a problem with the door in the domed room. I've opened and closed that doorway fifty times and never had a problem. Today, for some reason, the enchantment to close it did not work."

"I am sure it is a simple mistake on your part. Perhaps you should learn magic from someone other than that doddering Erceldoune. You must go back and try again."

"Yes, of course." Clacks wanted to tell him what he thought, that Thish only wished he had a tenth of Erceldoune's power, but he held his tongue.

Clacks sashayed between the patrons back to the table.

"What did he want?" Jake asked.

"Who?" Clacks followed Jake's dour glance at Thish. "He asked how you liked the mountaintop. Spilled our ale. Dolt."

"That's surprising. I don't think he likes me very much."

"Don't concern yourself with Thish. We have a saying about him, "Thish is Thish." Clacks's smile lightened Jake's heart. "Everyone loves you. There is a feast tonight in your honor."

"But I slept in these clothes."

"A shower is down the hall. Clothes are provided. I will come for you at seven. Now a toast to you, my new friend."

CHAPTER 23

In his room, Jake readied for the feast in his honor. The day had been weird, but wonderful. The people were great. Clacks was great. The Prince. Everyone. Well, almost everyone.

Jake hadn't been to a party in years. His mouth dried and his stomach lurched thinking about it.

The shower didn't cooperate. No knobs to start the water or adjust temperature. He waved his hand as Prince Lothian had done to open the doors. Nothing happened.

Jake stepped into the shower. A slot opened above his head and water poured onto him. The temperature was perfect. He stepped out of the shower. The slot disappeared. Like a kid playing in a waterfall, Jake jumped in and out of the shower to see if he could fool it.

On his bed lay a silk-looking shirt, his own cleaned and pressed blue jeans, soft leather boots, and a short, comfortable leather jacket, a little longer than a vest. He tried them on. A perfect fit.

Clacks was punctual. He and Jake traversed the hall staircase down to the foyer. Holly, magnolia, and pine with twinkling lights entwined the railings, giving the huge foyer a fresh outdoor smell. A giant chandelier lit with candles bathed the foyer in a soft glow. Tapestries of mountain and hunting scenes, different from before, decorated the walls.

As they descended the stairs, tall and wide doors opened on their left revealing a ballroom half the size of a football field. A twenty-foot ceiling shimmered in cobalt blue with white sparkles twinkling like stars. The walls shifted color from purple to green to blue with flashes of silver as fabulous as the northern lights. The floor was rich mahogany with inlaid portraits of the people standing on it. Jake looked down. A woody picture of himself stared back. *How is all this happening inside a mountain?*

The ceiling, walls, and floor intertwined to evoke a festive mood. Hundreds of people wearing bright colors of satin and silk, clothes similar to the ones provided for him, buzzed in small groups. When he and Clacks entered, every eye turned to gawk.

An unseen voice announced: "Clackmannan, Apprentice to Erceldoune,

Wyzard Extraordinaire. Jake MacCorkle, Son of Bard John MacCorkle, Friend to the Daione Sìthe."

People approached to introduce themselves.

"Well come. I am Minister Alfred, and this is my wife."

Jake didn't hear her name because the next person talked over him.

Jake shook hands and smiled. He bowed when they bowed. He laughed when they laughed. He knew why he avoided parties like this; he hated them. All this attention, it wasn't his style.

A face loomed on his left. Thish's mouth scowled as if he were about to scold a wanton child. In tow were a woman and younger man.

"This is my wife, Grezil, and my son, Afton." There was no "well come" or smile. Thish started to extend a hand. He withdrew it and nodded. Jake fixed him with a stare before returning a slight nod. *Meet force with force.*

A hand grasped Jake's arm. Grezil bounded into his face. Jake stepped into her, leaning close, as if they were old chums sharing a secret. *I don't know this lady. Why is she jacking me up?*

"Well come, Mr. MacCorkle. I am so pleased to meet you. I hope your earlier unpleasantness is forgotten." Her voice was melodic and sweet. She reached out, took Jake's hand, and folded it between both of hers.

Grezil was beautiful. She was taller than Thish. The package was near irresistible: a soft, oval face, oxbow mouth, sensuous and full lips, sharp chin with attractive dimple, smile with two more coy dimples, fitted black dress embroidered in silver and gold vines and leaves. His earlier thought evaporated as if she dimmed his wits.

Her greenish-gray eyes devoured Jake. A primitive corner of his brain screamed a warning. She seemed to be measuring him, grasping at him, sneaking her way into his mind, persistently pushing to understand his needs, his weaknesses like the tentacles of an octopus searching rocks for its prey. Given a chance, she'd take him over, body and soul. Grezil maneuvered him next to her side and entwined his arm with hers. Jake extricated his arm and stepped away from Grezil. Loose from the octopus grip, he breathed easier.

"This is my son, Afton." Afton was the poster child for faeries.

Easily, six-feet-five-inches tall, lean, and muscular, Afton was built like an Olympic swimmer. A firm mouth, clear-cut chin, and a strong Roman nose were highlighted by golden-brown, wavy hair and green eyes. Every aspect of him fit like an ingenious puzzle until Jake saw his clothes: spangled pants with large circles spinning and crashing together, topped with a lime-green shirt and yellow vest. His mother must have dressed him. Afton exuded a friendliness, a self-effacing good guy attitude. He grinned at Jake. He was sincere but dull.

"Here ye, hear ye. Lothian, Prince to the People of Peace."

All talk ceased. Fabric rustled as people bowed. Lothian veered to Jake, shook his hand, walked him to the dais, and seated him at his right side.

Music, strange and lyrical, commenced. Couples formed. The dance was a cross between the Virginia reel and hip-hop. Foursomes spun to music that stirred Jake's heart. His fingers strummed. His feet tapped. His spirit joined the rhythm and beat.

Servers brought tankards. The strong smell of ale floated up from them. Jake touched a cautious sip to his lips. He and alcohol had a love-hate relationship. He loved it but hated what it did to him. His past power drinking was a function of wanting to forget. Not tonight. He wanted to remember everything, to enjoy these people, and to participate, not in an inebriated state, but clear and sober. If he was going to become impaired, he didn't want it. But maybe just a swig or two. Despite the strong smell, his tongue swam in the liquid. Sweet, not bitter, and it carried no aftertaste. After two swigs, Jake felt refreshed.

"How do you like our ale?" Lothian asked over the music.

"Love it. But I shouldn't drink anymore. It seems different from human alcohol."

"It produces no sensation that the drinker does not want. It refreshes without filling. It relaxes without impairment. It is an elixir for the soul. It's okay to drink your fill." Prince Lothian raised his tankard, and Jake waved to the server for another round.

After the second mug, Jake was happy, not drunk, not even tipsy, but simply happy. His hands and legs joined his fingers and feet in appreciation of the music. Here he was, buried in a mountain surrounded by faeries and at a party he would normally hate, but was loving it.

Why was this so easy to accept? Was it part of a dream? Had he gone mad?

Across the room, Jake waved to Clacks. Clacks took the hand of his partner, a tall and beautiful woman with long golden curls and sharp blue eyes, and together they darted and feinted to the dais.

"My partner wishes to dance with you," Clacks said. Her winsome smile wilted Jake. He accepted.

Within minutes, Jake's self-conscious, awkward dance moves smoothed out. He jigged and pranced, hopped, and do-si-doed. He laughed. Lothian smiled from the dais.

"I haven't laughed like this since college. Since—" *Vivian.*

Jake zigged when he should have zagged and tripped hard into Afton Thish. Afton reached for his partner, who grabbed another, and the group crumpled in a heap on the floor. Everyone laughed so hard it became contagious—except for one.

A voice rose above the merriment. "It seems our Bard is a drunkard."

Laughter died out. Jake got up, helped his partner to her feet, and headed for Thish.

"He has no magic," Thish said, goading him.

Jake's temper flashed like gasoline thrown on a fire. His hands formed fists as he stalked toward Thish. His mind seared into a single scene from his youth. He lay on the ground, feeling smaller than usual. Always a head shorter than other kids his age, he withered to a smaller size. His classmates gathered around him. No one helped. No one wanted to lay next to him. No one had wanted to share his pain, be the next victim.

He was alone, again.

I'm gonna hit him so hard his mama will cry.

Clacks stepped between Jake and Thish. He placed a hand on Jake's forearm. Jake froze like a statue.

"He is baiting you. Let it go," Clacks said.

With a focused effort, Jake jerked his arm out of Clacks's grip.

"Ahhh." The crowd expressed collective awe. Looking neither left nor right, Jake stalked out of the ballroom. Outside on the street, he paced. *Where do I go?* He burned with shame. *Damn, Clacks.*

"Jake MacCorkle," Prince Lothian called him from the steps. "Thish took advantage of your enjoyment."

"Forget Thish. Clacks is the problem. What was he doing stopping me?"

"Being a good friend. Clacks protected you. Thish planned to hurt. You must know magic to fight magic."

"Okay, but everyone saw Thish put me down like he did this morning."

"Not so. You believe what you fear. The people bowed as you left."

"Bowed?"

"A rare honor. Faeries do not suffer human fools. Thish wanted others to follow him in believing that you were incompetent and incapable of assuming the Bard role. His gambit pushed you to challenge him. Clacks recognized his actions and stepped in to help. A magical grip is powerful. Few humans can break an enchantment through will."

Jake was caught short. "I don't understand. I thought Thish and Clacks shamed me."

"Nonsense, you proved Thish wrong."

"But I have no magic?"

"Magic chooses the person. Training develops ability. Consider a violin. The instrument does nothing until someone picks it up and pulls the bow across the strings. At that instant, it may make a sound like a tortured cat, or it may produce music that touches the heart." Lothian's words resonated for Jake.

"What does this have to do with me?"

"You can deny magic, but it will never leave you in peace. It is your destiny to—"

"To what, be a faerie wyzard? No way. I don't believe in destiny." *Look what it got Dad.*

"Denial changes nothing," Lothian said.

They sat on the steps without speaking. Long minutes passed.

"What happens if I decide to learn magic?" Jake said.

"You would train."

"And if I train?"

"Magic changes humans. Either for good or ill. Magic is power. Power doesn't determine its use for good or evil but requires a deeply personal and individual choice. When power first emanates, at that moment, a person decides how the skill is used—for personal gain, for the improvement of others, or both. The choice divines the future. The decision of that future rests with you. And it will come upon you unawares."

CHAPTER 24

Sleep came, but as Jake's body lowered into slumber, his mind identified places he'd never been and recognized people he'd never met. He knew he was dreaming, but the dreams were exciting, vivid adventures. Snatches of disjointed stories coalesced into a single theme, and he saw the next segment materialize.

Jake looked around. A military briefing. All men. Clothes were chain mail and leather. Weapons were swords and daggers. *What army is this?*

One man didn't belong. It was Corcle. Jake recognized him from the stream dream. He wore no armor, no sword, and was sorely out of place. He was dressed in green tights, brown leather leggings, a white silk shirt, and a supple leather vest.

The storyteller's voice began narration—the same voice that spoke in Jake's earlier dreams. But it was different this time. It was his voice. He wore the clothes. He was in the meeting. He was the one who felt out of place, an interloper. There was no separation. He was in the dream. He saw, heard, smelled, and felt every aspect.

Jake spoke as if he knew the story.

****

Despite my discomfort, I spoke: "I know the place."

"What of it, we all know the location. The problem is how to assault it," an older man with a no-nonsense military bearing said. "Do you know that, human?"

The older man acted like a general.

"I have a way."

"Go on," said King Torrinn. He sat at the head of the table, his purple robe surrounded by a thick white collar. Sunlight glinted off his silver crown and threw sparkles of light around the room.

"For many years, I fished that river. I know it well. My home is but a mile above the island. I have heard this council wants a quick end to war. War ends with the capture of the Orb. What a large army contending against another large army cannot do, a small group unseen can. As I heard the plan, the main army is to go into this valley and draw the opposing army toward these crags." I pointed to the map.

"Any attack by water is useless," the general said.

"If you had boats?" I asked.

"Boats would be seen," another man said.

"A small force, perhaps four men, drifting without sound, using the river currents, could land on the island undetected."

"We have no boats that can—"

"Corcle has such a boat." King Torrinn broke in. "I have seen it. It does all he says. It carried him silently on the water and brought him to my rescue. He was upon the Droch Sìthe before they knew he was there. If it works so in daylight, how much better in darkness?"

"Can this be done?" the general asked.

"It shall be done," King Torrinn said.

****

The dream and the storyteller's voice vanished. Jake lay still waiting for his breathing and heart rate to return to normal while he listened to the sounds of the castle.

He knew every squeak and groan of his father's house. He'd heard them over and over on the nights he'd lain awake. Tonight, in the castle, was different.

After midnight and the last person shuffled to bed, silence reigned. The castle became quiet as a churchyard. The Orb maintained a faint night light in his room and a brighter, but soft, light in the hall to avoid stubbed toes. As if it sensed, Jake preferred it dark.

CHAPTER 25

The whirlwind set Lucius and Simion down outside the Gleane gate. The road was pitch black. Simion chafed. Lucius refused to let him touch the key, unlock the gate, or lead down the trail.

"Lucius, you're not the boss of me."

Lucius snorted a derisive laugh.

The pair made good time up the mountain. Lucius found a large stone with a smaller stone set on top of it. Behind the totem loomed a dark opening in the mountaintop. As they entered, Simion stumbled against Lucius.

"Quiet, fool," Lucius hissed.

They froze, listening inside the small dome. Nothing. Lucius led down the circular stairwell. Simion seethed. *Wait 'til this is over. You'll pay.*

Inching down the narrow steps, Simion stumbled into Lucius for the third time. Lucius grunted, cursed in exasperation, and pushed Simion off him. Simion bounced against the wall like a rag doll.

Simion's hand went for his dagger. Lucius ignored him and crept down the steps. *This isn't over, fool.*

At a landing, a tall faerie appeared from the lower stairs. He withdrew a twelve-inch dagger and handed it to Lucius.

The dagger beckoned Simion, and he reached for it. Lucius knocked his hand away and stuck the dagger into his belt.

****

A noise, someone tripping against stone, echoed in the soundless night. Whispers ricocheted somewhere outside his room. Jake rose and opened his door a crack and listened. A muffled sound echoed down the stone steps. After opening the door wide enough to see into the hall, he backed himself in a dark corner of the room. The hall light's reach ended at the threshold. Jake could see out, but no one would see in.

Dim light outlined the hall like an oblong picture frame. Three shadowy outlines stood in black relief against the stone. Two separated and passed Jake's door. He counted; at five, he peeked out. Two shadows slunk ahead of him down the hall. The third was gone.

Jake entered military mode.

****

One, two, three, four. Fourth door on the right. Simion turned the handle. Unlocked. Lucius stepped past him into the room. A thrill raced up Simion's spine.

A soothing light gave the room a cozy quality. Soft snoring rose from a massive bed against the far wall. Lucius slithered toward the bed. The dagger was in his hand.

"Lothian!" a voice from behind him shouted. The Prince jolted upright and sprang out of bed.

Simion jumped. He hated being caught in the act.

"Kill him. I'll finish the Prince," Lucius said, all pretense of stealth gone.

Simion faced the voice. "MacCorkle."

His earlier rebuke from Isobel hardened his courage. He ran at Jake and drove his cruel, curved knife at Jake's chest. Jake caught his hand, spun Simion off balance, danced him into a tight circle, and slammed him into the wall. Simion bounced off the wall, and Jake turned him headlong into the edge of the doorjamb. The impact crumpled him to the floor like a sheet falling off a clothesline. Jake twisted Simion's wrist at right angles. The knife clattered to the floor. Jake's knee smashing into his face was the last thing Simion saw.

CHAPTER 26

Simion woke. He lay against the wall by the open door. Playing possum, he peeked through one eye. Lucius reclined against one of the upholstered chairs. His throat gurgled from a gaping cut. Blood covered his clothes and ran into an expanding pool across the stone floor. *I said you'd pay.*

Recovering his wits, Simion heard Lothian say to MacCorkle, "This treachery has the mark of the Droch Sìthe. Thank you, my friend. I did not see how you dispatched your man, but you saved my life with your warning. Where did you learn your fighting skill?"

"Army Rangers."

"Perhaps you will become my General instead of my Bard." Lothian smiled and embraced Jake. When he stepped away, blood covered Jake's clothes. A slash split Lothian's night clothes. They were filled with blood.

It was done. No one recovered from the cut of an enchanted dagger. Simion needed to escape.

"I will summon the guard. He will tell us all," Lothian said, nodding at Simion.

Simion shifted shape. As a large black dog, he rose and ran out of the door. Unsteady, he banged the door and thudded into the far wall before he got his footing. He heard footsteps close behind him.

He wobbled down the hall and across the landing toward the circular staircase. His four legs moved faster than the four behind him. Someone grabbed his tail. He spun, bared his teeth, snapped, and growled. They moved to either side. Simion lunged at Lothian's throat. Jake flung him back. He rolled and sprinted for freedom up the steps. A shout and thud behind him told Simion the dagger's poison won.

****

"Capture the dog." Lothian spoke in gasps. "There is no way out at the end of the steps."

Jake sprinted to the top of the stairs. The dog was gone. He sprinted back to Lothian who looked as gray as the residue ash in a fireplace. Jake carried Lothian down the steps. A group in night clothes, aroused by the noise, looked panicked.

"Get a doctor," Jake ordered.

"The Orb," Lothian whispered.

Jake threw Lothian over his shoulder in a fireman's carry and ran for the bedroom.

Lothian's clothes were soaked in blood. His wound was a deep gash that ran from his shoulder to the middle of his stomach. It gaped open like an ugly, toothless smile. A faerie placed the Orb at his bedside. Within seconds, it produced a thick mist that flowed around Lothian, covering him head to toe in a white mummy bag.

Minister Thish swept into the room. He motioned for Jake to step outside with him.

"As head of the Prince's council, I am in charge. I see blood on your clothes. Does it belong to our beloved Prince? Did you attack him?"

"What?" Blindsided by the false accusation, rage boiled. Jake's self-control hung by a thread.

"Answer my question."

"I saved his life."

"You say you saved his life. Do you have any witnesses?"

"Yes, but he went out a hole in the roof dressed as a dog."

"Best you answer my questions in a civil way, young man. Let me remind you, you are a guest. You came and we welcomed you. You walked the castle in the middle of the night, for what purpose, no one knows. You may well have killed your accomplice when you saw that your attempt on the Prince failed. We know you not. I am in charge until the Princess arrives. I will not tolerate you subverting my authority. Guards take our Bard," his voice dripped with disdain, "to the dungeon. I will question him at my leisure."

"Wait a minute. You can't lock me up because you want to. Listen to me. I helped the Prince. I stopped the assassination. I give you my word—"

"Your word. Your father was known to us, but you are not. You cannot ride his coattails and step into his role without earning it. Our Prince took your word, and he lies mortally wounded. Your word is worthless."

Thish raised his hands and spoke the language Jake did not understand. "*Ceangal prìosain*, MacCorkle, *seilear.*"

Starting with his feet and moving upward, each section of Jake's body froze like he was shrink wrapped. A scream caught in his throat, half uttered. Lothian's chamber, the people, the guards, and Thish whirled in a way that nauseated him, then they disappeared.

****

Briars tore at Simion's hide. Limbs smacked his face. He stopped for a second and chewed a painful pine needle out of his paw, but he kept moving. Panting and shaking, he stopped at the gate. Lucius had the key. The Prince's guards were coming. He had to get out and transform.

He poked his nose through. Nothing happened. No bolt of lightning. No thunder. He had come in as a man. What if the protective enchantments of the Gleane operate on humans, not animals?

Looking left and right, there was no fence. He trotted to his right, came to the end of the gate, and poked a nose across. Then a paw. Gingerly, he eased his body across an invisible boundary, expecting to be slammed back at any time.

CHAPTER 27

Stupefied, Jake knew neither where he was nor what was happening to him. Senses returned when he thudded against a stone floor. Muscles ached like he'd gone fifteen rounds with a prizefighter. A thin light eked through a single barred window in a massive wooden door. The room smelled of aging fruit, dusty vegetables, and onions.

"Well, at least I won't starve," Jake muttered sarcastically to himself.

An unexpected voice answered from the gloom. "No, you'll be well fed until the execution."

Jake jumped. "Who's there?"

Beyond the feeble light, the room was dark. Jake scowled into the blackest corner of his cell. Shadows flitted and danced into false shapes.

"Who's there?" Jake said again.

One shadow came together. A tall, gaunt figure rose and walked into the dim light. A pristine white robe caught the light and glowed. A tall cap rose to a point above his head. A wide leather belt decorated with gold and silver images hung around his waist. A windblown white beard was tucked into his shirt, and his hair ran wild around his ears as if he never touched it with a comb. His mouth seemed ready to laugh like life held some secret joke. When Jake saw his calm, comforting eyes, his mind jerked like a car out of gas, sputtering in fits and starts.

"Nathan Greenfield?" Jake's eyes sent the information to his brain, but his mind rejected it.

"Yes." The voice was calm with no trace of bother.

"You're—here?"

"Where else would I be?"

"But you're a lawyer."

"Sometimes. Right now, I have an important obligation to the Prince. Would you like to accompany me?"

"I can't. I'm locked in."

"That is not what I asked."

Jake reviewed the words in his head and nodded.

Nathan placed his hands on Jake's shoulders. "*Fly am prìosan gu lothian prionnsa.*" Nathan smiled at Jake and said, "Rough translation 'Fly the prisoner to Prince Lothian.'"

Jake's head rolled like he was on a tilt-a-whirl. When he stopped spinning, he stood at the exact spot from which Thish imprisoned him no less than ten minutes earlier. Nathan smiled, turned, and extended a hand for Jake to enter the Prince's chamber first. A small entourage of people, including Thish, gaped at him.

"How are you here? Guards!"

Thish raised his hands to intercept Jake. Nathan entered. Thish froze and bowed. Nathan ignored him and moved to the Prince's bedside. Nathan cocked his head as if he were listening for a personal message radiating from the Orb. Both hands dipped into the fog around the Prince's body. The room hushed. Satisfied, Nathan stepped away from the bed.

Thish spoke. "I am in—"

Nathan placed a finger to his lips as if he was shushing a child. "Please inform the Daoine Sìthe that their Prince's wound comes from an enchanted object. Thanks to the quick action by Mr. MacCorkle, he will recover."

Thish stepped forward. As bullying as he was to Jake, now he cooed like the most reasonable man in the world. Nathan waved him off.

"First, a message to the Princess that her brother is safe. I'll send it on the wind." Nathan closed his eyes. His lips moved making words, but he did not speak. He opened his eyes.

"Well come, Erceldoune." Thish bowed and tried to address him again.

Thish treated Nathan like royalty. Jake wondered what Nathan was to these people. Clacks mentioned Erceldoune, the Wyzard. *Is Nathan … Erceldoune? No way.*

Erceldoune ignored Thish.

"I am pleased you have come," Erceldoune said, smiling as he approached Jake. Thish sidled up behind him and talked to Erceldoune's back, prattling like a child needing parental approval.

"I have taken charge while the Prince is incapacitated and the Princess is absent," Thish said.

"Have you now?" Erceldoune did not turn or look at him. He grinned at Jake.

"I have. And I find this human may have had a hand in the treachery."

"Interesting. Your evidence?" Erceldoune turned on Thish, who took a faltering step backward.

"He moved about in the castle in the middle of the night." Thish spit the words out like hot soup. "He has the Prince's blood on his clothes. He admits being present when the Prince was wounded. I confined him until I can question him."

"Did you now?" Erceldoune became businesslike. "I praise your efficiency, Minister. Would you allow me to ask Mr. MacCorkle a question?"

"Of course," Thish stammered.

"Did you attack the Prince?" Erceldoune asked Jake.

"No. I warned him. There were two of them. They were going to kill him in his sleep. He killed the man who cut him. I disarmed the other guy, but he turned into a dog and escaped. I carried the Prince back here. That's how I got blood on my clothes."

"A plausible explanation, Minister Thish. I believe him. I take Mr. MacCorkle into my personal custody. I assure his availability for questioning, if necessary." Erceldoune turned a withering stare on Thish.

"If you guarantee it," Thish said. His words were mumbled.

"Do you have any doubt I can deliver on my word?"

"No, no, no, of course not."

"Thank you for extending me this kindness," Erceldoune said. "Come, Mr. MacCorkle."

Jake grinned, and Thish scowled. Erceldoune led Jake across the hall to a small room. In it were three straight-backed chairs and a small table. A window framed the patio and city outside. Studying Erceldoune, Jake felt an easy power ooze from him.

"Nathan, it is you, isn't it?"

"Of course, how did you like my entrance? But while we are in this world, best call me Erceldoune. I know what you saw and heard tonight. I witnessed Lothian's memory as I touched him. You saved the Prince. Before people know of your service, you will suffer some rough treatment from Thish. He is a crafty, ambitious man."

"He's a jackass."

"He can be that, but dangerous. Don't underestimate him. Now, tell me about your time here."

Jake relaxed. It was like chatting with his father at the breakfast table. Halfway through his story, it struck Jake—Nathan knew about his father and these People.

"Why didn't you—"

"I honored your father's wishes," Erceldoune said, anticipating Jake's question. "He requested I let you experience these People for yourself. Had I told you I was a Wyzard to a group of faeries … Your thoughts?"

Jake laughed. "I would have thought early Alzheimer's was kicking in."

"Have you considered your legacy as Bard?"

"It's over my pay grade. How can I help an entire people? I couldn't even—"

"Afghanistan?" Erceldoune asked.

"What do you know about it?"

"Possibly more than you."

"How?"

"The Orb has many gifts. One is following. As a child, you handled the

Orb. It followed you as you entered the military and went to war. War is nasty business. Things happened that called for you to be protected. I am not positive, but I believe it followed you and kept you safe."

"What are you saying?" Jake recoiled in shame. "What do you mean kept me safe? Why wasn't I taken when my men were captured?"

"I believe the Orb hid you."

Jake gripped the chair. Fear surged. His heart went blicky-blick. Breath strangled in his throat, and his voice cracked.

"Are you saying that Orb thing interfered in my life, and I didn't even know it?"

"Yes." Erceldoune waited for Jake's response.

"What does that even mean?"

"After the explosion, the Orb must have cloaked you, protecting you. I am unsure what happened next, but you went back to your men. Everything you did was honorable."

"Yeah, except abandon my troops."

"I have no knowledge of that. The Orb helped you."

"Why don't I remember any of this?"

"You demanded to be with your troops. You chose the responsible course. For that, your father and I were very proud."

"I don't want to be responsible for anyone but me."

"And yet, you fought for your Prince. He knows it. Before long, everyone will know. You will be a hero to the Daoine Sìthe."

Jake grew quiet. *Hero. I can't ….*

"Questions about the past are answered. Are you ready for the future?"

"I don't know."

Erceldoune waited. Jake delayed. A rush of anxiety clouded his thoughts. He felt defeated. *I can't ….*

"I want to go home." Jake said in a muffled voice.

"I will arrange it."

CHAPTER 28

A dim glow lit the hall. Guards stood outside Lothian's chambers. Others, including Thish, were gone. Erceldoune and Jake moved in silence across the landing and down the far hall. Outside Jake's room, Clacks paced back and forth like a caged tiger. Jake offered his hand. Clacks took it. Neither spoke. Jake went inside his chamber and closed his door, leaving Erceldoune outside with Clacks.

"Everything is my fault." Clacks's voice cracked. "I opened the entrance and failed to close it. I returned every hour, over and over, trying different enchantments, wracking my brain for an answer. Nothing worked. My faulty magic killed the Prince." Tears clouded his eyes.

"The Prince lives. As to fault, we shall see." Erceldoune and Clacks climbed the long circular staircase.

In the domed room, Erceldoune paused at the steps. He closed his eyes and touched the stone column with both hands. He sensed his way across every square inch of stone. He gazed at the right side of the opening and then the left. He ran his fingers along the edge. He stepped back and smiled.

"Show me your enchantment," Erceldoune said. Clacks stepped to the opening, moved his hands, and spoke the enchantment. The opening shrank a few inches before it popped back open. Erceldoune centered himself before the door.

"Be clear, show all here, now, appear," Erceldoune commanded.

Words in fiery gold letters glowed around the opening. In ancient Gaelic, it read: "Open is open. Close is open."

"Who knew you planned to open this room?" Erceldoune asked.

"No one."

"You told no other soul?"

Clacks thought.

"Minister Thish suggested it."

"A person inside the Gleane sabotaged the entrance," Erceldoune said.

"Someone inside our Clan helped assassins?" Clacks was incredulous.

"The person expected the intruders, came to the room, and enchanted the opening to do the opposite of your command."

"Minister Thish?"

"We cannot know without proof. What we do know is we have a traitor who wanted Lothian dead. We know how. We need to know who. A simple trap …" Erceldoune's voice trailed off as if he was speaking to himself.

"A simple trap, sir?"

"As to your earlier comment, Clackmannan, rather than cause the problem, you preserved vital evidence. The traitor had no opportunity to erase his handiwork. We will capitalize on your persistence. If you would be so kind, go to the hall outside Jake's chamber. Wait there and watch. Guard Jake until he is ready to leave. Guide him to the gate. Ask if you can accompany him home. If he will not let you, follow him, and intervene as needed. I fear he becomes a pivotal piece in a complicated chess match."

Down the steps and back to the hall they went. Clacks was so relieved he seemed to dance to his post. Erceldoune went to the other end of the hall, moved into a dark corner, and vanished.

Several people came and went, but no one ventured toward the stairs. Erceldoune rolled the events over and over in his mind. The conclusion was the same each time: the goal of killing a monarch is to rule.

****

In a twilight sleep, Jake recalled the dream. He was familiar with them now. It felt like he was walking through a door, becoming someone else, experiencing another life, and returning to his own body. His mind melded with Corcle as if they were twins, connected in body and mind during the dream but individual people when he was awake.

As Jake relaxed, the storyteller spoke.

****

"Can you train us to use your boats?" King Torrinn asked.

"Yes," I said. "A day at most. Since we travel downstream, you only need to balance and steer."

"You will accompany us," King Torrinn said. It was a matter-of-fact assertion, but I was shocked.

"Your Majesty, I am no soldier."

"No soldier is needed, only bravery. Courage, you have, but if you choose, you can wait with the boats. For this war, you will be our human." King Torrinn smiled.

I agreed to my small part. Our plan was to float the river, land on the island, and liberate the Orb. In the darkness, we would escape down river to the King's waiting army.

I returned to my room but slept little. In the morning, I left with two others. Our band consisted of myself, the King, and a slender knight who kept covered in a forest brown cloak. I could not see his face, and he had no interest in conversation. He carried a handsomely carved bow, beautifully made arrows, and a rich leather quiver. Beyond that, I discovered nothing of him. Our fourth member planned to join us later. I was boatman and lookout. Each person took a different route to a sheltered cove I knew above the island.

By horse, I traveled to my home and collected boats, rope, paddles, and other kit. With the small boats in a cart, I moved several miles upstream to our meeting place. This move required several disagreeable hours between the cart and a horse who refused to pull it. After more hours than I anticipated, I arrived at our training site.

In the remainder of the daylight, I taught each person to steer the coracles. No boat is easier to tip. One must stay balanced at all times, for it is a small circular craft, barely six feet around. I weaved oak saplings for a framework, stretched animal hides on the frame, and stitched it to the wood. Painted with pitch, it became waterproof. One man could sit safely in the middle and balance himself, but two needed to work together to keep it from tipping.

The slender youth did well. He managed the boat with ease and soon mastered steering. The King did poorly and was wet from the start. After one dunking, I walked into the water to help the King. As I raised him from the water, the King whispered, "We are watched."

I started to look, but the King dissuaded me. The youth overheard and slipped into the forest.

CHAPTER 29

In twilight sleep, Jake rested with the storyteller's voice resonating in his thoughts. Blinking eyes opened to an unfamiliar room. Momentary confusion flustered him until he remembered the previous night's incidents. The good times and friendship he'd felt faded away. Despite Prince Lothian's words, thoughts of shame and anger crept in. An urgency overtook Jake. *Before the town wakes up, before I have to face anyone, I want to be gone from here.* Jake jerked out of bed, gathered his few belongings, and headed out the door. Clacks surprised him.

"Have you been here all night?" Jake asked.

"Yes." Clacks behaved as if his waiting for him all night was the most natural thing in the world. The straightforward response took Jake by surprise, but his resolve returned.

"How do I get out of here?"

"Come. I will guide you." Clacks turned left and took the circular stairway down. Delicious smells drifted up the steps. Jake's stomach rumbled.

The kitchen, a large square room carved into the farthest back wall of the mountain, buzzed like a beehive. Young faeries in aprons bustled past them. One carried a leg of lamb. Another toted sacks of potatoes up from storerooms below. A third side-stepped past them with a hot pan of bread.

To the right, atop a wood-fired stove, water boiled for porridge. Biscuits and breads baked in the ovens below. Blue and white tureens, plates, cups, and saucers sat on an eight-foot, open-faced Welsh china cupboard that nearly touched the ceiling. An open door next to the cupboard revealed a deep storage room lined with shelves full of spices, sugar, flour bins, and barrels of all shapes. On a stout central table, twelve feet long, were bowls and a dusting of flour. Copper and silver pans hung from hooks above the table. Across from the steps, straight ahead, was a small, round-topped green door.

In organized chaos, one stable point existed: a large, cheery woman in an immense food-stained apron. She sat on a stool, bowls mixing before her, snapping orders and adding ingredients, a pinch here, a spoonful there while the huge bowls spun. Wisps of flour dotted her face, hands, and hair. She was the axis on which this world turned. She smiled and spoke to Clacks.

"Oh Clacks, it's good to see you, dearie. How are you keeping? Have you had your breakfast?"

"No. Would you be so kind?"

"You look to be traveling. We'll get you a bread with trimmings to carry in your hand."

"Have you heard our Princess is home?" she asked and busied putting two immense sandwiches together.

"When did she arrive?" Clacks asked. He hefted a sandwich of warm homemade bread, cheese, and ham slathered in mustard with both hands. He nibbled around the edge, looking for a place to start.

"She left Scotland as soon as she knew about her brother. Got here last night. I was her nanny, you know." The old woman beamed with unmistakable pride.

"The Princess?" Jake asked, both hands filled with his huge sandwich.

Clacks swallowed. "Prince Lothian's sister," Clacks said. "She's in graduate school at the University of Edinburgh."

"The attack happened last night. How did she get here from Scotland?"

"With magic, things you imagine are possible." Clacks smiled.

From the corner of the kitchen, an unmistakable voice raised over the din. "Jake? I heard you were here."

Whirling toward the voice, his breath caught, and his heart banged in his chest. Blood rushed to his ears and nullified the kitchen noise. A knot seized in his throat. *No way. It can't be.* Her last words to him leaped to his mind: "War is not a job with prospects." And it was over. Jake searched for the voice's owner. "Vivian?"

From across the room, she smiled and opened her arms. His sandwich hit the table. He wanted to swallow, but his throat was too dry to get anything down.

In four steps, he entered the cocoon of her warmth and rested there. Snuggled to her cheek, he forgot where he was. Forgot Thish. Forgot he wanted to leave. He pulled away, looked into her eyes, and drew back to her embrace. *Vivian. I love you.* If I could stay right here, be in her arms forever … The comfort of her arms transformed to shocked incredulity.

"How are you here?" Jake pulled away.

"Where else would I be? This is my home."

"Home?" His mind flashed to when they met at the library in undergrad. It took him weeks to get a date with her. She had been studying history … Celtic something. Myths and legends. Boring stuff. His mind skidded on a rough patch of reality. He'd taken her life, her love, for granted. Can she forgive me?

Vivian laughed. "Don't worry, Jake. Being a faerie isn't catching."

The kitchen work slowed as everyone eavesdropped. Like a cue from a movie director, the old nanny said, "What's everyone gawking at? Get back to work."

The clang of pots and scurry of feet picked up. Vivian stepped near him, while the others couldn't hear, and whispered, "Please, don't leave until I have a chance to talk with you—alone."

Jake tingled as her hair touched his ear. A chance to see her alone made his heart soar.

Clacks touched his shoulder. "Are you ready? I can show you a quick path to your truck." Clacks pointed the remainder of his sandwich at the small green door.

"No, I need to wait for a few hours." Vivian's urgency bothered Jake. It wasn't like her. "I want to avoid Thish. Where's a good place to hang out?"

"Outside the town would be best." Out the green door they went. Clacks turned right, away from the town and down a narrow alley carved behind the castle. The alley dead-ended at a stone wall. Clacks felt along the left side of the wall until his hand disappeared into the stone. He turned sideways, smiled at Jake, and slid into the mountain. A disembodied hand reached out and motioned Jake to follow. Feeling his way like a blind man, Jake pushed his hands into the section of stone where Clacks had disappeared. He detected an opening and glided inside.

CHAPTER 30

As Jake and Clacks left the tunnel north of the large field, daylight kissed the mountain peaks and twilight clung to the low places. An old road, part of the rail system to haul gold and timber out of the mountains, lay in front of them.

"How well do you know the Princess?" Clacks asked.

"We were in undergrad together. Those incredible eyes. She's amazing."

"Everyone in the Gleane would agree. I knew she followed you to university, but I never heard about her time there."

"Followed me?" Jake asked.

"It is legend how Princess Vivian followed you and your father around in secret each time he came for training. When you went to university for your undergraduate, she requested to attend. Her brother agreed. Everyone knew her real reason was to be close to you."

Vivian wanted to be close to me? The thought didn't fit his perception of her. He had pursued her. Undeniably, something happened when they were together. Not chemistry; that was too trite. More. A naturalness, a belief, unspoken, that they were connected. It was almost spiritual, and he knew she felt it the same as he. They never talked about it. She tried, but he wouldn't go there. And then, it blew up. *No. I blew it up.*

"The road passes a private sanctuary where you may wait for the Princess," Clacks said.

"How did you know I was waiting for the Princess?"

"What passed between the two of you in the kitchen was lost on no one."

"I guess I was kind of obvious." Jake grinned.

"Kind of." Clacks smirked.

Jake laughed as memories crashed in on him. Every time he saw her, she stole his breath. Auburn hair in a perpetual French braid, creamy skin that needed no makeup, tall, precise, but relaxed like a swan gliding across water.

Why had it never occurred to me she was a Princess?

****

Afton loved the fresh morning sounds and smells of the forest. Dew wet his boots as he ambled across the field and followed the small stream bed east. He was the Minister's son. No one questioned where he went or what he did. He liked it that way. A confusing question flitted at the edge of his consciousness. *Where am I going?* The thick parchment in his pocket reminded him. Important paper. Daft thing to do. Stick a paper under a rock. He wasn't sure why he did it, but mother knew.

Leaving the streambed, he approached the gate skirting the inside boundary of the Gleane. Since the attack, no one entered or left without a key. A key. Another perk. Few people had keys. Most keys belonged to Clan members working in the human world on Clan business. But he got a key any time he wanted. Mother was very clear about that. Being the Minister's son, he earned it.

Afton walked out the narrow lane to the junction where the cove road met the paved road. He restacked the stones.

From his pocket he took the rough, thick paper, raised the top stone, and placed it underneath. He retraced his steps, entered the gate, and got distracted by fresh deer signs. He tracked them north, eased into a thicket, and saw a doe and her fawn grazing. He was ten feet from them before they noticed. They ignored him. He left them and returned to the castle to complete his last errand.

****

All night, Erceldoune had sat in concealment at the far end of the hall. Before daybreak, he had watched Clacks and Jake leave together. Midmorning, Erceldoune's patience paid dividends. Afton Thish meandered down the hall. At the circular stairs, he pretended to admire a tapestry, checked the hall, saw no one, and sprinted up the steps. Minutes passed. Afton returned and ambled down the lower steps toward the kitchen, whistling like he hadn't a care in the world. Erceldoune rose and walked up the steps to the mountaintop room.

****

An old thirty-foot railroad bed cut a flat track around the base of the mountains. As it made a gradual right turn, Clacks swung left into a compressed thicket of trees, brambles, ferns, and mountain laurel. He faced the thicket, raised his hands, closed his eyes, and chanted several words that were inaudible to Jake.

A scraping, swishing, hissing scrunch came as plants pulled back their branches to open a crooked passage. Clacks stepped inside. Jake held back, unsure he trusted his eyes.

"What just happened? How did you do that?"

"One way we protect our sacred places," Clacks replied over his shoulder. The dense compact plants formed a darkened tunnel of foliage as if a hole had bored into the thicket three feet wide and ten feet tall. Jake reached out to touch it. It was as solid as a massive hedgerow.

The trail zigzagged through the underbrush and ended against two massive boulders, triple Jake's height, standing like silent watchmen at the entrance to a small meadow. Unlike the winter outside, the meadow was sheltered. Winds were calm, and greenery thrived. As soon as he stepped into it, Jake sensed a magical quality pervaded the place.

To the right, seven chest-high stones stood in a circle around a central pillar of equal height as if they were planted in dark green periwinkle. Manicured grass grew in all the open spaces. Clumps of flowering plants dotted the meadow. Trees, tall enough to offer shelter, but small enough not to overpower the space, spread across the lea as if placed by a master horticulturist. At the far end flowed a sparkling stream that pooled into a small pond.

Jake's hand rested on a pitted stone worn by centuries of weather. His fingertips traced the gray-green lichen dents and creases. "These stones must weigh tons. How did they get here?"

"We have our ways." Clacks's vagueness didn't bother him.

A sacred place. The words popped into his mind. Instinctively, Jake pulled a long satisfying breath deep into his lungs. As he exhaled, his body shuddered and his shoulders, freed from years of stress, dropped. Posture straightened. Peace descended in his mind. *If this is magic, I want some.*

At the shallow pond, water bubbled up from an unseen spring. Fond memories of the mountains overtook him. Opening the gate for Dad. Hiking the trails. Dad teaching him how to shoot. The plink sound when he hit the tin can. The water's white froth when a trout hit his fly. Hours spent talking and laughing around the campfire. Each long-absent thought rejuvenated him.

Jake roused as if he'd been sleeping. Clacks was gone. "How long have I been here?"

His heart thudded; Vivian was walking up the meadow. *I want to hold her. Touch her.* As if she read his mind, she turned aside before she reached him and sat on a dark gray boulder. He crossed to her. Fidgeting with a button on her dress, she asked, "Will you stay in the Gleane?"

"Why would I do that?" He grinned, thinking she would say to be with her.

"Because my brother is incapacitated."

Wrong answer. What's she playing at?

"What's that got to do with me?" *Why am I talking to her this way? I need to hold her. Apologize.*

"We have a traitor in the Gleane."

But he wanted her to say she needed him.

"Again. What's that got to do with me?" Harsh. *Not how I want to talk to her. Tell me that you need me to stay.* In his mind, he was pleading with her, but his words were scornful, aloof, and uninvolved.

"Your family has been Bard and Adviser to our leaders for six hundred years.”

“So I’ve been told. Since I’ve been here, I’ve been insulted, humiliated, locked up, attacked, and accused of murder. I discovered my lawyer is a Wyzard, my ex-girlfriend is a faerie Princess, and my father was murdered. My life is a lie. And you want me to hang around for the next act of this bizarre play. No thank you. I’m going home.” *What am I doing?* His heart pleaded with him to shut up, listen to her, stop being an ass, and apologize. His mind overrode his heart and demanded she beg. She didn’t.

“As you wish.” Her head dropped.

No. No. No.

He hurt her—again—and he knew it. She wouldn’t tell him what he wanted to hear, and he’d punished her for it. All his life he’d pushed people who love him away. Why?

Vivian kept her head down.

Was that a tear?

“I—” Jake started, but she vanished. He spun around, looking left, right, even overhead. Where did she go?

Regret throttled him. The same stubborn, hard-nosed, do-it-his-way attitude produced the same result. Vivian was gone.

Idiot.

“How did it go?” Clacks asked as he walked past the stones.

“Not well.” Jake shook his head. “How stupid can I be?”

Clacks shrugged as if no answer was needed.

When they reached the gate, Clacks said, “Erceldoune believes you are a critical player in an upcoming conflict. He wants to ensure your safety.”

“How does he plan to do that?” Jake’s voice retained a couldn’t-be-bothered tone because his mind was still on Vivian.

“He requests that I accompany you into the world of man. He does not make this request idly. He senses danger.”

“I can take care of myself.”

“No doubt that is true in your world, but you have entered the world of magic.”

Jake had backed into a position and couldn’t see an option that didn’t involve capitulation. He doubled down. “Magic or not, I think I’m done with this place.” Rather than admit the sadness that hurting Vivian caused him, he became numb and belligerent.

Clacks tried another tack. “I wish it were that easy. You thwarted an assassination. You dismantled a plan involving a traitor who knows who you are.”

Jake hadn’t thought about that. Defensive anger rose in his voice. “I don’t care. I’m done.”

“So be it.” Clacks vanished.

CHAPTER 31

On the Ministry's main floor, a type of court convened. Erceldoune entered.

Behind a heavy oak table in large, ornately carved, upholstered chairs, the three top ranking ministers, dressed in matching somber dark brown robes, took their places on a raised dais. In some ways, the scene looked like an old-style tiny high school auditorium, in others like a kangaroo courtroom.

Behind the dais hung a large, sky-blue flag depicting a man passing the Orb to a faerie with the inscription *Truth in Everything*. Beyond the table and chairs for the ministers, the room was bare except for one rather uncomfortable-looking, straight-backed chair provided for Erceldoune. Witnesses stood.

"I call this investigation to order," Thish announced in a loud voice. "We are here to discover the person or persons responsible for the attack on Prince Lothian. Presiding are Ministers Thish, Elliott, and Campbell."

From his surveillance, Erceldoune knew who and how. What he lacked was why. Why would Minister Thish's son help assassins attack Prince Lothian?

As a formality, Thish asked Erceldoune, "Would you like to sit on the platform with us?"

"No. I will be comfortable here." Erceldoune sat to the side of the raised dais. He asked no questions. Within five minutes, he closed his eyes. His breathing became calm and rhythmic.

Irritated by Erceldoune, Minister Thish pushed on. "Before you, I enter the following facts. The dead person is a faerie, unknown to the Clan. A second person escaped. A key with a chain was found, belonging to Bard John MacCorkle, taken from him when he was attacked and killed by Isobel, Wyzard of the Droch Sìthe. The assassins entered the gate using Bard John's key. How they found the mountaintop entrance, how they knew it would be opened, and how they knew the position of the Prince's chamber inside the castle are unknown."

"The dagger used was captured, an enchanted blade, sinister and evil. Our protections on the gate and forest would never allow an enchanted dagger in;

therefore, the dagger was given to the assassins after they entered the Gleane."

"There was one witness to the attack, Mr. Jake MacCorkle, son of our deceased Bard. His room was at the base of the stairs where the assassins entered. He claims he followed them down the hall and thwarted the attack by warning the Prince. He admits being awake and 'hearing sounds in the hall' prior to the attack. He admits being in the room during the attack. He had the Prince's blood on him. He resisted questioning and was allowed to remain free under supervision of Erceldoune, Wyzard to the Daione Sìthe."

"Furthermore, Clackmannan told me personally that he opened the mountaintop room and was not able to close it. Clackmannan may be a co-conspirator in this plot."

"Minister Thish," Minister Campbell said, "you present no evidence. We have not heard Clackmannan's testimony. Before you condemn an honorable personage of our Clan, who has no slur against his name, we should hear his testimony."

"Here, here," Minister Elliot agreed. Thish relented.

One by one, the Ministers interviewed everyone in the Prince's wing of the castle. Each suffered the same questions.

"Where were you when the Prince was attacked?"

"What time did you go to bed?"

"What did you see?"

"What did you hear?"

"Can anyone confirm your story?"

"Do you own a dagger?"

Nothing came of it. Within the hour, the interviews stalled but plodded on until lunch. Thish saved Clacks and Jake for last.

"Call Clackmannan," Thish said. The request was repeated outside the room and throughout the town as if on a loudspeaker. No response. They waited. Nothing. Erceldoune awoke.

"Where is Clackmannan?" Thish asked.

"I released him. MacCorkle also."

"You what?"

"Mr. MacCorkle asked to go home. I sent Clackmannan with him for protection."

"But I need to interview them both. I need to know if MacCorkle attacked the Prince. I need to know how he opened the mountain door."

"He did not. Clackmannan opened it, as you well know, Cornelius. I went there yesterday with Clackmannan and found it enchanted not to close on his command. This work was done by someone inside the Gleane." Erceldoune smiled as a beet-red color arose in the Minister's face.

Thish changed tactics. "I understand the family connection, but he is under suspicion for attacking our Prince. Clackmannan may well be his accomplice. How do we know he is an innocent and not a traitor?"

"Interesting question." Erceldoune stared at him like a parent expecting a guilty child to confess.

Several moments passed. The room was uncomfortably silent. Erceldoune asked, "Who suggested Clackmannan tour the mountaintop with Jake?"

"It was suggested to me, and I suggested it to him." Thish looked down before he rushed forward. "I don't recall who made the suggestion, but it was reasonable, and I passed it on. I was not in the castle but at my home. I have not been to the mountaintop room in months. Mine was a simple suggestion. I thought our guest would enjoy it. I did not have blood on my clothes. I have no dagger. I demand to interrogate Jake MacCorkle." Thish raised his voice.

"You took my word once regarding his innocence," Erceldoune said. "Have you changed your mind about me?" Thish squirmed under the Wyzard's gaze.

"I did not have an opportunity to question him." Thish's petulance rose.

"Question me," Erceldoune said, his voice rising ever so slightly.

Thish hesitated, feeling the full force of a powerful Wyzard's scrutiny.

A door opened. Grezil, and her son, Afton, entered carrying a basket with Thish's lunch. She softened the situation in a sweet sing-song voice like she was talking to children. "Of course, there are no questions for a person of your stature. But such a puzzling situation. Assassins enter our sanctuary, a place protected by your own powerful magic. They find the castle within thousands of acres, know the Prince's chamber, attack the Prince, and Jake MacCorkle is the only one present. It is most confusing as to what is true or not."

She reminded Erceldoune of a spider spinning a web. He said dryly, "Confusing for some, perhaps."

Erceldoune eyed Afton Thish, who looked like a schoolboy daydreaming in class. Erceldoune smiled at him, and Afton returned a dull grin.

"The Minister is correct. We have a traitor," Erceldoune said. "To work!"

Erceldoune rose, strode from the chamber, and left the Gleane. He made sure no one saw him leave and ensured it was widely believed, particularly by Thish, that he remained nearby. As he traveled, his appearance changed. His robe shifted to a blue pinstriped Brooks Brothers suit. His beard vanished. He stepped into his office on Piedmont Road in Atlanta as conservative lawyer, Nathan Greenfield, coming to work.

CHAPTER 32

Sitting behind the partner desk, Weir's fingers flexed like a spider doing pushups on a mirror. He trusted Lucius, but Lucius did not return, only Simion. Simion was expendable; Lucius was not. Simion was here; the Orb was not.

Simion stood before Weir's desk. A folded parchment lay unopened. Weir picked it up and read. "P lives." *Is my spy known?*

Isobel took the lead. "Well?" she asked. She moved around the desk to get in his face.

Before he answered, Simion sucked a deep breath and blew it out. Weir attended to every twitch. A brief, twisted smile flashed across Simion's face.

He thinks he controls this meeting. Weir sat back, waiting for the circus to begin.

"I killed the Prince as you ordered," Simion said in one exhaled breath.

"Where is the Orb?" Isobel's eyes gleamed like an addict anticipating a fix.

"MacCorkle interfered before I could search for it."

"MacCorkle? Why was he there?" Isobel asked.

Simion didn't answer the question. Weir's patience thinned. *Now comes the merry-go-round.*

"I used the key like you told us. I led Lucius up the trail to the mountaintop and entered the castle. I met the boy and got the knife. I found the Prince's chamber. I directed Lucius to keep watch, but the fool couldn't handle that simple job. I slipped into the Prince's chamber and was ready to strike when MacCorkle shouted to the Prince. I was quick. I struck a killing blow while Lucius fought MacCorkle. MacCorkle killed Lucius and attacked me. With my superior skills, I overcame him and would have killed him, but others came. I escaped."

Weir considered Simion's story. Simion's standard fare when he wanted to keep secrets was to offer some small truth and mix in lies until who knew which was truth and which was lie.

"You waited at the gate?" Isobel asked.

"Yes. No message came. I found this one under the stone on my way out." He indicated the parchment on the desk.

Isobel narrowed her eyes. "You are confident you killed the Prince?"

To Weir, Simion's hesitation spoke louder than his words.

"I saw him bleed," Simion said.

Weir tore a small piece of parchment from the note, crushed it into a ball, and hid it in his hand. "Your words tell me little. Is the Prince dead?"

"I saw—"

"You falter, Simion," Weir said. He opened his hand. The crumbled paper ball spun on his palm. He flicked it at Simion. Simion's eyes grew wide, but he was too slow to avoid what was coming.

"I—" The dart hit Simion in the chest with enough force to lift him off his feet and throw him into a chair across the room that cracked under the sudden impact.

"Now, I need the whole story. I enjoy a little incentive. Don't you?" Weir said.

Paralyzed, Simion saw a second dart coming in slow motion. Striking his forehead, it lodged there like a well-flung spitball. A sudden jolt like a Taser shook his body and arched it into a banana curve. When the charge subsided, muscles relaxed, and he slid to the floor like a rag doll. Before breath returned, another spasm struck. The second contortion twisted his face into a wind-tunnel grimace.

"Speak the truth," Weir said.

Simion jabbered the truth from the gate to his escape in exact detail.

"Where did you get this note?" Wier asked.

"After I escaped, I hid under the house on Karland, watching for MacCorkle to come back like she told me. I went back and found the note this morning." The Prince was not dead. Weir's upside-down smile deepened.

The agonizing interrogation over, Simion lay in a fetal position, unsure he could stand, with his long arms and legs wound around himself like a dead spider. Weir removed the second dart. Simion sucked short gulps of air.

Weir stood and touched Isobel's shoulder. As if she were mesmerized by Simion's interrogation, she struggled to take her eyes off him. Several seconds elapsed. Weir recognized the gleam in her eye. She roused. He motioned her outside.

"It seems the Daione Sìthe entertain a new Bard," Weir said. "Have we had other communication from the Gleane?"

"No, security has stiffened."

"We need to know with confidence that the wound killed the Prince. A new Bard hurts us. Summon our spy."

CHAPTER 33

Long branches screeched against his truck as Jake drove the narrow road away from the gate. At the junction of the cove and the paved roads, he turned right.

Next he knew, he woke, at home, in bed, fully dressed. He had no recall of the drive, arriving home, or lying down. The storyteller's voice rang in his ears as another dream occupied his mind.

****

The small expedition—myself and the youth in one boat, the King and Clackmannan in the other—rocked gently into the current. The float to the island was uneventful. As we landed, I knew guards must be nearby. We lifted the boats, carried them ashore, and turned them over to expose the black tar under-skin. We lay branches over and around them to change the shape. Into the long shadows along the bank, we crept.

Excitement grew, and I forgot to stay with the boats. At the crest of the first hill, we lay on our bellies examining the terrain. King Torrinn motioned for Clackmannan and the youth to circle right while he and I went forward. Bending low, sliding through waist-high grass, we crawled. The grass made a swishing sound that clogged my ears. I feared it screamed our presence to the enemy, but all remained quiet.

Sounds winged on the night air. Voices came from the center of the island. A flicker of firelight showed. We crept toward it.

A large fire blazed a dozen yards from a small tent. Warming around it were sixteen men at arms—too large a force for our little band to engage. The others returned with the same report. We withdrew to talk.

"Lazy dolts," King Torrinn whispered. "Separated, we may have overpowered them. As it stands, we die in the attempt."

"Perhaps the Orb is in the tent, and they guard it," Clackmannan said.

King Torrinn and Clackmannan crawled to the back of the small tent. They slit an eye hole in the fabric. No one inside. They widened the hole, entered, and searched the tent.

No Orb.

****

Jake opened his eyes. Each time he dreamed, the story advanced like a serial comic book. He looked down. He slept in the clothes he wore home. *Home from where? Oh, yeah, I went to the mountains.* "Didn't I? No. Couldn't have." Recent memories evaded him as if he were trying to tune in an indistinct radio station.

The house felt like the same quiet sanctuary he'd known since childhood. His room remained familiar, right things, in right places. Mangled covers indicated a rough night. Nothing new. Clock ticking loudly. Water and pills on the nightstand. The Corcle dream provoked other thoughts. *Faeries?*

"That's crazy ... a group of faeries living in a mountain I own. And Vivian's a faerie Princess? And my lawyer's a Wyzard." *Yeah, right.* Needing proof, he checked the house. The alarm was on; doors locked. *This is way stupid.*

In the kitchen, Jake started coffee. Bacon grease coated his hands as he pulled strips from the package and made his hands slip when he twisted the stove knob to four and threw the bacon into the frying pan. He cracked an egg over a mixing bowl. Bacon sizzled and popped. A thought tugged at him, ran away, and came back. If he didn't go to the mountains, then it's all dreams, those stupid ancient-time dreams. But if he did—

He cracked the last egg. *Dad's ashes?*

The urn was on the mantle where he'd left it. "I spread the ashes in the river. Or did I?"

He unscrewed the lid. No ashes. Was it true? Maybe ... or another bizarre dream?

Jake reached for his cell phone. Dead. In the kitchen, his finger walked down a list of numbers next to the home phone: *Nathan Greenfield.*

The number rang three, four, five times before the familiar voice spoke.

"Hello, Jake."

"How did you know it was me?"

"Caller ID."

Jake laughed. Hearing Nathan's voice soothed him. "I need to talk to someone."

"Who do you have in mind?"

"I hoped you."

"I would be delighted. What time and where?"

"Here. Is now, okay?" Jake asked.

"See you in thirty minutes."

Jake ate, showered, and dressed. Nathan's car pulled into the drive. From the front porch, Jake watched him get out. No robe, no beard, a lawyer visiting his client. He followed Nathan's glance toward a large black dog who slunk under a house across the way.

In the kitchen, the acrid smell of coffee percolating and sputtering filled the room. At the oak table, Nathan sat like a sphinx.

I can't read him. "Something happened to me, keeps happening to me, and I don't understand it."

"How can I help?" Nathan asked.

"I inherited the property where Dad and I used to camp? Right?"

"Yes."

"I went there to spread Dad's ashes?" Jake halted before he said the next part. *If I'm crazy, I might as well get on with it.*

"Yes."

"Living on that property inside the mountain is a Clan of faeries."

Nathan didn't hesitate. "Correct."

"I forget the name?"

"Daione Sìthe."

He knows. It's real. "And they have this glowing softball?" Jake heard and felt his excitement rise.

"The Orb."

"You are Erceldoune, a Wyzard?"

"Yes."

"Vivian is a Princess?"

"Yes."

The answers were simple, as if this truth was the most obvious thing in the world. Details of his visit flooded his mind. "Why am I having these vivid dreams about ancient times?"

"The Orb trains you to become Bard. Your first lesson is your heritage. Corcle is your ancestor who saved the King of the Daione Sìthe." In some deep recess, Jake knew it was true. The dreams were teaching him without his knowledge or participation. His stubbornness reacted.

"What? I didn't ask for any training. Why is it happening to me?"

"Had John lived, he would be teaching you, training you. The present Bard instructs the future Bard. Since your father died, as heir to the Bardship, the Orb recognizes your openness to learn, to train for the position. The Orb chooses the training method. Yours is dreams."

Jake leaned back, resting his head against the hard oak of his dad's chair. "You know about Afghanistan?"

"Yes. As I told you at the Gleane, the Orb followed you and protected you. Do you want to talk about it?" Nathan smiled at him with a gentle caring look that made Jake consider it.

Jake stared away, the ten-thousand-mile stare some veterans have when memories of combat arise.

"I'm not ready," he said in a murmured voice. *I can't … Can I?*

His mind raised the visage of Vivian's face yesterday. The single tear. Embarrassment boiled to his face. He would train. He would help her. But he couldn't go back now, untrained, helpless, useless against magic.

"Can I train here?" Going back to the Gleane was unthinkable until he had something to offer her.

"Perhaps. I advise against it. The Gleane is safer and the resources greater."

Jake's mind was set. "I'll do it here."

"As you wish; dreams can happen anywhere." Nathan continued. "Your first task is to learn the history of the Clan and your family. Your training will come in dreams. Once you have an orientation, you will need to move to the Gleane. There, you will use the Journal."

"A journal?"

"*The* Journal. Here, let me see, I have a library card somewhere." He patted his suit pockets as if he was searching for it. The twinkle in his eyes was unmistakable.

CHAPTER 34

Simion again stood before the expansive partner desk in Weir's office. The trauma of his earlier report reverberated in his body. Weir fiddled with a scrap of parchment, which made Simion wary. Isobel draped her small body on a tufted, orange leather couch to his right like an old-time movie star on a fainting couch. Simion read Weir's mood. *Dangerous.*

"MacCorkle has returned home," Simion said as he backed toward a chair in the corner. Before a response came, a chime rang in the hall.

"Answer the door," Weir said.

Simion went. Errand boy, that's all he was around here.

A tall, striking young man, exceptional even by faerie standards, stood on the step. Simion gazed at him. *I know him from somewhere.*

"Yeah. What do you want?" Simion growled.

"I was summoned." The voice was clear but there was something off, like the guy was half-stoned. Simion stared at him for a long instant to let the man know who was in charge before he pulled the door back and led him to the office.

Standing before the desk, the man shifted back and forth like a schoolboy waiting to report to the principal.

Simion could smell bad news coming, and bad news meant pain. Pulling deeper into his corner, he watched Weir with a caution that bordered on paranoia. If Weir started to spread the pain around, he didn't want to get any on him.

Weir looked up.

The young man began. "Greetings, Laird. I am Afton, Son …"

"You failed me." Weir's mouth slid into the upside-down horseshoe that bespoke disgust.

The young man staggered back as if someone slapped him. Simion knew how this dance worked. Weir would tighten his control like a thumbscrew. The man's spirit would shrivel until Weir's path was the only decision. Every person was grist, and Weir was the grinding stone. Pleasant in the early stages of a relationship, he positioned people like pawns on a chess board: cajoling, manipulating, and pushing them to take a position that appeared to be to their advantage. If they refused, he gutted their dignity, demoralized them with insults, and surgically removed their sense of worth. Offering power, fame, sex, wealth, or whatever fantasy they desired, he let it ride until he needed something, a return for the favor he granted. In truth, faerie gifts were all he offered, gifts that evaporated like mist when he had no further use for the person. This young man was about to lose—badly.

"Very well. How am I to know you can deliver the kingdom?" The young man recovered and spoke brashly.

The fool expects to negotiate?

Weir's right finger twitched. Simion's muscles shuddered in rich anticipation. The young man's breathing tightened, and his eyes widened like a weasel caught in a trap.

Nobody's gonna help you now, brother.

Weir's face contorted into a deeper frown, not a simple disapproving look, but a scowl where the corners of his mouth drooped so low that it looked like an upside-down "C" touching his jawline. Simion saw Isobel sit up, intent. He recognized the gleam in her eye as she waited for the hammer to hit the glass.

Here it comes.

"The Prince lives. Isn't that what you wanted to tell me?" Weir said in slow, measured words.

The statement disarmed the young man. Like a child afraid to tell a parent of a wrongdoing, he wheezed to get words out. "Lothian lives … Yes … The Orb heals … MacCorkle interfered—"

"Tell me." Impossibly, Weir's scowl deepened.

Simion loved this part. Weir knew, but he'd listen, compare, and skin every scrap out of him.

The young man's report ended.

"Finish the job."

The young man's jaw dropped. His voice became high and groveling. "Laird, we were not to kill him, only to grant access and deliver the dagger. We cannot—"

Weir wagged a finger back and forth like he was correcting an overstepping child. The upside-down "C" stayed at his jawline. Simion watched with glee as the young man, who moments before was a tall, striking figure, now shrank and twisted to avoid Weir's fury.

"What family standing will you have," Weir spit the words at him, "when it becomes known you opened the mountaintop, let assassins in, and a Thish enchantment lays upon the dagger?"

Begging was the best part.

"No, please—"

"Everyone makes choices. Yours is made. It is simply a further step along the same path." Weir closed his eyes. "Get out."

The young man froze to the spot. Weir didn't move. The man bowed and bungled out of the house.

Simion savored the tension like a fine wine.

"Who was he?" Simion asked Isobel.

"Afton Thish. Our spy."

"Bungling fool," Weir said.

"Will he do it?" Isobel asked Weir.

"When the time comes, his pride will evaporate. He is not the master," Weir waved his hand in a dismissive gesture, "only a stuffed puppet. Jake MacCorkle trains to become Bard. I feel it. As yet, he remains uncommitted, or he would not have returned home, but he's still an impediment. End the family line."

CHAPTER 35

After Nathan left, there was nothing for Jake to do but wait. The day dragged on. He tried to relax but was too excited. He wanted the vision to come now. Nothing.

After an early dinner, he checked the house security and went to bed. Sleep came at once—and so, too, a dream, accompanied by the now familiar voice of Corcle. Jake slipped into his story.

****

Clackmannan watched the King slit open the tent canvas and slip inside. He followed. A thorough search revealed no Orb. Hidden within the tent's folds, Clackmannan and King Torrinn listened to the men around the fire.

"I don't like being around that thing," a heavy-set soldier said. "My cousin told me it would strike you deaf and blind if you look at it. I'm glad we buried it."

"Where is it?" a young recruit asked.

"Never you mind about that," the heavy-set soldier said.

"Over that way," a third man said, inclining his head to the south.

King Torrinn and Clackmannan crept from the tent.

"How will you find it?" Clackmannan asked.

"It will find me."

****

Corcle's voice faded, replaced by another. Jake willed Corcle back, to experience more of the dream, but it and his voice, swirled away.

A different, distant, woman's voice called him. Nearing consciousness, Jake reasoned, *Nathan said the Orb would use dreams as my training method. This new dream must be training.* He let his awareness slip away, but his body tensed, unlike earlier dreams. The faint voice amplified.

Sweet and beckoning, she said, "Awaken, MacCorkle, awaken. Be here with me." Trudging up toward consciousness, away from Corcle, felt like swimming through molasses as he sought the new voice. Awake and out of the dream, senses worked, but body movement was non-existent, like the motor connection from his brain to his body had short circuited and he lay paralyzed.

"MacCorkle, you wish to be Bard, a Wyzard?" Soft and gentle, she prodded him. "Here in your bed lies your true power. Alone. Unable to move. Think of your parents. Picture them in your mind. Mother dead many years ago, father dead only a few months. I. Killed. Them. Both. Your mother. And your father." Harsh and taunting, her words ripped into him.

Jake strained to open his eyes. His eyelids flickered open briefly, and he could just make out a black shadow mixed among shards of gray light. The words screeched in his mind. What did she say? *Killed … Dad … and Mom.*

Whispering to him like a lover was his father's murderer. Shock waves jolted his mind awake, but his body didn't react. Completely defenseless, he begged to get up, protect himself, exact retribution, but his body lay inert. Fear turned to agonized rage. He wrestled to open his eyes, kick his legs, flail his arms, but his body lolled as if paralyzed by a powerful anesthetic.

"Soon, very soon, tonight even, I might kill you."

A panicked scream rose to his throat, but his ears heard only a stifled grunt. A nauseating reek of perfume assaulted his nostrils as she taunted him like a cat toying with a mouse.

"MacCorkle, you chose badly. The People of Peace cannot protect you. They cannot protect their Prince. They are deluded fools." She knows about the Prince. Does she know about Vivian? Helpless images floated to mind. He fought them. *I can't … Must … get free.*

Dimly pulsing, the Orb flashed into his mind. The chain around his neck warmed like metal left in the sun. Blocking her voice and stench, he focused on the chain. The Orb's light brightened. Jake willed his right index finger to move. Nothing. Memories of the Orb arose, the light in the dark tunnel, the healing cocoon around Lothian. A sensation burned the back of his hand like a concentrated ray from a magnifying glass. The warmth from the chain moved across his body to his right shoulder. Unnoticed in the folds of the cover, his right index finger jerked.

On she droned, baiting him in a confident, singsong voice. "Once upon a time, a family joined a Clan—the wrong Clan. From the beginning, bad things happened. A disease moved through the family tree, cutting off the limbs. First, the mommy limb died. Then the daddy limb died. And the baby limb was left all alone. The baby limb didn't die right away. No, not right away. The baby limb withered, grew weaker and weaker. So sad. It withered away." Her whining, pitying voice that had wounded him earlier now strengthened his resolve.

Jake's eyes fluttered, and he demanded they open. They half-complied. Through slits, he saw a woman bending close to him as if she were attending the bed of a sick person. A dim light from the bathroom backlit her odd-shaped head, but her face remained shadowed. Keep talking, I just need a little more time.

"While the baby dithered, waiting for something to tell him which way he should go, while he played at his life, the world moved on and left him behind. Poof—it all disappeared. The poor, poor thing was left helpless, lying in a bed, unable to move a finger. In the end, even his body abandoned him."

Closer and closer, she moved toward his face.

"MacCorkle is home. Alone." An inch from his ear, her voice changed from singsong and patronizing to sarcastic and caustic. She goaded him in a harsh, rage-filled whisper. Spittle smacked his face. "No help will come for you unless …"

Jake wasn't listening anymore. He begged his arms and legs to move, but except for his finger, his body responded like he'd had a spinal sedation. The Orb, King Torrinn, Prince Lothian, Clacks, Vivian, healing mist, his father's murder, even Thish spun through his mind, strengthening the Orb's connection to him. Warmth traveled to a second finger.

"The moral is choices kill people. A choice comes for you." Her sarcasm rose and fell, but she hadn't attacked him yet. One moment more …

Jake concentrated again. Three fingers moved. Clearly in his mind, the Orb brightened. The warmth progressed to his hand, wrist, and forearm. A sharp warmth flowed down his shoulder to his elbow.

"For centuries, your family was servant—and slave—to that worthless rabble. Would you prefer to be a King?"

Inch by inch, feeling came into his right side. Almost ready. One arm was all he needed.

"Now, it ends." She moved her head back.

Like a rattlesnake striking its prey, his right arm grabbed her throat. The woman thrashed like a pinned worm stuck on a hook. Jake squeezed her neck until a gurgled shriek eked from her throat.

Inch by inch, he dragged her face forward until they were nose to nose. A deep, guttural growl came from him. Her eyes widened, and terror seemed to consume her. While she flailed at his head with her fist, fingernails dug deep into his forearm.

"That ain't gonna do nothing. I got you, bitch." He spat the words at her, tightened the vise on her neck.

She twisted and struggled to rise. Jake slammed her back to the bed. His left arm came alive. Reaching back to punch her, he aimed as strong a blow as he could muster. Before it landed, she drove her nails deep into his right forearm and jerked free. The sudden release rolled her off the bed and bounced her against the far wall. Coughing and gasping for breath, she steadied herself.

"You touched me! Pay!" A dagger appeared in her hand. She shrieked toward him. Running footsteps reverberated down the hall.

A massive explosion blew her through the drywall into his father's bedroom. Sprinting through the doorway came Clacks, a small spinning disk loaded on his hand.

The woman lay unconscious. Jake put out a hand to steady himself against Clacks. A noise came from the hall.

Over Clacks's shoulder, Jake saw a huge, black dog lunge for Clacks's neck. Jake dragged Clacks down. The growling beast sailed six inches overhead. Without stopping, it bounded through the hole into his father's bedroom. It skidded across a throw rug, legs scrambling, nails clicking as they cut the hardwood. The next instant, the dog became a man.

Clacks aimed a spinning object through the hole. Before it struck, the woman and man melted to mist. In his father's bedroom, all that remained was her horrid perfume.

Still unsteady, Jake sat back on the bed. "Who was that?"

"Isobel, a hunted person," Clacks said.

"She entered my dream and paralyzed me. She said she killed my father … and mother." Loss touched Jake's heart. He shoved it away. When he was four years old, his mother had disappeared. The first loss of many that decided how he would handle others who might have loved him. *That bitch murdered my mother?* Jake's rage shriveled his loss like fire consumes paper.

"How did you break her enchantment?"

"How? I don't know. I kept thinking about the Orb and trying to move until it happened. Why didn't she kill me when she had the chance?"

"She meant to wither your will to live and turn you to evil, but the chain your father gave you is enchanted. She could not touch you while you wore it. When you touched her, the chain's protection was nullified. Breaking a paralysis enchantment is difficult, even with the help of the Orb, and you have done it twice as an untrained human …" Clacks shook his head.

The adrenaline wore off. Jake's arm ached. Several deep gouges showed in the meat of his right forearm. Blood dripped down his fingertips.

"Is this enchanted?" Jake held out his bleeding arm.

"No. As you crushed her throat, the last thing on her mind was enchantment."

"Where did you come from?" Jake asked.

Clacks smiled. "I will strengthen the protections on the house."

CHAPTER 36

Grezil brooded as she sat and waited, surrounded by things she loved: the sewing box that belonged to her mother, the famous writing table that had been in the family for centuries, and her favorite upholstered chair that Cornelius had given her on their first anniversary. Her fingers absently rubbed the tufted buttons. It was an overstatement to say she loved this life, but she enjoyed it and the status it offered. Until recent events, to give it up would have been unthinkable. Now, her regret was resigned. It had to be done. The grandmother clock, another gift from her husband, clanged ten unmelodic times. The tone aggravated her taunt nerves.

Afton's simple task took longer than she expected. *Did he make a dog's dinner of it?* On edge, she waited like a coiled spring. Erceldoune circled and drew nearer. She knew it was a matter of time before—

The latch click-clacked in the kitchen.

"What did he say?" Grezil asked as Afton hurried into the parlor.

"He thought the Prince was dead," Afton said. Grezil knew better but waited. "He was angry when I told him the attack failed. Mother," Afton's voice cracked, "he wants us to kill Lothian. It is one treason to open the entrance but another to kill the Prince by our own hand." His voice raised into a high-pitched wail.

Grezil put her finger to her lips to shush him. She walked to the door, opened it, and looked out. No one. She motioned him into the farthest corner of the room away from the door and window. "In all things, mind your tongue. We risked opening the entrance and planting the knife. We must measure a new risk. No one knows what we did unless they hear you babble it out."

His face reddened.

"My beautiful boy, as your father does, you sag under pressure. Let me consider his proposal. Tell it to me again."

"It was no proposal. It was a demand. I have never felt such power. He wants it done and soon."

"Where is Erceldoune?"

"How should I know? I was away." Grezil tolerated his outburst but found it beneath him.

Simpering child. "Go and find him. I want to know where he is and ensure he is not nearby. Bring word back to me." She grabbed his face and turned it to look directly into her eyes. "Do not—I repeat, do not—speak to him or go near him."

Resigned, Afton leaned forward. She kissed his forehead.

Afton meandered through the town, asking after Erceldoune. Everyone had seen him, but no one knew where he was, exactly. What report should he make to his mother? *Erceldoune was everywhere … and nowhere … like a Wyzard.* Afton smiled.

****

Barely conscious when they transported, Simion carted Isobel in his arms like a child. He did it for Weir. Had he left her to her own devices, she would have been captured. Her capture would be blamed on him. And no amount of sniveling would have saved him.

Isobel leaned on him as they staggered up the drive like drunken people. As if Weir were expecting them, the door opened.

"What happened?" Weir asked.

Simion set Isobel in a chair. "She attacked MacCorkle, but a faerie, a Wyzard, intervened. He hit her with a dart. I got her out before she was captured."

Weir stared at Isobel. Her head bobbed slack against her chest. Fresh cuts covered her face and arms. Blood dappled her clothes. Her legs splayed open like they wouldn't support her and she wasn't going to ask them to. Purple finger marks discolored her neck. She didn't speak.

"What happened?" Weir asked her.

Without raising her head, she spoke into her chest, "Everything is as Simion says."

Simion watched Weir's mouth curve down. Stepping away in case Isobel was about to catch his wrath, Simion waited for his attaboy.

Weir paced. "Our spy is in jeopardy," he said.

"What do we do?" Isobel asked.

"It is out of our hands. Our spy is resourceful. We may yet …" He hesitated, thinking, before he said, "Let it play out."

No praise coming to him, Simion slunk from the room like a disheartened child.

CHAPTER 37

The bell twinkled and bounced as Grezil opened the door to the butcher shop. Sausage, lean ham, and ground meat were displayed in the glass butcher case. The sparkling white porcelain was immaculate. Behind the counter stood an old man with bright, quick eyes, a wool touring cap, and a bloodstained leather apron. To his right behind a desk sat a gray-haired woman sorting papers with the pleased look of a grandmother.

Grezil approached the counter and overheard the butcher tell his wife, "When I delivered the meat this morning, Nanny told me that the Prince is receiving visitors."

"I am so pleased to hear it. Erceldoune said he would recover. And, I am happy to see our Princess home. She was gone too long." She beamed at Grezil.

"Good morning, Grezil," the butcher said. "How may I serve you?"

"I need some stew bones to make broth. Leave some meat on them this time. Not like the last ones."

The butcher gave her a hard look. Grezil ignored him. With meaty stew bones wrapped in white waxed paper, she left the shop.

Shoppers flowed by her as she walked the five minutes to her home. The finest house in town, near the castle, easily recognizable as a home of distinction, with all the opulence of a mansion, she'd insisted on it. Opening the gate, she entered the white picket fence, the only house inside the mountain that had one, and went to the kitchen door around the side. She handed the package to her cook. "Prepare a broth for the Prince."

As the soup boiled merrily, Grezil hovered in the kitchen. She tasted the soup and added a seasoning here and there. At eleven o'clock, she said to the cook, "Take the rest of the day off."

"Who will serve the Minister his lunch?"

"I will manage it today. Enjoy your afternoon." Grezil dismissed her.

At twelve sharp, Thish arrived for lunch. Grezil ladled the soup into his bowl but held it back.

Afton arrived. "The soup smells delicious."

"Before you eat, you must take this soup to the Prince. No dawdling. Go straight to the castle. I want him to enjoy it while it is hot. Be sure he eats it and share some with the Princess."

"But I'm starving," Afton said.

"Do as you're told." Grezil turned and poured broth into a small pot. She noticed Afton slip a spoon into his pocket. *It's just as well.*

Afton picked up the pot and started for the door.

"Ahem," Grezil said.

Afton stopped and dropped his forehead for her kiss. She gave it and pulled him into her breast for a long hug.

"What's that for?" Afton stepped back and looked at her oddly.

"I just wanted a hug before you go. Do as I told you. Do not eat before the Prince does. You may eat with him if he permits it and be sure and save enough for the Princess." Afton nodded and left on his errand.

"Where is my soup?" Thish asked. "The Prince gets his before I get mine in my own house."

"It was too hot to serve." Grezil placed his soup, a slice of cheese, a loaf of bread, and a mug of ale on the table. She stepped back, removed her apron, glanced at Thish as he ate, and left the kitchen.

A large multicolored carpet bag was behind her chair in the sitting room. She picked it up and walked out the front door. The streets bustled. Several people spoke. She smiled and nodded. Looping behind the castle, she exited the upper entrance.

Once in the forest, her pace quickened. Through the woods she hurried until she came to the gate. The key fitted the first lock. It was the same key taken from the intruder who attacked the Prince. The same key that had belonged to John MacCorkle. It was her key now, stolen from her unknowing husband.

The red clay dusted her shoes as she stepped off the road, found a rock, placed a minor enchantment, and left it there—just in case she may need it later.

"A wind to travel. A wing to ride. O'er the distance make great stride. Bring me home where he abide."

A gust of wind rose around her, and she rode it away.

****

At his desk, Erceldoune, disguised as Nathan, ruminated. *Why not go to the source?*

He took a deep breath and, as he exhaled, pictured an old enemy, one he rarely thought of, but one he trusted, in a vigilant way.

A gruff voice spoke to him, "Erceldoune, what do you want?"

"I have a question."

After a pause, the gruff voice responded in a controlled manner like a cautious banker assessing a poor risk. "Ask."

"Are you prepared for war?"

"War. What war?"

"War with the Daoine Sìthe."

"We want no war."

"Then, the truce remains satisfactory."

"Yes." Contact ended.

Nathan placed his fingers to his temples and hailed Vivian.

"Can you talk?" Within seconds, a reply came.

"Lothian sleeps. Is he the one you want?" Vivian said.

"I wish to speak with you. Use the Orb. I want a record."

A quarter-sized dot of light appeared six feet in front of him. It expanded until it was the size of an oval vanity mirror. In the space was Vivian's face.

"I know the spy," Nathan said.

"Who?"

"Let me give you some information you do not have. After the attack, Clacks reported to me that he opened the mountaintop and could not close it. As you know, it was the entry point for the assassins. When I investigated, I found it enchanted. The assassins received the enchanted dagger after they entered the Gleane. The assassins came from outside, the dagger and mountaintop enchantment inside. Afton Thish removed the enchantment from the mountaintop."

"No … Afton?"

"Both enchantments, door and dagger, are beyond Afton's skill. Jake's involvement and timing made him a logical suspect. Thish seemed eager to convict him. I spoke with the Droch Sìthe. They deny involvement. Your thoughts?"

The blood drained from Vivian's face. "Our Minister betrays us?"

"Yes," Nathan said. "Or someone close to him. They failed once but will try again."

"I will strengthen enchantments on the Gleane. Set patrols on the parameter. Command the Orb to protect Lothian, and call a Council for tomorrow morning. Then I will question Thish, Grezil, and Afton."

"A strong strategy," Nathan said. "Vivian, someone wants the Gleane and the Orb. To have it, they need to remove both monarchs." Nathan waited for his last words to sink in.

Vivian's color returned. "Let them come."

CHAPTER 38

Vivian acted swiftly.

"Strengthen the perimeter enchantments to the highest level," she said to the Orb. "No one enters or leaves except by key."

She left the room to organize patrols and sent for three skilled fighters. She met them at the castle steps.

"Come with me." She led them down the wide staircase. At a trot with Vivian in the lead, they moved like a military unit two blocks to the Thish house. People stepped out of the road to let them pass. All was quiet.

She pointed to one of the men. "Go to the kitchen door."

Another banged on the front door. Nothing.

"Break it in," Vivian said.

Both men put a shoulder to the door, and it splintered. The front room was empty. They searched the house.

In the kitchen sitting at the table was the Minister. His frozen eyes looked into a place miles beyond this life. His left arm was in his lap. His right arm hung limply by his side. A spoon lay on the floor in a small splash of soup. His face showed only a trace of soup that ran from his gaping mouth. Dribbled drops were on his chin and jacket. The jacket showed his rank as Minister, one he would never hold again. Grezil was gone. Her belongings, except for a few items, remained in the house.

An alarm went off in Vivian's head. She hitched up her dress and ran.

****

Afton was unhappy. His mother denied him food, basic sustenance. He would do as she asked, but not now, not right away. He would show her. He dawdled. He window-shopped his way across the city. Crisscrossing the streets under the Swan Pub, he headed in the general direction of the castle, but he killed time to show he was his own man.

Both the saddle maker stitching brown leather saddlebags and the silversmith putting the finishing touches on an elegant gown for an upcoming ball nodded to Afton. Smells of fresh baked bread stole around the corner and summoned him. He ordered a sticky bun, sat at the counter, and stuffed the sugary treat into his mouth. The soup pot steamed next to him. He glanced at it. He licked his fingers and took the purloined spoon from his pocket. One spoonful of soup wouldn't hurt. An odd, guilty, urgency clutched him. Afton changed his mind and hurried to the castle, seeing Princess Vivian hustling with several men in the opposite direction. None of his business. The castle was near.

CHAPTER 39

"Afton Thish," the herald announced.

Prince Lothian sat up in bed, bandages looped around his torso and over his left arm.

"Afton, well come," Lothian said and smiled at him.

"I am glad you are better. Thank you for letting me visit. Mother sends soup to mend you. She demands you eat it while it is hot." Afton grinned.

Lothian understood this bit of humor about Afton's mother. He laughed and waved him to his bedside. Afton bowed and carried the pot to the Prince. He handed Lothian the pot, stepped back, and waited.

Lothian opened the lid. A fragrant aroma filled the room. He called for a spoon, dipped it into the soup, blew on the steaming liquid, and moved to take the first mouthful.

The entire room turned a deep scarlet color. Surprised, Lothian hesitated with his spoon in midair.

The Princess came at a run, dashed to the bedside, and lowered Lothian's hand. She put the spoon into the pot and took it away from him. She turned on Afton.

"Guards," she shouted.

Two men who accompanied her to the house came in.

"Arrest him for treason."

Afton didn't flee. He stood with his mouth hanging open. "What have I done?"

The guards pinned his arms against his sides.

"Your treachery is known, Afton Thish," Vivian said.

"What? I've done nothing."

The guards dragged him away.

Alone with Vivian, Lothian looked as shocked as Afton had been. "How could this happen? One of the most respected families in the Gleane. My friend. A trusted Minister to the People. How did Erceldoune know?"

"He has his ways. He told me Afton was the spy and to prepare for a second attempt on your life. I left your bedside to improve our defenses and almost lost you. His father is dead, killed by the same broth." She trembled.

"Minister Thish? Dead?" Lothian stared at Vivian, a feeling of horror creeping up his throat.

"I saw him dead in his kitchen minutes ago." Vivian sat down on her brother's bed.

"Did Afton kill him? Where is Grezil?"

"Grezil is missing. Her housekeeper says Grezil prepared the soup. She is the spy. I placed Afton in the cellar. I need to understand his part in this. I plan to interview him. Would you like to come? Do you feel up to it?"

Lothian leaned on Vivian. "Why did he betray us?"

****

Vivian helped Lothian down the stone steps, past the kitchen level, and into the storerooms below. The Orb's light guided them. The earthy smell of freshly plucked vegetables met them. On the left, dusty and disused items cluttered shelves that extended from floor to ceiling. On the right, a heavy oak door with a small window led to a vegetable storage area that doubled as a hardly used dungeon.

Afton sat on sacks of potatoes with his back against the wall. He paid no attention to the light and did not look up when Lothian and Vivian entered.

"Afton," Lothian said quietly.

"Why am I in this cellar?" Afton asked.

"You tried to poison me." Lothian's feelings leaped out.

Afton reacted like Lothian spoke a foreign language. "Kill you?" he asked, his voice clear. "No, the soup was to heal you."

"Where did the soup come from?" Vivian asked.

Afton stared at Lothian with the face of a child, not comprehending. "I don't understand why you did this to me. We are friends, aren't we? Didn't we play together as children? Didn't I court your sister? Isn't my father your closest adviser?" Afton's face expressed honest confusion.

Lothian changed tactics. "When did you see your father last?"

"At lunchtime, he was home for his midday meal. Then, mother sent me with the soup."

Lothian glanced at Vivian.

"And your mother, where is she?" Vivian asked.

"She's at home serving him his meal. What's this all about?"

"Will you tell the truth?" Vivian asked.

"Truth about what?"

"The soup you brought to Lothian."

"It smelled wonderful, didn't it? I was so hungry, but I was to bring it to you." Afton said, nodding to Lothian. "And, I had strict instructions not to eat any myself, even if you gave me some, until I offered it to the Princess." A sincere, earnest look radiated from him, showing no deceit.

It was becoming obvious to Vivian that he had no idea what he'd done and that the soup was to kill both monarchs. "Afton, did you know the soup you brought was poisoned?” Vivian asked.

“Poisoned? No, it couldn't be. It smelled too good. I started to eat some myself, but it was forbidden,” Afton said with the wistful innocence of a hungry child.

“It was,” she said.

“No, I would never hurt Lothian. He is my friend.”

“Do you know that your father is dead? Poisoned by the same soup.”

“No, he's probably back at work by now.”

“Did you know your mother has left the Gleane?”

“No, she's at home.”

He denies everything. He can't be that thick. A deep enchantment? Vivian became direct. “Afton, hear me. Your father is dead. Your mother has fled. And you delivered poisoned soup to your Prince.”

“No. Everything is all right. Everything is fine. You'll see.” A boyish grin shown from his handsome face. “Can I go home now?” He eyes blinked drowsily.

“You must wait here for Erceldoune.”

Afton accepted her words, leaned back against the wall, and appeared to sleep.

Vivian rose and motioned to her brother. “This is beyond my skills. Erceldoune will have to sort it.”

At Lothian's speed, they moved back to his chambers. Vivian sat on the bed next to him.

“You saved my life. To repay you, take my half of the Gleane,” Lothian joked.

Vivian did not laugh. Lothian was all the family she had. “Don't turn those ghost eyes on me.”

She trembled. Her mind raced. Who would want her brother dead? Grezil? Another?

Vivian slowly shook her head. “I need to speak to Erceldoune.”

CHAPTER 40

Cold water stung his ripped skin as he washed his arm over the kitchen sink. He dabbed the oozing blood with a flat pad of paper towel. After treating it with antibiotic ointment, the marks looked like an old roadmap leading to dead-end canyons.

"We must get back to the Gleane," Clacks said.

"How? Drive?"

"Faeries have other rides." Clacks placed his hands on Jake's shoulders. He spoke several odd words. The kitchen disappeared. Jake's head went tilt-a-whirl, but he maintained his bearings. Unlike his travel with Erceldoune and earlier inside the Orb's fog, he kept his eyes open as they traveled. To the side, the world flashed past like the view from a supersonic train. To the front, the land, roads, trees, and rising sun were clear and bright. The turn to the Gleane gate appeared and disappeared. Movement slowed. Clacks motioned for him to put his feet down, as they landed twenty feet from the gate. Cold air rushed to fill the space vacated by their travel cocoon. Amazing. Rather than confused and disoriented as earlier magical travel had left him, Jake felt exhilarated.

Jake pulled his key. The chain clanged, a disruption to the still morning. With the gate secured, they retraced their earlier route to the alley behind the castle.

People, many voices, talking at once echoed up the alley. The noise sounded like a bumblebee trapped in a jar. Around the wide ministry steps, the entire population of the Gleane stood, each wearing a black armband, buzzing in hushed tones.

Did the Prince die?

In unison, the people bowed. The Prince, with his arm around Vivian, walked onto the patio above the crowd. *Thank God.*

Lothian motioned for silence and spoke to the crowd. "On this sad occasion we mourn our fallen Minister, Cornelius Thish. He was a loyal servant to the Daione Sìthe. He managed our fortunes. He never shirked his duty. We are saddened by his untimely death. Our Clan celebrates his life and accomplishments."

"Let's wait inside," Clacks said. The kitchen was oddly silent. Pots and pans, trays and dishes waited for workers who were listening outside. The dull smell of metal, soap, and food pervaded the quiet. At the circular steps, they went up and across the landing toward Prince Lothian's chambers.

"What do you think happened?" Jake asked Clacks.

"I don't know. The spy? But that makes no sense. Why would he kill Thish?"

Through the round kitchen door, they walked upstairs and found Erceldoune, Lothian, and Vivian in the small conference room across from Lothian's chambers, looking grim.

Clacks bowed to his Prince, Princess, and mentor. Jake bent at the waist but didn't pull it off. *I don't know how to do this.* Lothian embraced them like prodigal brothers.

Vivian and Lothian wore small silver crowns. Lothian was dressed in a deep purple tunic, a vest embroidered with gold threads, and gray pants. A substantial gold chain garnished with squares embossed with ancient symbols lay around his neck.

Vivian's sky-blue dress was inlaid with silver garlands of leaves and vines and flowed to her ankles. A loose, thin, silver belt adorned her waist. Vivian, more beautiful than he had ever seen her, gave him a slight nod but no smile. Jake gawked. They looked like a Prince and Princess. *How can I make it up to her?*

Erceldoune wore his white robe and cap, his normal glow dampened by the circumstances.

Lothian relayed recent events in the Gleane, and Jake told his story. Erceldoune concentrated on every word and nodded, but made no comment.

****

Simion sat in the corner. *I'm sick of this.*

Isobel limped to the orange couch and gingerly sat. Weir said nothing—no greeting, no question after her health, nothing. The less Weir and Isobel spoke, the more left out Simion felt. When they talked, it was about inane issues. Did the gardener come? Who called earlier? *Blah, blah, blah. Another day in paradise.*

Bored, Simion stepped to the window. A whirlwind crossed the wall into the garden. Trees shook and leaves flew. From the tempest's center stepped a handsome woman, hair windblown, carrying a carpetbag. Simion gawked. "Uhhh ... a woman just landed in the yard."

"What are you babbling about?" Isobel asked.

"A woman rode a whirlwind into the yard. She's headed to the front door." *No one transported directly into the compound. Who is she ...? How does she dare ...?*

Isobel struggled to her feet and stood next to him. "Go let her in, fool."

Simion trotted through the hall to the front door. He arrived before the bell rang and swept the door open to see a tall, striking faerie woman reaching for the brass knocker.

Before Simion asked her business, she blew past him and headed for the office. Simion loped behind like a short-legged child running to keep up with a parent. He reached to grab her arm but pulled his hand back. Maybe she was a Wyzard and would strike his hand off if he touched her. A closer look told him to be wary. She acted like she owned the place. She looks like … him.

The woman marched into the office. Looking neither left nor right, she strode straight to Weir. Simion watched with glee. He drew away, awaiting the strike, waiting for Weir to pulverize her for breaking into his sanctuary.

Weir rose and walked around his desk. Closing on her, grasping both her forearms, and gently kissing her cheek, he said, "Well come, Sister."

CHAPTER 41

Long black drapes hung over the door to the Ministry offices. Black crepe paid tribute to the fallen Minister along the top and sides of the flag. A small gathering of five sat on the dais at the end of the room.

"The people in this room are my trusted advisers," Lothian said. "The problem confounds me. I understand Grezil was a traitor and worked with an outside force to kill me. But why? What does she gain?" He turned toward the group. "Have the Droch Sìthe risen? An assassination after centuries of peace?"

Every eye turned to Erceldoune.

"I do not have a complete answer," Erceldoune said. "Parts of this thing remain murky. Three issues are clear. First, my source reports that the Droch Sìthe are absolved. Isobel left the Clan and hid after she attacked Jake's mother. She remains hidden. No one knows where. Second, to kill one monarch and not the other does nothing. A crown reverts to an heir. The Orb remains with the Clan. Nothing is gained. Third, the planning and execution was meticulous. Isobel is a blunt force with little guile. This attack was planned and executed by a cunning alchemist. For me, the key is Afton Thish."

"Lothian and I spoke with him," Vivian said. "He remains deeply enchanted, appears to know nothing, and shows no concern about his actions. We seek your help."

"I will do what I can."

****

In the dank, poorly lit, cool, spud cellar, Afton wasn't uncomfortable. He wasn't anything. He waited. For what, he didn't know.

From outside, snatches of words floated in to him. "Poison. Dagger. Traitor. Spy. Droch Sìthe." For the briefest moment, fear, anger, or shame would erupt in him, but each emotion dissipated as quickly as it rose. Memories were the worst. They flitted into and out of consciousness like fireflies he couldn't catch.

Footsteps sounded down the cellar stairs. The great wooden door creaked back. Erceldoune and Vivian stepped into the dim light.

Afton stood and reached for them like a man grabbing a life preserver. "What is true? Father is dead, mother a traitor?" His eyes bored into Erceldoune's. An urgency to escape his limbo hell of not knowing overrode his compliancy.

Erceldoune held his reply so long that Afton wasn't sure he would answer.

"All is true," Erceldoune said in a gentle and mild tone.

Horror assaulted Afton. His body shook like an icicle icepick had been plunged into his heart. Before the full impact hit him, the emotions ceased as if neutralized by a powerful tranquilizer. He knew what Erceldoune had said, knew it was horrific, knew he had shamed his family, his friends, and his Clan, but his emotions would not rise to meet the intellectual understanding. He felt slammed back and forth like a sliver ball in a pinball machine.

Erceldoune continued. "From the night the Prince was attacked, I suspected a traitor. Someone placed a powerful enchantment on the mountaintop entrance. I waited and watched. You came and removed the enchantment."

"Noooo," Afton moaned and buried his face in his hands. He wanted to wretch, to vomit out the past as if it were a poison, to release the sickening sensation. As hard as he fought to release it, it clung to him like a stench.

"Are you prepared to hear?" Erceldoune asked. The words were patient and kind, but belied a firmness. Not a demand; rather, it was as if Erceldoune requested him to make a difficult, considered decision.

Several moments passed. *Did he really want to know the truth, the worst truth, of his life?* Afton required his brain to answer the question. Slowly, he reclaimed his wits. "I have to know."

Without a second's hesitation, Erceldoune began. "The enchantment on the door was complex. Your skills were not up to the task. I attended your father's investigation. It was an able job. He was sincere in finding justice. Your mother appeared unconcerned. Both your father and mother were accomplished Wyzards. She was the logical choice."

The white noise in his head lessened a few degrees as he forced himself to concentrate on every word. "But what could she hope to achieve?"

"I suspect theft of the Orb," Erceldoune said, "but am unsure. I desire your help."

"Me? What can I do?"

"I believe your mother enchanted you, dulling your awareness to the tasks she required from you. She used you as a messenger and minion. She scrambled your memories. When I closed on her, she made one last effort to kill Lothian before she escaped. Here, the motive becomes murky."

"What else?" Afton asked. He suspected the worst but wanted to hear it.

"She sent you in a final attempt to murder the Prince and, rather than have your father endure shame and ridicule, she killed him. Flawed logic. But there it is."

Afton heard the terrible words. Matching emotions didn't follow. He was in a place beyond Erceldoune's truth.

"Would you like me to withdraw Grezil's enchantment?"

"Yes," Afton said, but his expression waivered. *I can't have done these things. I can't* … He willed himself to remember, but only fuzzy vague images came and danced away.

Erceldoune spoke with a grave warning. "The full knowledge of what was done, how it was done, and your part in it will fall upon you. Be aware. Withdrawing a protective enchantment leaves a mortification, unlike anything you have ever experienced."

"I never meant to harm anyone. For what I did, I own my part. I am afraid …" Afton wasn't sure he could survive total recall.

Erceldoune waited. Afton wavered. He sat on the potato sacks and fell back into a dark corner, pushed himself to sit up, and withered again. With finality, ready to take the blow, he pushed himself to sit up straight facing Erceldoune. Whatever came he would endure it. "I am ready."

Erceldoune placed both hands over Afton's head. He circled them in opposite directions like he was erasing a blackboard. With these movements, he spoke: "Confuse the knowing, embers glowing, spark the light and clear the cloud, the one who seeks the truth, unshroud."

Once an overly proud faerie with no worries, Afton's world evaporated like a water puddle on a hot day. Awareness flooded his mind. The room whirled. A gut-wrenching cry tore from his throat. Wanting to purge the feelings, vomit them out, he wretched. But his emotions clung to his insides like burning, sucking leeches.

Afton shrank to the floor. He opened and closed his mouth, gulping for air. He attempted words. Nothing came. Air exited in a gagged scream. He fell forward to his knees, curled in a ball like a terrified child, and wept.

****

Vivian and Erceldoune climbed the steps from the cellar. Vivian couldn't shake Afton's excruciated image. A friend since childhood, his mother's enchantment robbed him of honor, dignity, and Clan relationships, and for what?

"How will he recover?" Vivian asked.

"Deep enchantment etches the soul. His body will recover; as for his mind, we shall see."

"Sad. He was a friend," Vivian said. Pangs of loss surged through her.

"We need to understand who we are fighting. Would you do some research for me?"

"I will do whatever I can to help." Any activity was better than waiting.

"Go to the Journal and research the Thish family," Erceldoune said. "We need to understand Grezil's history and discover her motive. I fear she has lived among us for years without anyone understanding who she was."

"I begin now," Vivian said and left for the Ministry offices.

CHAPTER 42

Jake and Lothian sat in the comfortable chairs at the small table in Lothian's chambers. Clacks, arms akimbo, leaned against the unlit fireplace. Lothian's white bandages showed inside his open shirt collar; one arm was in a sling, but his eyes held a grim determination.

Waiting for Lothian to speak, Jake leaned forward, elbows propped on his knees, hands relaxed one inside the other, as if he were in a military briefing awaiting the commander's orders. Minutes passed.

Lothian looked at Jake and said, "I want you to train in earnest. I am unsure what challenges us, but I want you ready to fight when the time comes."

"What do I do?" Jake was eager but unsure. "What kind of training?"

"Magical. But first, find your way in the Journal. Allow it to lead you." That's what Erceldoune said.

Lothian turned to Clacks. "Will you mentor him?"

Clacks's calming smile came out like sunshine on a cloudy day. "I would be delighted."

"What's first?" Jake asked.

****

Jake and Clacks passed every dull-colored door in the ministry wing until the hall dead-ended. Written on a final door in a beautiful script was *Library*. Greeted by a ten-by-ten room with slanting gray stone walls curving up to a rounded ceiling with sparse, simple furniture that included a brown straight-backed chair and matching writing table, Jake hadn't known what to expect, but this wasn't it. No windows. No pictures. No shelves. No books. Clacks motioned for Jake to sit. *How can this place hold the entire history of the Clan?*

"What do you know?" Clacks asked. It seemed a casual question, but it made Jake squirm like a schoolboy who can't answer a teacher's question. *What's he doing?*

"What?" Jake asked in surprise. A moment before Clacks had been a friend. Now, he was an interrogator.

"A simple question. What do you know?" Clacks asked. Jake felt trapped.

The question was vague and non-contextual. *What does he want me to say?*

"I don't understand what you are asking me."

"What do you know? It's not a trick question."

"Know? About what?" His surprise slipped into frustration and headed toward anger.

"Anything. Everything. All is connected. Tell me what you know." Clacks didn't smile.

Jake's confusion rose and fell as he tried to think. *An empty room. Stupid questions. I don't know anything about magic.* He struck on a simplistic response, "I know if this is a library, there should be books. I don't see any."

"Ah, a small connection. A start. Think, Jake, think."

Jake's frustration wrestled against his intellect. Pressure didn't bother him, but something was tugging at his core. A deep hidden fear. One he wanted to avoid, even now.

Jake never wanted to look "less than" others, like he was unprepared, like a failure. He struggled for options. A powerful urge grabbed him. *This isn't fair. Get up and walk out. So what if people were trying to kill him. So what if he didn't understand magic and couldn't defend himself against it. So, what …* He took a deep breath and another. As his fear dimmed, thoughts formed. A library, books, writing, Bard. His father's job. A library belonged to the Bard, to him.

"Nice beginning." Clacks peered at him like a bug under a microscope.

Did he just read my mind? "Where are the books?" Jake asked.

Clacks reached behind his back and placed an ancient tome on the table before Jake. The thin wood cover was overlaid with leather. Gold engraving formed Celtic symbols and writing. The binding was string sewed through the pages and tied against the covers.

Jake, gently, opened the cover. The pages held bold handwritten words in a strong, slanted style, but in a language he couldn't read. The yellow paper was bucked and curled while the handwriting was crisp and preserved. He glanced at several other pages looking for clues. Nothing came to him.

Jake closed the book. *This must be The Journal.*

"What do you know?" Clacks asked as if the answer were obvious.

"This is the Clan Journal. A Bard's job is to record Clan history. This volume is about an inch thick, very old, leather cover, wooden front and back flaps, string binding, hinges, and leather straps. It looks fragile. I can't read the title because it's in some weird language."

"Use all your senses."

Jake flushed. Frustration boiled. His hand touched the book again. Closing his eyes, he sensed the book in the same way he lived through the dreams. An odd sensation rippled up his fingertips and coursed into his body, as if he knew the book, knew what was in it, and was a part of it, or it was a part of him. *Wow.*

Smells rose. Old paper and ink, at first, followed by scents of a forest, a fire in the grate, and animals. Sounds echoed: a roaring river, clashing steel, shouts, cries of joy, a baby cooing, and a spring rain in a forest.

"What do you know?" Clacks smiled. Jake opened his eyes. Staring at the pages, no understanding came.

"Nothing more. I can't read it." Jake wasn't sure why, but he kept the sensations and images of the Journal to himself.

"You do not answer my question. Think, Jake, think."

"What do you want from me?" Jake's anger bubbled.

"Some display of what you know."

Enough. Jake pushed back from the table and stood. Clacks dissipated through the wall like a movie ghost. Being angry at a wall made Jake feel like a fool.

"What do I know?" *I don't know anything.*

****

Jake remained at the brown desk until evening. A medico visited him in his room and checked his arm and gave him a salve. The question ran around his brain like it was a hamster wheel. Sleep was fitful.

Clacks had come at dawn, lead him to the Library, and again, asked him the interminable question. When Jake sputtered, he left. After hours, the Journal hadn't changed, the room was the same, and the chair was uncomfortable. Jake circled the small space. Bored, his mind wandered. He came to himself after what seemed like minutes but could have been days. *How long have I been here?*

A daydream tugged at his consciousness. He sat down and let it come. Corcle's voice spoke as if he were sitting next to Jake.

****

As they left the tent, Clackmannan whispered, "Your Majesty, the Orb is buried. How do we find it?"

"The Orb will find me," King Torrinn said.

Moving in darkness, Clackmannan tripped on a hidden rock and fell into a tangle of underbrush. The crash resonated in the still night. The guards, lounging around at the fire, reacted.

"At the ready," the captain ordered. "Move!"

They stood as one and ran toward the sound. They may have been lazy guards, but they were well-trained soldiers. They closed on Clackmannan. Stealth was useless. Clackmannan and King Torrinn ran.

"Light the Orb!" The King shouted.

Twenty-five paces ahead, a dull light showed in a thinly covered pit. They reached the spot. The guards crossed a small hill behind them.

"Enter my hand," King Torrinn cried as he ran. His voice held the command and tone of a true king.

The ground shifted. The light brightened. An arrow whizzed near Clackmannan. He drew his dagger and closed on the closest soldier.

CHAPTER 43

The three of them sat in high-backed leather chairs around a small wooden table in one corner of Weir's office. Simion, nearby, missed nothing.

"Is he dead?" Weir asked.

Simion knew that blunt question wasn't Weir's style, but he needed a swift answer, a reassurance. He didn't get one.

"I don't know." Grezil looked into Weir's eyes without shrinking.

"Why have you come?"

"Erceldoune knew. Within a day, he would trap me. I sacrificed my family for you, dear brother."

Weir nodded. Simion searched his and Grezil's expressions. *Neither seems to care much.*

"As the minister's wife," Grezil said, "I had access to the Orb's power. Now I am blocked from it. I sent one final present but could not stay for its opening."

Grezil showed no sign of worry or fear. *Strange.* Simion watched the interaction between Weir and Grezil. She wasn't afraid of failing Weir. No desire to whimper or placate. *Gonads of steel on this one.*

As if a nerve pinched in her back, Grezil stiffened and winced.

"Damn Erceldoune," Grezil said. "The enchantment that kept Afton chained to me is released. I felt it slip from him. I needed him to become our spy."

"You failed me," he said.

"Perhaps," she replied. "Your plan to kill a monarch in his castle was bold. I fulfilled our agreement. Your people were inept."

That stings. Simion shifted and tried to fade into the woodwork.

"Today," Grezil continued, "I sent poison to the Prince."

"But is he dead?" Weir demanded.

"It was my time to depart," Grezil said with no hint of regret.

Weir pushed her. "With you here, I lose my spy."

"Would you prefer I be imprisoned where the Orb could loosen my tongue? Then you would have no plan," Grezil responded, meeting Weir's gaze without flinching.

"Can we turn your husband?" Weir asked.

"He turns no more."

She killed him? She kills her husband and enchants her son to do the dirty work. I need to watch this one.

Weir sat back, thinking. Simion watched to see when he would crush her. No one in his experience had the gall to talk to him as she had and not pay the price. Weir rose and came around the desk. *Here it comes.*

Weir took both her hands in his, smiled, and kissed her cheek. "Sister, I rejoice to have you back with me."

Isobel looks like she could chew iron and spit nails.

"Formulate a plan to take the Princess." It was an order and not a request.

"I shall," Grezil said, "but first I will reclaim my son."

CHAPTER 44

Jake needed a break. While his body wandered the town and he spoke to people who spoke to him, his mind remained on the Library. *How does it work? What do I know?*

Flowing with the crowd, Jake glimpsed auburn hair, braided and flipped around a shoulder. He picked up his pace. At the next intersection, one lane over, was Vivian. Looking neither left nor right, she walked with intent, as if she stalked unseen prey. From one lane over, Jake followed her.

She turned right under the pub, took a shortcut through an open shop, and climbed the castle steps two at a time. No hiding place between them, Jake stayed back. Castle doors swung open for her and closed behind her. Running up the steps, Jake tripped, scrambled to his feet, and made the foyer in time to see her enter the black-draped Ministry door. *Do I go in? She'll think I'm following her ... I am.* Jake dithered in the foyer. *If I want to see her ...*

The hall was empty. Acting like he was going to the Library again, Jake ambled nonchalantly down the hall. When doors were open, he glanced in. When closed, he hesitated and listened for her voice. Nothing. *Maybe she left.* Disappointed, Jake continued to the Library.

He entered the small gray room, resigned that he had missed her. Sitting at the dark oak table in the straight chair was Vivian. She did not look up, so she could have no idea it was him, as she raised a finger signaling that he should wait and remain silent.

****

Having spent a long morning visiting people who would know or should know about Grezil, Vivian resolved to find what the Journal would offer.

She concentrated as the Journal's pages flipped like cards shuffling. Once the shuffling stopped, she placed her hand on the page, closed her eyes, and sat still as if she were meditating. A vision came to her.

"Isn't there another way?" King Torrinn asked his council. The group sat around a long table cluttered with parchments and cups. Men in medieval garb unwilling to add to the King's turmoil looked across at one another but did not respond.

"Your Majesty, my honored friend," Corcle said, "I learn much from you.

122

One lesson is that there is but a single answer to any question. Yes or no. This is such a question. If you held no great love for your brother, the answer would be the same. If you cushion his punishment, he learns nothing."

"Sire," a Minister said, "we could banish him from the Gleane to live in the human world for the rest of his life."

Both King and Bard knew it was no great punishment. Corcle, loving King Torrinn, wanted to spare him unneeded grief. But as a true Bard, he said, "His banishment will not curb his appetite for power. It may be we are putting him exactly where he wants to be. The other option is placing him between worlds where he has no power."

King Torrinn shuddered. "I will consider it."

****

Jake watched Vivian. Her eyes were closed, concentrating on the Journal. "Continue," she said aloud.

What's she doing?

****

Torrinn, Corcle, and Corraidhín stood in a forest.

"I commit you and your progeny to the world of man," King Torrinn said.

"Would you send me there helpless?" Corraidhín asked.

"I strip you of assistance from the Orb and of magic, but not of the knowledge of magic."

"Damn you. I'm your brother, your flesh and blood. How will I survive?"

"By your thieving wits, no doubt."

****

Jake willed Vivian to open her eyes and turn to him.

"I won't be long," she said, but she did not look up to see who waited. The pages whirred. She closed her eyes again. Pages whirred. After several minutes, she looked up.

"Hello, Jake." Her greeting was neither warm nor welcoming.

"How did you do that?" *I have to apologize. Say it!* Jake knew he'd hurt her. He shifted on his feet and leaned against the door frame. *I am so sorry.*

"I can help you for a few minutes, but I have to talk to Erceldoune at noon." Vivian answered as if helping him was a chore.

Anything to keep her here for one moment longer.

"What do you know?" Vivian asked.

Not you too. "Nothing." Jake felt her eyes on him parsing, examining, and weighing.

She sighed. "The Journal works differently for different people. I assume you do not read Ancient Scottish Gaelic." Vivian's tone was sharp.

"No."

"I do not know how it teaches you. You must discover it for yourself." Vivian got up.

Say something to make her stay. He had nothing. He hurried to the obvious. "I saw it flipping pages when I came in. How does that work?"

She looked through him again. "When you find your way into the Journal, you can request information, and it provides the page."

"Like an automatic index?"

"Yes. I can't help you until you find your way."

"What were you looking up?"

"A private matter."

What else can I say to make her stay? He wavered.

She left.

CHAPTER 45

In the small hours of the morning, Grezil stood on the road before the gate to the Gleane. She called for the key. A rock nearby flipped into the air. The key floated to her hand. She opened the gate and locked it behind her.

Quiet as a fawn, she slipped down the old railroad bed. The cloud-covered moon painted her as an inky apparition. She plucked a thin branch of mountain laurel and stripped away the leaves to form a crude wand. She held the twisted stick in her left hand.

"Light be here, light be clear," she said. The tip glowed and lit her way to the alley behind the castle.

The town slept. From shadow to shadow, she passed familiar landmarks, came to her home, and peered in the front window. The old housekeeper slept in Grezil's chair by a dying fire. *How dare she?*

Where was Afton? He should have been home by now. A nanosecond of fear gripped her. She ignored it.

Grezil sneaked to the kitchen entrance and found the house key's hiding place unchanged. *Stupid woman.* The kitchen was spotless, much cleaner than when the old woman had worked for Grezil.

Grezil peeked into the living room where the old housekeeper dozed. She crept forward until she was inches from her sleeping face. She pinched the sleeping woman's jaw in a vice grip. Startled, the old woman's eyes flew open, and seeing who held her, terror filled her face.

"Making cozy in my house," Grezil said as she saw the terror spread. *That's better. I have you now.*

"Your son gave it to me," the housekeeper mouthed through her squeezed lips.

"Where is he?"

"The castle."

"Where?" Grezil squeezed harder.

"Basement."

Grezil released the terrified woman's face and raised her right hand. The woman shrank away.

"Sleep like night, forget all fright," Grezil chanted.

The old woman's face sagged. Her breathing deepened. Grezil obliterated the memory of her visit.

Leaving all as she found it, Grezil marched to the kitchen entrance of the castle and entered the round green door. Pots and pans glinted in a dimming firelight as she crossed the empty kitchen and descended the cellar steps. *The fools never lock anything.*

Afton sat reading. When she saw him, a soft feeling arose, but she crushed it. *This is business. He will thank me later.*

"Afton," she whispered. He turned. She sensed a difference in him. He was not the frivolous boy she enchanted. He was a man. A calm openness showed in his manner. *I don't like this.*

"Why are you here?" Afton said, his tone icy. The distant way he addressed her set her aback.

"I came to see you." Grezil knew she lied but she worked to sell it, twisting her face into the facade of a smile.

Afton said, "Bright the light." The candle flame flickered and brightened. Grezil felt exposed.

Looking around the converted storage closet, disgust arose. *Allowing yourself to live in this hovel. I raised you better.* "I wanted to see how you are doing."

No response. The silence unsettled her. He had never acted this way before. I need a response, something I can manipulate, a way to twist him to my will. She sought an opening. "I regret the things I did, but they were necessary. Your father would never have withstood the scrutiny of an investigation. You know that. I knew they would let you go after they discovered it was my enchantment. I did it for us, son. For you."

Afton did nothing, said nothing. Grezil soldiered on. "For a long time, I wanted more for our family. Your father was satisfied as Minister. I pushed him into the job. I made him a force in the community. I moved him in the right circles. It was always me, pushing behind the scenes, making things happen. He was weak. He enjoyed the position, but he never strove for the next step. My brother suggested another way. I took it." Grezil heard disgust slip into her voice. "You helped me and will share in what's coming. I need your help one more time."

Afton remained silent, and it unnerved her.

"A trifling thing really," she said, "a message when the Princess goes back to Edinburgh. That's all I need. Please, son, this will get us the power and prestige we deserve. I have the support of my brother and his entire organization. Only this one thing: I need to know when the Princess leaves. Then if you want nothing to do with your old mother, so be it. But you can rule with me and take over when I'm gone. You can be king of the Daione Sìthe, owner of the Orb, and ruler in the world of man." Pleading irked her. Once again, she pushed her face into a smile.

Afton stood and walked to her.

I don't like this. She drew back.

He touched her shoulder and looked into her eyes. "Go."

Her grip was gone. A fury tore into her. *How dare you? You can't deny me. I'm your mother.* "Now, look, Afton Cornelius. I—"

"Go," he said.

Shock flooded her. If not by manipulation, then by magic. She raised her hands. *You cannot resist my will.* As she started an enchantment, she felt it. He was protected. But she felt more—a trap!

Grezil dropped her hands and backed away. Fear rose in her throat. Cold hands clutched at her chest. She backed out of his cellar, ran up the stairs, out the round door, and down the alley to the forest tunnel.

****

Afton fell backward into his chair. His breath caught. His heart thumped. He sat stock still, waiting for the feelings to pass. *I defied mother.*

An hour later, he climbed the circular stairs to the second floor, entered the room, and stood before the Orb.

"I have done as you asked."

"Where is your mother?" Erceldoune's voice came through the Orb. Afton breathed and concentrated. A picture grew in his mind. A tall stone wall came into view. As if he were watching a movie, Afton saw his mother walking up a curved driveway, clothes disheveled, and hair windblown. A house came into view. Without Grezil's knowledge, his touch allowed him to track her. An old enchantment, unknown to most, lay on her.

"I know the house," Afton said.

CHAPTER 46

Vivian found Erceldoune and Lothian in the small room across from Lothian's chambers.

"Is your research complete?" Erceldoune asked.

"As far as I was able to go. I asked the Journal for all references on Grezil but all had been deleted from the Journal. I found nothing that helped. On Minister Thish, the records were complete, showing he was not the traitor. On Afton, the record stopped three years ago, which indicates to me that is when he became her minion. Has he added anything new?"

"No, his mind remains blank for that period," Erceldoune said. Vivian shuddered. To lose three years of your life …

Vivian said, "The Journal provided one odd tidbit. When I asked for Grezil's ancestry, it took me to the banishment of Corraidhín. I found no direct connection because it appears the only knowledge we have of her genealogy is what she told us. She deleted her following almost the day she arrived. The Journal holds no record of who she saw or where she went."

"What we know is Grezil passed information to someone outside the Gleane who plotted to kill Lothian," Erceldoune said.

"But why?" Lothian asked.

"The answer lies in Scotland," Vivian said. "I could be over and back before anyone knew I was gone."

"A dangerous trip," Erceldoune said, considering her offer. "Perhaps there is a way."

****

"Are you quite recovered, my dear?" Weir asked Isobel.

"I am well enough to find MacCorkle and send a steel dart through his skull."

"Rest. Post a small force, our best around the Gleane, to keep watch. Ensure they are not seen. Let the Gleane relax before out next incursion."

Isobel nodded and left.

"I have work for you." Weir turned toward Grezil.

"The Princess lives and studies in Edinburgh. In time, she will return. Find a way to trap her. Don't kill her." Weir added in a conspiratorial tone,

"The brother will come to her rescue. When he does, we kill both."

****

Jake stared at the Journal, trying to force a vision. He touched it, caressed its pages, demanded information, read passages in ridiculous pronunciations, and spoke made up incantations until his eyes crossed. Nothing happened. Changing course, he reviewed the question everyone kept asking him.

"What do I know … about this book? What do I know about this room, this place, and these people?"

Walking off his frustration, he battled to fit it together.

He started again. "I am in a room, in a town, inside a mountain. I have a book with writing in it. Writing can be read if someone understands the language. I don't. Languages can be translated. Translation means converting one form of communication to another."

Convert? How?

The book lay open. The first page summoned him. The words were gibberish. He leaned back, rubbed his eyes, and quit thinking. He inhaled a slow, deep breath and exhaled. He inhaled and exhaled again and again in the same deliberate way.

For a brief second, a colorful collage gyrated on the wall. Jake froze and his breathing became stilted. *Vivian touched the book.*

Reaching a hand for the Journal, the sensations returned. The veneration for the Journal's age, the awe of growing power, and the immense possibility it represented surged at him.

Jake's first instinct was to capture the sensations and control them. To do so, he stalked every twitch, sound, and color. He cradled the color in his mind, trying to make it do something, become something. The collage began to swirl, but the more effort Jake made to force it, the more the color dimmed. When he made a final push to force a whole picture, it vanished.

He placed his hand on the page. "I did it," he said. "Kinda. But how? What do I know?"

"At last." Clacks stood to his left.

"Where did you come from?"

Clacks did not answer.

Clacks stepped forward, smiling, comforting. "Prior to this moment, I began to think you were a clod unearthed by a dull plow."

"Thanks," Jake said, feeling Clacks's comment was a backhanded compliment. He knew he was close to discovering how the Journal worked. Taking a deep breath, he relaxed, saw colors on the wall, tried to manipulate the hodgepodge, and it vanished.

Imitating Vivian, Jake put his hand on the book, at the top of the first page. He closed his eyes and took a breath. *Don't control it. Let it happen.* His father's statement popped into his mind. *Experience it for yourself.*

Red, blue, and green swirled in his mind. His eyes opened. The wall transformed to a smooth, white screen. Outlines formed. He blinked. Forms dissipated. He started again. Summoning all his patience, he relaxed, letting the event unfold without his oversight.

The scene returned, a swirl of multicolor paints mixing, shifting, and flowing together. Edges formed. Shapes emerged. He took his hand off the book. The scene disappeared.

Become the book.

He touched the page. Vivid colors rushed together like a wave on the beach. Sounds emerged. Birds, water. The edges of his vision blurred into a scene. The storyteller's voice spoke.

****

This is my first Journal entry for the People of Peace. The year is 1342, day and month, 28 February. Edward II rules England. David II rules Scotland. Bilbo Baggins has returned to the Shire. England contends for rule of Scotland.

I am Corcle, a humble builder of small boats. Until this time, I knew nothing of my destiny or how it intertwined with the Faerie Clans of Scotland.

To my past mind, faeries were a mixture of long-ago legends and nursemaid tales to make children behave. What I know now is different. I tell this story, simply, as it happened.

Scotland is a bonny place to live. The highlands, rivers, and lochs afford a fair life to any man willing to work. My life is on the River Gress. I build small boats that I use for fishing and trade.

It was a brisk morning. I went out early to set my nets when I heard a sharp cry. Clearly, a man was in trouble. Shouts followed. He was pursued along the riverbank toward me. With care, I paddled around the bend and saw three men attacking one man. I believed they meant to kill him.

****

Jake pulled his hand off the Journal. The scene faded. The vision ended. The white screen misted and dissolved. The skin of his face was cold. Brushing his hand across damp tousled hair, Jake knew he had experienced the wind off the river and heard the men's shouts ring in his ears.

"My dream; it's my dream."

CHAPTER 47

Grezil transported to Scotland. She dressed as a middle-aged teacher. She moved around the University of Edinburgh as if she were a lecturer.

From past conversations, she knew Vivian was in graduate school for Celtic History. The university map showed the languages building at 50 George Square. She found Vivian's department on the fourth floor and walked to the department's front desk with a predesigned lie. The young woman was child's play.

"Hello, I am Samantha Foggarty. I am visiting Scotland for the first time. I am looking for a dear friend from the US, Vivian Harman. But she divorced. I don't remember her maiden name. Do you have a graduate student named Vivian?"

The girl's dark hair and chestnut eyes smiled up from the desk. "We do. I didn't know she was married before."

To cement the lie, Grezil added: "She's tall, has long auburn hair, wears it in a French braid, and has two different colored eyes?"

"Oh yes, that's her, but she is in America. A family emergency."

I know. I created it. "Do you have her address here in Scotland? I would like to drop her a sympathy note."

The graduate assistant hesitated. "I'm not supposed to give out that information without permission from Vivian."

Grezil glanced around. No one. She raised her hands. The girl's chestnut eyes grew wide. *This will be as close as you'll ever get to Celtic enchantment, dearie.*

Patrick Geddes Hall in Old Town, Milnes Court, minutes from Edinburgh Castle, was built of ancient eighteenth century stone. Large white windows overlooked the city. The sound of truck tires, knocking and jouncing in an irregular rhythm over the paving stones, faded as Grezil entered the locked doors with no problem.

In the hall, Grezil shifted her clothes to khakis, a green blouse, a rust-colored sweater, and a denim jacket. She hiked up the steps to the third floor and found the room but hesitated. She closed her eyes and concentrated, checking for enchantments. Nothing. Inside, no one was home. *Good, much easier.*

She discerned which room was Vivian's. A class schedule lay on the desk. Clothes were thrown about as if someone packed in a hurry. Grezil sat on the bed, thinking. She needed to know when Vivian would return. Scanning the room, her eyes locked on the pillow. *If she lays on this bed, I will know.*

****

Magic knowledge came fast; application lagged. Clacks assigned Jake simple skills to master. Spark the tip of a stick to make a light. Spin a small stone on his hand. Hear and speak without talking. He witnessed them in the Journal, but to craft them was different. The spark glimmered on occasion, stones lay on his hand, happily inert, and no telekinetic messages reached him through the airwaves. Frustration rose and waned. One moment he garnered hope; the next, hope was dashed when nothing he tried produced results.

"Show me Create Light," Jake said, forcing a deep commanding voice. Journal pages flipped and directed his hand down the page. A vision came, showing a faerie deep in the forest picking a live branch from a tree, holding it aloft, pronouncing an enchantment, and a tiny fire lighting the tip like a match striking before turning into a bright, glowing ember. It didn't help. The harder Jake tried, the less light he produced. "What's wrong? Why doesn't this work for me?"

Jake conjured a thousand reasons for his failure. He wasn't a faerie. He wasn't paying attention. He wasn't holding his mouth right, holding his hands right, saying the words right.

Connections between enchantments, ways to strengthen or weaken an enchantment, and counter enchantments were all in the Journal. To make them work, and work consistently, demanded connection, intuition, and insight. Jake was flummoxed, but he refused to quit. He practiced everywhere. He stalked the skills like a hunter after big game.

As he walked down the street staring at his hands like a person absorbed in texting, cobblestones tripped him, people dodged him left and right. *Come on. A spark, a glow, anything.*

For the fiftieth time, Jake ordered the little stick to glow. A faint reddish ember showed. A growling frustration filled with self-critical anecdotes transformed to wonder and excitement. People around him clapped and slapped his back. He hadn't noticed that they were watching.

Jake danced toward the pub with the glowing stick held in front. *Don't go out. Don't go out.*

The Swan door swung open. People stepped back to let Jake and his stick in. Smiles followed him, celebrating his tiny triumph. Clacks was late. The place was slammed. All the four-top tables were full. Except one.

Sitting alone at a back table was Afton Thish. *The rumors are true. He's out.* Afton appeared mesmerized by his ale. Jake jigged through the patrons until he got to the table.

"Is this seat open?"

"They all are," Afton responded. He rose to leave.

"Where are you going?"

"You wanted the seat, not the company."

"I'm so excited. I need to talk to someone."

"About what?"

"Magic, enchantment, what to do, how to do it. I just lit the tip of a stick." Jake joked, pointing to his twig. Wanting Afton to smile, he stuck his warmest, gentlest, kindest, most concerned look on his face and gave it to Afton, who stared back and seemed to struggle to determine if Jake was for real. He looked like the last kid waiting to be picked for dodgeball.

After a prolonged silence, Afton said with a thin smile and a flat monotone voice, "That's great."

Jake ordered an ale.

"I am a baby at enchantment. I know it's natural for you. Talk to me."

"I'm not sure I can help you." Afton seemed to shut down like a series of doors slamming one after the other. He stood to leave.

"Please stay."

At the threshold of the final slam, Afton hesitated. "What do you want?" Afton asked in a quiet voice. He seemed desperate for a connection, any connection, but nothing fake, nothing patronizing.

Jake knew the feeling. "You look like you could use a friend."

Afton's face dropped.

Jake knew that pain. It squirmed into his body for the first time when he was four years old and he had asked his father, "Where's mommy?" Jake had never seen his father cry, but that day, a tear rolled down his cheek. It scared him.

Jake blinked the image away. "As odd as it seems, I do understand what it's like to be alone."

Afton sat back down.

****

Wind tossed bare limbs in the inner circle of George Square at the University of Edinburgh in Scotland. In the early hours, no one was awake to care about a freak windstorm.

Vivian landed and walked between the trees toward the multiwindowed library. At a row of empty computers, she went to work.

Around nine in the morning, Vivian stretched her hands overhead. Bending left and right, she flexed unused muscles. *Get a shower and a few hours' sleep.* Her huge leather handbag carried everything from notebooks to a change of clothes. She placed her notes into it and hefted the bag over her shoulder. She needed a more complete database and knew where to find it. Typing a final order for the information she needed, she hit Enter.

Out the back steps, the twelve-minute walk to Geddes Hall was welcome exercise. Vivian loved Edinburgh—the old town, the castle, the cobbled streets. Anything ancient and historical captivated her.

At Geddes Hall, her home for the past three years, the front door opened, and familiar smells of students, Lysol, fruit, and hard work drifted to her.

Her room was open. Something felt off. Too tired to investigate, she tossed her everything-handbag on the desk, lay down on the bed, and drifted asleep within minutes.

****

Jake's routine varied little: sit in a cabinet meeting with the Prince and Princess, go to the Library, and discuss magic with Afton and Clacks.

Outside the Ministry offices prior to another boring meeting, Jake's eyes followed Vivian. His heart lurched as he watched her walk behind Lothian. *It's driving me crazy. I have to apologize.*

As the meeting dragged on, Jake glanced at Vivian. She seemed to hang on every dry word. *How does she do it?* Jake nodded, trying to catch her eye.

Vivian never spoke and kept a blank smile on her face. When the meeting broke up, Jake touched her elbow. Vivian turned and faced him with a look of innocent curiosity.

"Vivian, I …"

She stared through him, gave him a dull smile, and wandered away like she hadn't heard.

Jake stopped Clacks in the hall. "I keep trying to apologize to Vivian, but she ignores me."

Clacks took Jake's elbow and walked him to a quiet corner. "Princess Vivian is not here," Clacks said, his voice low. "She is in Scotland on a task for Erceldoune."

Jake's reality skidded like a truck in the mud.

Down the hall, he saw Vivian following Lothian like a dutiful puppy. "No, she's not. She's right there." Jake pointed.

"That is a stock," Clacks said as he smiled.

"A what?"

"Princess Vivian returned to Scotland to gather information for Erceldoune. The people would worry if they knew she was not safe in the Gleane. A stock is an enchantment. A person's duplicate. Not a perfect replica, but good enough for appearances. Stocks cannot reason; they simply obey. Princess Vivian's stock makes brief appearances to forestall questions."

"I've been trying to talk to her and thought she was ignoring me."

"True. Her stock has no interest in you." Clacks grinned, and Jake laughed out loud.

134

CHAPTER 48

Jake sat at the now familiar brown table in the gray stone library.

"Continue Corcle's story!" Relaxing his hand, it hovered over the Journal. Rustling pages flipped to the correct entry. The coarse parchment crackled when he touched it. The wall misted white. *I know they get the Orb. But what happens?*

****

From my hiding spot, I saw Clackmannan run toward his attacker. The Droch Sìthe soldier, surprised by light rising from the ground, hesitated and lowered his guard. Clackmannan drove his dagger into the soldier's chest. He grabbed the sword from the fallen faerie's hand, scampered uphill, and felled two more. Soldiers encircled him.

An arrow struck the captain in the chest. A second hit another soldier in the thigh. A third arrow skinned close enough to draw a yelp. Men dove for cover, scanning the dark for the hidden archer. The circle broke. Clackmannan fled down the hill.

Torrinn's face flushed in the Orb's light. His voice boomed, *"Light turn bright, cease all night!"* With this command, the Orb's glow brightened, bringing light until no shadow hid.

"I'm blind!" one soldier screamed, prompting others to fall to the ground and cover their faces. King Torrinn and Clackmannan ran between the cowering figures. The youth and I abandoned our hiding place, and we all ran for the boats.

"Cease the bright, release the night." With this command, the Orb's light transformed to a shadow-filled dark.

Stumbling, we fell against each other.

The King gave another command. *"Light before, dark no more."* A single beam showed before us like a sunray, lighting our path. All else remained black as pitch.

The beam led us over a small rise. The boats showed ahead. Running with all my might I reached them and threw the limbs from the boats, flipped one over. Wading into the cold river, I steadied it for King Torrinn and Clackmannan. Shouts came. The Droch Sìthe guards had regained their wits and were seeking us.

In haste, I flipped the second boat, grabbed the boy, settled him in it, and pushed into the river. I stepped in, kneeled, and paddled for my life, striking hard for the channel.

King Torrinn and Clackmannan, unable to escape the shoreline current, drifted back toward the island. The soldiers sprinted into the water, slipping and falling, but missed the craft by inches when it gained speed and moved to deeper water.

"Damn you, bloody thieves!" A heavy-set soldier yelled.

When capture was futile, the soldiers sent arrows whizzing into the darkness at the sound of our paddles. The arrows came within a hair's width of striking our boat.

Clackmannan stood and draped himself over his King, nearly upending their little boat. One arrow pierced his side clear through and passed into King Torrinn's shoulder. Had Clackmannan not deflected the strike, the arrow would have pierced the King's neck. Knitted together, shoulder to side, they floated toward freedom.

"Corcle," King Torrinn called. "We are wounded and have lost our steerage."

I dug my paddle into the river and strove for them. The boats knocked together. I tethered my boat to theirs and steered both through the dark water.

Below a curve, King Torrinn's troops waited.

"I see them!" a sentry cried out. "River right. Prepare!"

A line of men roped together ran into the river, caught our boats, and swung us to shore.

As if handling a chick, the soldiers raised Clackmannan and the King from their craft. The youth broke the shaft and removed the arrow. A cart carried the wounded companions to the castle.

For the first time, I saw the power of the Orb. As King Torrinn and Clackmannan lay side by side, a healing fog rose from the Orb and wrapped fully around their bodies. Within days, their wounds healed. A minor scar remained, but no remnant of a wound.

After a day of rest, we traveled to King Torrinn's castle. Feasts lasted for weeks. Our tale was told and retold and grew in the telling.

The Droch Sìthe sued for peace. King Torrinn requested I record our adventure. I protested. I was a poor man who could neither read nor write. The King dismissed my argument. Bringing the Orb before me, he bade me place my hand upon it. I forced my hand not to tremble. It is one thing to see magic touch others and quite another to touch it for yourself. The King laid his hand atop mine and spoke the most beautiful words I have ever heard. A calm swept over me. And, from that day on, using a strange magic, the Orb produced the pages for me. As I witnessed it, I envision it, and it appears, handsomely written in a thin volume that never grows no matter how much information is placed within its pages.

From that day to this, I live with the Daoine Sìthe. King Torrinn is my true friend. I had thought my life empty—no family, no wife or children. But I was changed. I was loved and respected by an entire people—the People of Peace—and I returned their affection.

To my surprise, the youth of our adventure had not been a young man, but a fair lass, Lulie. Without her warrior garb, I looked on her with new eyes. I end with this pleasant nonsense; I am smitten with Lulie. She smiles on me. This records my first adventure with the People of Peace: The Reclamation of the Orb.

****

"Wow." This vision was his longest. Jake felt exhausted. He needed an ale.

Through the rabbit warren of winding alleys, past city shops, Jake made for the Swan. At the top of the stairs, the red door opened for him. The pub was nearly vacant. Afton sat at a corner table and grinned as Jake crossed the room. Jake smiled back; he enjoyed Afton's friendship.

"Well come, Jake. How go the studies?"

"I finished the Corcle story. Exciting stuff."

"Corcle was a great man. He became a Wyzard in his own right. So, how goes enchantment?"

"Slow."

"This may help." Afton slid a small stone across the table.

"What is it?"

"A dart my third-great-grandfather picked up from a battlefield. It has been in our family for centuries. I want you to take it in recognition of your accomplishments."

"Accomplishments?" Jake wasn't clear what he had accomplished. Knowledge about the Clan, okay. Minor understanding of enchantment, maybe. But accomplishments? Yeah, right, like there was more than one. Despite his misgivings, he didn't want to disappoint Afton, so he accepted his friend's gift.

The stone was quarter-sized, a deep green color with flecks of red, brown, and purple sprinkled throughout. Jake turned it over. He bounced it on his palm. The small weight lay oddly heavy. As in the Library, his eyes closed, and he relaxed. Energy, raw energy, pulsed. His mind pictured the stone zinging at an enemy. The force struck like dynamite.

"Jake. Stop!" Afton's voice called from light-years away.

Jake opened his eyes. The stone spun on his hand but stopped and fell into his palm when his concentration broke. "Yow. That's hot!" Jake bounced the stone out of his hand and onto the table. The stone pulsed and glowed.

Jake looked to Afton. "What happened?"

"This stone's power is evil. Once activated, the stone seeks to kill. Your magical abilities advance more than you recognize."

Abilities? I don't have any abilities. But something had happened. What he thought was beyond him a moment ago had happened in the blink of an eye. *How did I do that? I was practicing what I do in the Library.* The display frightened him. Magic happened. He caused it. Frightened, no … excited. A thrill grabbed him that was akin to joy but was followed quickly by a worry. *I don't have control of it.* I almost unleashed a deadly stone on my friend.

"What do I do with it?" Jake's concern was honest. "I don't know how to control evil."

Afton sat back. "Why not make an amulet?"

"An amulet?" The ordinary stone lay on the table.

"An evil object, converted to good."

CHAPTER 49

The Journal lay on the library table next to the stone. An amulet was perfect. Jake would give it to Vivian as an apology. *But how do I make it?*

Jake requested the information, and the Journal provided. Corcle created an amulet for his eldest child. Sir Michael Scott created the Orb. Reference after reference appeared. Each was slightly different, but all were essentially the same. Jake practiced the enchantment, hand movements, and words. He reviewed them over and over. He was ready. He knew the place, the time, the procedure. He would do it tomorrow night.

****

Grezil landed inside Weir's compound. The wind whirled the trees and bushes as she set down. A shiver pulsed though her body. Someone had disturbed the enchantment in the dorm room. "The Princess is in Scotland," she announced as she entered the office.

"Go now. Take her," Weir said. "And use any means available, but she must have a heartbeat, or the Orb will know. Block her following when you take her."

Grezil took Simion, Isobel, and two others with her.

****

Above the field standing on the old railroad bed, Jake picked up a small branch and lit its tip to guide him. A gray robe cloaked his clothes. The moon shown clear and bright, making a solid circle of shimming white around him.

A few weeks ago, I couldn't do this.

Jake shook with excitement, making a small pot rattle in his pocket. He followed the old railroad bed to the small meadow where the circle of stones stood. Mimicking the word and hand movements Clacks used, Jake watched the foliage open, revealing the path to the sacred valley. *Am I really doing this?*

Moving to the stone circle, Jake said, "I ask for a blessing on my task tonight." Entering the circle, a ripple of energy surged up his legs into his chest and shot down his fingertips. He hadn't expected that. The surprise of the energy jolt confirmed his belief. *I am doing the right thing.*

The lighted tip of his improvised wand illuminated the top of the central stone. Jake sighted along the edge until he located a small nick marking the exact center, where he placed a four-inch brass bowl with three short legs. From a small leather bag, Jake removed Afton's gift and placed it in the bowl.

Replacing the lid, he said, "A stain it caused, ugly and black. A pain it caused, a death direct. Evil restrained, move to collect. Good become, its final effect." His hands performed the correct exhortation accompanying the words.

Cool moonlight brightened inside the circle like someone had directed a spotlight on the space. Blackness deepened outside. It was working.

Moonlight coalesced into a single beam over the bowl, intensified, and ceased when its light sucked under the lid. The intense moonlight in the circle snuffed out like a candle. Still night returned. Jake's eyes adjusted. A bright reddish-purple light glowed beneath the lid of the bowl. A joy swelled in his chest. *Magic, I did real magic. Did it really work?* Like a stage magician conjuring a new illusion for the first time, Jake's pride swelled.

With the lid off, Jake beheld his success. Knowing it was his handiwork, he was seized by a sense of power, a confidence he'd never felt before.

Afton's gift shimmered white, completely transformed from its old color, with specs of gold. The red glow diminished. Cool to the touch when he picked it up, it pulsed in his hand like a beating heart. The amulet touched his skin, and it transfused a secure sense, a healing calm, throughout his body.

A single nagging thought interrupted the marvelous sensation. *Should I have told someone I was doing this?* Jake excused it, convinced himself that he did it for his training. They would have wanted me to do it.

I've done nothing wrong.

He danced back to the castle with his treasure.

Jake entered the round green door, ran down the steps to Afton's chamber, and entered without knocking.

"I did it," he said, holding out his treasure for inspection like an excited school child with his first drawing.

Afton jerked from a sound sleep with a start. "What time is it?"

"Late. Look. I did it."

"Good. Go to bed."

"No. Look at it now."

Afton accepted the amulet. "I feel the protection you put into it. Have you shown it to Clacks?"

"Er … no, maybe tomorrow."

"Nice job. Go away. Let me sleep."

Jake was too excited; he had to get it to Vivian now. Handing it to her would give him the courage to apologize. He would go to her that night. He would fly. No, he didn't know how. *The Orb …*

Deep in the night the castle lay quiet. Jake went to the second floor, across from Lothian's quarters. He entered the small room where he first talked with Erceldoune. The Orb glowed, maintaining a soft, steady light throughout the mountain. *It won't hurt anything if I borrow it for a few moments.*

A small silver stand cradled the Orb. Still in his robe, Jake caught his reflection in the glassy ball. He looked like a Wyzard. *I am a Wyzard.*

Transferring an object was child's play compared to creating the amulet. *I will travel to her and present it personally.* Jake stepped to the Orb, placed both hands on it, and pictured Vivian.

Nothing. Jake closed his eyes.

"Transport to Vivian!"

No tilt-a-whirl. He opened his eyes. Erceldoune and Clacks stood in the door. Guilt slashed Jake's soul.

****

Even in sleep, Vivian felt the Orb reach for her. Nothing happened. She drifted back into a caressing slumber.

CHAPTER 50

Jake was alone. The Ministry meeting room was quiet. Black fabric draped over the flag. Its motto glowered at him: *Truth in Everything*. Ordered to stand and wait, he shifted his weight back and forth from his left leg to his right and back, waiting with a wretched sense of nausea in his stomach. An old feeling he dodged and danced around clung to him like the stink of a skunk: disappointment. *I failed everyone, like I did in the Army.*

Erceldoune, Lothian, and Clacks entered together. No one greeted him. No one smiled. The chilled atmosphere in the room grew colder than the mountain stone walls.

Prince Lothian wore his crown and regal clothes. Clacks wore his gray robe. Erceldoune wore pristine white. The trio took seats on the dais. Lothian, in the middle, presided. He pointed to a spot in front of the dais for Jake to stand.

"Jake MacCorkle, we are here to understand your reasons for misuse of magic and misappropriation of the Orb."

"Misuse of magic?" Jake played the words over and over. "I didn't misuse anything. I created magic. I thought that's what you wanted me to do."

"Please, withhold comments until you are asked directly," Clacks said. Jake looked at the faces. Clacks showed worry but resignation. Lothian conveyed a stern, severe look. Erceldoune, a man he'd known all his life, showed the keen interest of a hawk assessing its dinner.

"The first allegation, misuse of magic. Your Prince commands you to speak."

What can I say to them?

Jake pushed air through his throat to speak, but it came out as a wheeze. He started again. "I regret my actions but not the reason for them."

No one moved. No one spoke. Jake hesitated. *Slow it down. Begin at the beginning. Tell them everything.*

Jake swallowed hard. He collected his thoughts, ordered them, and said, "I desired to protect a person I love. She is absent from me. I am new to magic. When presented with an opportunity to protect her, I took it."

"Go on," Lothian said.

Jake retold how Afton gave him the dart and suggested he make it into an amulet. He reported his research on amulets and the creation of it.

"I intended to send it to Princess Vivian with my apology." Jake didn't add why he needed to apologize.

"Your actions sound like selfless acts," Erceldoune said. His eyes bored through Jake.

Selfless? To apologize by giving a gift, was it selfless or a distraction from what I really needed to do?

"Your use of the Orb?" Lothian asked.

"It was the only way I knew to get the amulet to her." His voice dropped. He had to get it to her.

Jake's breath caught and his throat froze. "I hadn't thought …"

"Speak!" The warmth in Lothian's voice was gone.

"Did you ask anyone for help?" Clacks spoke up.

Caught. "No."

"Show us the amulet," Lothian said.

Jake handed it over. Each touched it, felt its weight in their hands, and passed it to the next without comment. Erceldoune, the last to handle it, set it on the table.

"I—"

"Answer only questions put to you," Lothian snapped before Jake could say anything.

Dismissed to the hall like a child waiting on his father to get a ride home, Jake was humiliated, his armpits soaked. Anxiety smothered him like a stack of blankets. Old feelings, feelings he tried to keep buried, surfaced with a fury. *I failed my friends … my men … again.* No real memory of Afghanistan existed for him, and his imagination got the worst of him. Hours passed.

The door opened, and Clacks waved for him.

Jake feared his new family would banish him, and he'd go home alone. *But to what?*

Dread shook him like a terrier shakes a rat. Jake's hands trembled. His breathing was short and strained. He waited for the verdict, expecting the worst.

"I have asked Erceldoune to sum our findings," Lothian said, "and I will pronounce my verdict."

No one smiled. Jake faced Erceldoune.

"Jake MacCorkle, you are accused of misuse of enchantment and misappropriation of the Orb."

Jake had no saliva but wanted his throat to swallow.

"Nevertheless, this Tribunal recognizes attempts to use enchantment for the help of another. Also, we see progress in your training despite the unconventional way it was achieved. We recognize independence in your thought and practice."

Erceldoune paused.

"However, your application put the Gleane, and all we hold dear, in jeopardy. Had you succeeded in leaving the Gleane, you would have opened a magical portal in our defenses that could have been used by our enemies. At a time when we are under attack, this was a dangerous undertaking. Your lack of trust, lack of acceptance of supervision, is a flaw that is dangerous to our way of life and security."

Jake blanched. *I didn't know. I didn't know.*

Lothian took over. "These are your options: leave the Gleane today with no memory of your time here or offer this tribunal an alternative that will ensure you are no threat to our people. Present your decision to this Tribunal in one hour."

Jake said nothing. The judges rose and filed from the room. Jake bowed. His legs wouldn't hold him. He collapsed to the floor.

****

Jake faced the Tribunal.

"Prince Lothian warned me when I first arrived about a choice that came when humans learned magic. I did not heed his warning. Small enchantment successes blinded me. Erceldoune said my actions were selfless, but this is not true; they were selfish."

Jake spoke from his heart. "I refused opportunities to face Princess Vivian in person and give her a true apology or change in insensitive behaviors. Instead, I apologized with a trinket that would show my achievement rather than take responsibility for my behavior. With all my heart, I regret my arrogance and cowardice. With your permission, allow me to remain in the Gleane. Give me an opportunity to regain your trust. Permit me to continue my relationship with the Daione Sìthe."

"How do you propose to accomplish these goals?" Lothian asked.

Jake was shaking like a leaf in a high wind, but he went on. "Intensify my training. Serve my apprenticeship under Clackmannan. Increase my time at the Library in the early morning and evening and, with your permission, I request a training partner. Afton Thish is my friend. If he is willing, his knowledge would advance my training both in cultural understanding of the Clan and application of enchantment. On my father's honor, I will use no enchantment without permission from whosoever this Tribunal orders. I take these actions to reclaim your trust and friendship, which I value above life."

Jake waited in the silence. *Would they accept it?*

"We will consider your proposal."

CHAPTER 51

At daybreak, Jake stood alone in the large field outside the mountain town. A muted breeze swayed the brown grass. Fresh, clean air filled his lungs. Dew stained the toes of his boots. He paced, worried how they would treat him.

His memory of Lothian's words was tattooed in his brain. "Mr. MacCorkle, this Tribunal places you on probation," Lothian said. "Any infraction of your training, any lack of communication, results in banishment. Train under Clackmannan. Train with Afton Thish. We accept your proposal."

Clacks arrived first. He grinned his infectious smile. Jake's jittery nerves calmed. Afton walked in from the opposite end of the field. He offered his hand, nodded, and smiled. Jake's worries eased.

Clacks waved his hands and spoke. "A blanket of white. Cover the sight. As thick as night."

A thick fog rose.

"A word of caution before we begin," Clacks said. "Be on guard while outside the gate. Several faeries were attacked in the forest." He turned to Jake. "Create a light."

Jake picked up a small, crooked branch. "Light be here, light be clear."

Jake's jitters returned as he waited for the tip to glow.

It glowed. Delight and pride surged through his chest. Afton and Clacks smiled at him.

Using Jake's light, they moved across the field to the railroad bed and down to the gate. Jake used his key. The forest was a new playground. Clacks and Afton peeled left and right.

"Find us," Clacks called over his shoulder. "Sense where we are. Use your light."

Anxiety gripped Jake. He didn't know his way around out here. He didn't know how to sense people. *I need to look it up in the Journal.* He froze and stared at the small glowing tip of light. *What do I know? I lit this without thinking. Sense them?*

He pictured Clacks in his mind. That comforting smile. A joy came to him. In his mind, Clacks, with his smile, stood beside a group of three trees to his left. Twenty feet maybe, no thirty.

Jake turned where his sense pointed him and felt his way along a self-discerned path. Ten feet farther, he saw the trees. Clacks leaned against one, grinning at him.

"Well done. Now, Afton," Clacks said.

Jake inhaled and exhaled a deep breath. He thought about Afton sitting in the Swan's back table, waving his hands, giving a Clan history lesson. Afton's passion was Jake's connection, and he sensed Afton, fifty feet ahead, almost a straight line. He doubted his senses. Afton had turned right. He saw that with his own eyes. He had to be somewhere right and not straight ahead. Jake turned to his right and started back to the gate. He stopped. *What do I know? My sense tells me he is straight ahead. Trust my intellect or my sense?* Clacks followed, saying nothing.

Jake slowed his breath and pictured Afton. *Straight ahead. Fifty feet.* Sensing a path, he started forward. Fifty feet later, Afton sat on a stone.

"Very well done," Afton said.

Very cool. "How did I do that?"

Clacks didn't answer. He handed Jake a small bag. Jake took a single, small, smooth stone from it.

"What do you know?" Clacks asked.

Jake calmed his thoughts and studied the stone. His breath slowed and became steady. A shift occurred. A sudden feeling of dread arose.

"I fear I don't know the right answer." *That was a first for me.*

"Consider. If fear was going to kill you, you would have died years ago." Clacks smiled, pointing to the stone.

What do I know? Sense the stone. Turn it with my mind. He set the stone on his palm, relaxed, and sensed it—size, weight, color. It turned in his mind.

"Each entity has an existence," Clacks said. "A story. See its pattern. The pattern is the gift."

Jake pictured a stone used to grind corn, used for trade with another person, used to kill. The stone never changed. Its purpose changed depending on a user's intention.

"Connection refines belief and sustains reality," Clacks said. "Live with the essence. Sense the character. Know the pattern. Connection defines magic."

I get it.

"Rise," Jake commanded the stone. Nothing. It lay inert. Jake looked away. Out of the corner of his eye, he saw it hover. He faced it. It fell onto his hand. It was no good if he couldn't see it happen. *Try harder.*

"Harder may not be the answer," Afton said. "Do by not doing."

How does he know what I'm thinking? Confused, Jake put the stone on his palm. He dropped his hands. The stone floated.

"Disappear," Jake said.

The stone disappeared.

"Where is it?"

"It did as you commanded," Clacks said.

"Reappear." The stone fell to the ground. He put his hand out, palm facing the stone, and imagined the stone in his hand.

****

Jake and Afton sat at the back table in the Swan. A raucous darts game played out in the corner.

"Do you know what happened?" Jake asked.

"No. Only that I was summoned and asked to train with you. I am honored."

"Can I tell you something I've never told anyone?" Jake asked.

Afton waited, watching with a kind, open face.

"When I was in the Army, my unit was assigned to clear a village. The intelligence was faulty. We got attacked by a superior force. We were pinned down. I called in air support, but it wasn't coming fast enough. An explosion took me out. After the explosion, I remember nothing. I believe I betrayed my men, left them, abandoned them. Erceldoune told me as much. He said the Orb protected me. My men were captured. I have to know … I have to know if I left them. I have to know if … I'm a coward."

Afton remained silent for several minutes.

"If the Orb helped you," Afton said, "a record exists in the Journal."

Afton was right. Jake had looked for enchantments, not information. But he would need permission to search for the truth.

"Thank you." Jake rose and went to find Clacks. He found Erceldoune.

CHAPTER 52

"I need your permission to look myself up in the Journal," Jake said to Erceldoune.

"To what end?"

"I need to know what happened in Afghanistan."

"As you wish. You need supervision only to act, not to investigate."

"I have your permission?"

"Of course."

Erceldoune had a twinkle in his eyes. *What's he thinking?*

****

Jake parked himself in the brown chair. The Journal lay open. He had never looked up current history, and his nerves frayed. His secret tormented him.

"Show me MacCorkle." As soon as he said it, he recognized his mistake. *No.* Way too broad a request. *Dumb idea.*

The pages flipped. He laid his hand on the page. A scene arose and Jake recognized the voice—it was his father, John MacCorkle's voice, telling the story.

****

I forced a car through Atlanta traffic.

Easing at red lights, horn blaring, I barreled ahead. The car fishtailed around curves. As I drove, I issued a summons over and over: "Come. Come at once. Come. Come at once."

I felt an evil ooze from the house as I drove into the driveway. Entering the back door, the foreboding grew. I peeked through the small square serving window into our living room.

Isobel sat on the couch with her right arm around Mary, hugging her close like a dear friend. In her left hand, a dagger thrust against Mary's ribs. As I entered, Isobel pulled Mary closer. The knife point cut her, and she cried out.

I couldn't attack without endangering her. Helpless, I waited.

"Give me the key," Isobel said and held out her hand.

I took it off and held it out from across the room.

Isobel pressed the knife tip to Mary's side. "Throw it to me!"

I hesitated.

Wind toppled lamps and blew pictures off the wall. Erceldoune appeared, hands raised, ready to battle.

Isobel drove the dagger between Mary's ribs. She screamed. Laughing like a banshee, Isobel vanished. Mary passed out.

Erceldoune closed his eyes and held out his right hand. The Orb appeared. A white cloud flowed around them. It flew us to the Gleane.

"She'll recover, won't she?" I begged Erceldoune.

"If it were a normal wound, even without enchantment, yes, but the tip of the knife broke off near her spine. It cannot be removed without risking death. Do you want to risk it or have her stay where the Orb can treat her daily to prolong her life?"

"Where is Jake?"

"The King sent for him. He is playing with Lothian and Vivian. He knows nothing of what happened."

"Thank God. I see no alternative. She must stay."

****

The vision dissolved. *Mom left when I was four. Dad said she died.* The revelation rattled Jake. Information he sought all his life was now at his fingertips. His original quest forgotten. He pressed on.

"Show me Mary MacCorkle."

The familiar routine began. Pages fluttered. The rustling stopped. Jake put his hand on the page. A woman's voice came.

****

The Orb restores me, but the dagger's poison drains me within a few days, and I must rest. My physical pain is bad but being away from John and Jake is worse. I watch Jake through a prism the Orb provides. But it's not the same. I ache to hold him. I miss him so much!

When I feel good, I get bored. These people are so kind and gentle. They fret over me constantly. Their Library and Journal are my refuge when I need time alone.

Reading their history, I found one who is lost, Ly Erg, a soldier like my Jake. Trapped by his own wicked actions, I feel his life must be continuous torment. I want to help him.

Today, after lunch, I'm going to Ly Erg.

****

"What was she up to? Who is Ly Erg?"

Questions outweighed answers: *If mother didn't die, then why was she kept from me? Why did Dad lie? Is she still here somewhere?* Jake had to know the truth. "Mary MacCorkle, continue." Jake pondered all the things she might do as the Journal pages flipped. He relaxed his hand over the page. A mist formed on the wall. His vision opened. His mother's storytelling voice was loud and clear, and he entered her life as it played out on the pages.

****

The Orb provided my way. I walked down a tunnel into a small cave that led to an opening next to a large field. Turning away from the field, I walked a trail that wound next to a forty-foot river. A small brook meandered into the river from the right. I jumped it and kept right, away from the rushing water, into a darker part of the forest. A butterfly lit on my sleeve. On the south side of an open meadow, I uncovered a five-foot cave opening covered by ivy, where the Orb said it would be. I entered.

The cave floor was flat and straight. Ten feet into the cave, a small indention housed a tall prism like a full-length mirror.

I reached out a hand. It disappeared into the prism. Steeling myself, I stepped into it. The picture went tilt-a-whirl. When it stopped, I stood in a different, darker cave that emerged in a different forest.

Tall trees, hundreds of feet high, composed an ancient forest. Yellowish-green heather grew everywhere among interspersed rocks that stuck their heads out like sleepy giants.

From my vantage point, small streams flowed down to broad valleys toward long lakes. At this height, the valleys looked like elongated balloons attached with many strings. Pausing a moment, I turned right and walked up a dirt trail worn deep by many feet.

Branching right, the trail curved gently down into a small, isolated cove. Stone outcrops grew tall, surrounding a small lake at the bottom of the cove. Pine trees grew in sparse clumps, not tall, but hardy, gripping the soil with firm patience. I threaded down through the trees. At a bank beside the small lake, a young man sat on a log staring out into the clear, turquoise-green water.

"Ly Erg?" I asked. The question lingered, and for a moment, I believed he wouldn't answer.

"You intrude on my solitude. Are you here to fight?"

"Not to fight."

"Are you the dead or dying?" Ly Erg's voice sounded tired.

"Dying."

"Do you want me to end your pain?"

"No," I said, "I came for your pain."

"I cannot be healed."

"Neither can I. May I sit with you?"

Ly Erg never turned. He never faced me. He hesitated. His shoulders hunched forward; his hands hidden under his armpits. He gazed into the pool for a long time.

"Yes, for a time," he said.

I sat on a rock ten feet behind him and talked to his back.

****

"I don't get it," Jake said.

Pages flipped. Visit after visit had been recorded between Jake's mother and Ly Erg. Most were the same. His mother talked. Ly Erg listened. An odd relationship.

During the Journal record, many single entries popped up over and over.

"Traveled to see Ly Erg. Away."

She never complained. Ly Erg never explained.

With daily care from the Orb, Mary lived seventeen more years. She visited every week, sitting on the same rock, Ly Erg on the log facing the lake.

Jake had to attend his afternoon training. Jake left the Library, rattled by these new revelations.

CHAPTER 53

Three men and two women emerged from the trees behind Ross Bandstand. Simion was pumped. He loved a chase.

Grezil, tall and beautiful, oversaw her crew. Two men were heavy built, solid, and dangerous, looking like refugees from the Sopranos. Simion's tall, wiry frame seemed out of place. Isobel, short and meaty, rounded out the odd company.

"Through here." Grezil brought them out on Princes Street. They headed for Geddes Hall.

****

Even though only a select few knew she was in Scotland, Vivian recognized it wasn't good to stay in one place too long. Her thoughts followed her through a quick chat with one of her roommates, who she tried to politely dodge. She knew she had to pick up the research and get home to America. But right now, she was famished.

Out the front door of Geddes Hall and up the Mound toward Princes Street, she hunted food.

****

After a fifteen-minute walk, Simion and the others reached Geddes Hall.

"Take the back," Grezil ordered one of the Sopranos. He headed off at a trot.

Simion smiled at Isobel. *I guess we have a new boss.*

"Wait here," Grezil told the other Soprano.

Isobel, Simion, and Grezil ascended to the third floor.

"No enchantments," Grezil told them at the door. A young man with glasses and a leather book bag strapped across his shoulder opened the door before they tried the handle. Isobel shoved him back.

"What? Who are you?" the young man protested.

Isobel sauntered toward him, closer and closer, until her face was within inches of his face. Putting a finger to her lips, she shushed him.

Simion grinned. *Someone else is getting a dose of her.*

"Silence," Isobel whispered to the young man. Shocked, he backed away, tripped over a chair, and fell on the floor. His glasses went askew across his nose. Isobel shook her head at him like he was stupid. Grezil pointed to Vivian's door.

"She's—"

Isobel took a step toward him. He dropped his head and went quiet.

Isobel and Grezil placed small stones in their hands and said a word. The stones spun, slowly at first, but by the time they crossed to Vivian's door, the stones were a whirr. Simion transformed. As a lean black dog, he padded to the door.

In a slow, gradual movement, Grezil opened it. Simion sniffed. He knew Vivian was not there. The trio eased down a short entry hall in single file. They peeked around the corner. No Vivian.

Simion transformed again. "Gone within the hour," he said.

"Who are you people?" the young man asked. "How did you do that stuff—"

Isobel crossed to him and slapped him hard. Despite her diminutive size, the strike raised him off the ground and bashed his head against the wall.

"Kill him?" Isobel asked.

"No need." Grezil reached for him. After a short enchantment, the young man's face sagged.

Grezil said, "He'll have no idea where those bruises came from when he wakes."

Isobel laughed.

Simion kept his thoughts to himself. *He's lucky he's not dead.*

****

After a quick lunch, Vivian headed up Princes Street. As she passed the gray-green Duke of Wellington statue reared on his bronze horse in front of the General Registry building, a renewed feeling nagged at her. The feeling had been building since she woke up, but it was nothing she could put her finger on, just a growing urgency to finish this task and get home. Was it Lothian … Jake … the Gleane? No clear overriding impression held her, only a prodding sense she needed to hurry.

Up two sets of wide stone steps two steps at a time and through tall double doors, she felt excitement stirring; research was her world. She knew the drill. After examining her reader's card, taking her pound coin, giving her a clear plastic bag to store her belongings, the clerk passed her into the building. The catch-all handbag went into a locker, and she headed straight to the archive room.

The information she ordered last night was not ready. "By half past," the research assistant assured her. Grezil's ancestry would have to wait.

An hour. No problem. Erceldoune had given her two other leads: the house Afton visited and the owner's name.

Vivian studied her notes. After Thish's murder, the house where Grezil went was the same house Afton visited, at Grezil's behest, in Atlanta.

Erceldoune located the house and the owner's name: Weir.

In Scotland's People section, she searched for the name Weir. Afton reported that Grezil referred to Weir as brother. Was he a biological brother or a member of a clandestine organization that referred to its members as "brother" and "sister"?

Multiple ancestry lines contained Weir. Several brother and sister combinations. Some dated back to the Kings of Scotland. *Which one?*

Thirty minutes passed before she found the answer.

"Weir Dismantles Kirkton House." A newspaper picture showed a crane removing huge stones from an old building. "Thomas Augustus Weir, an American millionaire. Weir family ancestor … moves great house to Atlanta, Georgia, USA … built in 1662 … torn down to make way for community housing …" *Big money to move a massive stone house across the pond.*

Using Kirkton House as a starting point, Vivian followed Weir's line. In the seventeenth century, the owner was Thomas Weir who had a sister named Grezzel. The spelling was close. Grezil may have been named for her. *An odd coincidence?* Vivian doubted it.

In the record of deaths, there was an obscure reference to the Laird of Kirkton dying, causes unknown. The widow remarried within months. The new Laird took the same name as the deceased owner. *Very odd.*

In the same year, the new Laird was accused of murdering Lord Darnell, the husband to Mary, Queen of Scots. He was never tried for murder. *Why not?*

Later, the government accused his descendants, a brother and sister, of witchcraft and burned them. "Weird family, unless … magic?" Vivian whispered.

A single piece of information completed a connection. The first Laird died, and the second arrived within the same year as Corraidhín's banishment.

"What if Corraidhín's lust for power drove him to kill a Laird and take his land, title, house, and wife? What if he used magic to influence the Scottish monarchy? What if the Weir in Atlanta descends not from King Torrinn but from Corraidhín?" *And Grezil is his biological sister.*

The pattern fit like a glove. "If Lothian and I died," Vivian's voice rose, "Weir has a legitimate claim to the throne. What if it was the Gleane itself he wants, and the Orb was secondary?"

"Shhhh." The person across her table shushed her.

Vivian sensed the Orb reach for her as it had the night before. Again, no message. But this time, a small purple drawstring bag materialized in the clear bag on the table. *What's this?*

Loosening the drawstrings, a long-handcrafted silver chain connected to a beautiful white stone fell into her hand. She knew all the craftsmen in the village. This workmanship was exceptional. A powerful amulet sparked and emitted a warm, calming sensation.

Vivian unclasped the silver chain and placed it around her neck. A note read: "Jake's apology." Jake's love flooded her heart. A warm flutter ascended to her chest. It grew. Tears welled. The amulet's strength teemed through her body. *I've waited so long.*

****

Outside Geddes Hall, the five split up into pairs. Simion was the odd guy out.

"You stay here," Isobel said to Simion.

He always got the crappy jobs.

"If anyone finds her, signal," Grezil said. "We need to subdue her, alive."

Isobel and Grezil took the University. The Soprano twins took Old Town.

Simion waited. When they were all out of sight, he walked up the stairs, transformed, and went to the door. Moving around the apartment, his educated nose sought Vivian. Knowing she had been on the bed, he started with the pillow.

Her scent. *I've got it.* He put his nose to the ground and followed the scent from the apartment and into the street. He sniffed left, back right, and left again. Up Princes toward New Town, he tracked her. If she kept walking, he'd have her.

Twenty minutes later, he contacted Isobel: "National Records of Scotland building, 2 Princes Street. She is here."

The Sopranos arrived first. Isobel and Grezil followed within ten minutes.

"She is in that building," Simion said.

"How do you know?" Isobel demanded.

"I tracked her here."

"You what?"

"I got her scent from the room. Followed it here. She's in there." He pointed to the General Registry building.

"Are you sure?" Isobel almost shouted.

Quit questioning me, bitch.

"Circle the building," Grezil said. "Cover as many exits as possible—No, wait. Let's do it a different way." She scrutinized Simion.

CHAPTER 54

Mammoth trees captured all but the most determined rays of morning sunlight. Blackened trunks and the absence of low foliage bespoke a forest fire. Jake and Afton moved quietly across the forest floor seeking a cave entrance.

"Let's split up," Afton said. "I'll send you a thought message when I find it."

"Like seek and find," Jake replied. Early in training, Jake learned no one was hiding, so he changed the name of the old children's game.

"Yes, but without sensing. I want you to practice receiving messages at a distance. I'll contact you when I find the cave." Afton moved off to the right.

Jake's ability to sense others was advanced. Without substantial effort, he found them. Sending and receiving messages had improved. Nearby others, Jake comprehended messages. At a distance, words garbled. After training, Afton sent mind messages when they were apart. The last message Afton sent was, *Get me an ale*. What Jake received was, *You're looking pale*.

Jake focused on Afton, waiting for his communication. Picking up a pebble, he spun it on his hand and flicked it toward a target. His use of darts advanced, but not as quickly as he wanted. Stones, sticks, and larger objects like pinecones, spun on his palm and became weapons. In early training, Clacks hit him with tiny pebbles so many times his chest became pockmarked with tiny bruises. It was weeks before he learned how to deflect the small stones. Then Clacks used larger ones. Deflecting them became critical before they drew blood.

On his own, Jake experimented with darts. Early in his thinking, he believed larger objects would do more damage, but the problem was they moved slowly through the air and were easily deflected. A pinecone looked like a grenade but when it exploded on target it did little damage, bouncing its tiny petals off the target like a water balloon. Size didn't make a difference. Speed did. Days and days of practice taught him how to vary speed of an object as it struck a target. Once he did it right, the target exploded with the force of C4.

Jake received a thought message.

Nothing. Afton was having the same luck as he. Drifting toward the south, he followed a small creek into a swampy area. Skirting around the water, he got another message.

Come … a missing word … *strang* … the word garbled. Maybe Clacks had joined them. No. Something about the message was off. An urgency. Jake stood and sensed Afton. He was to the right at two hundred yards.

Transporting was still beyond Jake's skill, so he ran, driving himself toward Afton until his legs burned and lungs stung.

A hundred feet ahead, Jake heard muffled cries. *Afton?* In a fast and low combat mode, Jake snaked forward. A thrashing noise like deer battling, pushing each other back and forth, sounded. A large stranger pinned Afton to the ground, grabbed his throat, and a glint flashed.

Closing the gap, Jake's belt made a slapping sound as he whipped it out of his pants. He doubled it around his hands into a garrote. Slipping it over the unsuspecting man's head, he put his knee in his back, and jerked upward against his neck. The man grunted as the belt cut into his throat.

Jake tightened his stranglehold, jerking the man off Afton. Afton grabbed the knife hand and wrenched the weapon away.

Afton's attacker clawed at the belt. He struck out wildly trying to hit Jake. They fell backward to the ground. Jake twisted the belt and held on. Within seconds, struggle ceased.

Shaken, Afton got to his feet. "Is he dead?"

****

Standing before the attacker in the cellar were Jake, Erceldoune, Lothian, and Afton.

"Tell me your name?" Lothian said in a voice that carried the authority of a Prince.

Head down like a penitent child, he said, "Edwin."

"Edwin, tell me why you attacked Afton."

"I did nothing. I was minding my own business. Camping. And this fellow," he pointed at Jake, "throws a rope around my neck and tries to kill me."

Erceldoune straightened. "Enough." The voice was quiet, but so powerful that Jake felt the room quiver. Erceldoune held out a hand, and the Orb appeared.

"We have no patience for interrogation," Lothian said.

"I agree." Erceldoune placed the Orb before the prisoner.

The prisoner's eyes grew wide. He shrank away from the iridescent colors and averted his eyes. But he couldn't help himself. He looked again, stared into the Orb's depth, and his jaw slackened.

"Why were you in the forest?" Lothian asked.

In a slow, methodical, monotone voice, the attacker answered.

"Kill MacCorkle."

Jake flushed. *I was the target?*

"What is your Clan?"

"I have none."

"Who sent you?"

"Isobel."

"Was she in the forest with you?"

"No."

"Where is Isobel?"

"Scotland." Jake's breath caught like someone had punched him in the gut.

Erceldoune stepped away and messaged Vivian: "Beware. Isobel in Scotland."

Within seconds, a response came, "Safe. Headed home."

****

The amulet radiated a cozy comfort against her chest. Reaching to touch it, Vivian forgot her mission for the moment and basked in the love-imbued token. *I need to get home to Jake.* Pushing to finish, she opened the last paper about Weir.

Weir's Odd Take on Capitalism. She scanned it.

Weir proposed homage, "… the bond of inferior to superior … a weaker man pledges servitude to a stronger lord in return for protection … must be friend to all his friends, and foe to all his foes."

According to Weir, homage was necessary for capitalism to survive. That was a direct reproduction of Corraidhín's belief that humans needed domination and domestication by faeries. The same opinion led to the theft of the Orb and the Nine Years' War. *Weir advocates slavery.*

A chill ran down her spine. Her brother was attacked to eliminate him. Grezil was sister to this crazy loon who thought faeries should enslave man. *He's straight out of the Middle Ages. I need to get home.* Vivian dug the locker key out of her clear bag, collected her papers, and headed for the front desk.

Taking her big bag out of the locker was quicker than putting it in. As she stood at the desk, the front doors swung back. Turning the corner and coming up the gray steps was a person wearing sunglasses, holding the lead of a large, black dog.

They're here. Vivian's hand trembled. Shock gripped her gut. The one-pound coin, returned for her locker key, rolled away. *How did Grezil find me?*

Turning away from the desk, she hid her face and moved far enough back into the building to watch the entry doors. A heavyset man and a dyed-blonde woman with a weird hairdo entered behind Grezil. Vivian stepped back and raised her hands. Four was too many to fight. *I want to be…* She started the enchantment to become invisible but realized Grezil would sense her even if she could not be seen. She had to run.

An argument ensued. "What reader's card?" Grezil's voice raised.

That would take a few minutes, but would it give her the time she needed? Offices were dead ends. The public traffic came and went through the front entrance where Grezil stood. Vivian headed deeper into the building, looking for an exit. At a trot, she zigzagged between two tables and around a third. The guide dog jerked off the lead.

****

Simion put his educated nose to the floor and sought Vivian's scent. Crisscrossing the room several times with the others following, he found the trail. Not long, and he'd have her.

A perturbed patron protested. "Get that animal on a leash."

Grezil glanced at the man and he quieted.

The path went toward the back of the Registry.

Run, rabbit, run.

****

Vivian crashed through the back doors. Still running, she started the enchantment to transport. Before she had spoken three words, the dart hit with the force of a tree falling on her. Her knees slammed into rough pavement. Pain jolted through her shoulder. The strike flung her body against the cobblestones. Before she could rise, a stout man was on her. Running feet sounded on the pavement behind her.

Half sitting, propped on an elbow, Vivian swung her immense handbag in a wide, looping arch at Grezil's face. Leaping away, Grezil tripped and smashed into the woman behind her. Both went down. Vivian was on her feet. Adrenaline surged. She raised her hands to attack.

The blow popped her head forward and back like a bobble doll. She saw stars. Her legs buckled. Hoisted by her armpits, her feet dragged. A metal door slid and banged to a stop. Rough hands threw her body into the air. Like a rag doll, limbs splayed, she landed hard on a steel floor and passed out.

CHAPTER 55

At midafternoon, the Swan crowd thinned. Jake, Clacks, and Afton sat at their back table. Time slowed. Anxiety jacked Jake up to a point he couldn't follow the conversation.

Clacks said something about Vivian. Half listening, Jake caught the name but missed the content. "Err, what?"

"I said, Princess Vivian should get here this evening. The trip from Scotland takes time."

Jake couldn't focus, not until she was safe. All morning, odd impressions cascaded through his body. Over the last few months, he learned to trust his instincts. Today, those intuitions drove him in ever-changing circles. First, an image of Vivian came to him with warm, cozy feelings. When the perception shifted, he felt fear, not a tepid fright, but a terror. None of the emotions assaulting him made any sense. Vivian was fine. Her message said she was coming home. But the perceptions continued to buzz around him.

Trying to push the confusion away, Jake changed the subject.

"Who is Ly Erg?" he asked.

"Ly Erg? Your studies venture far afield." Clacks smiled.

"What do you mean?"

"Ly Erg is a nasty piece of work. He was a very young soldier who succumbed to blood lust during battle. He does naught but challenge anyone and everyone, faerie or human, to fight. If you engage him, win or lose, you die. He fights like a rabid dog but cannot be killed. Anywhere there is carnage, he appears. Where did you hear about him?"

"In the Journal," Jake said without elaboration. Jake wanted to ask why they let his mother befriend him? Did he kill her? But he changed the subject.

Bewildered by the devilish dispositions, he had to say something. "I'm having strange impressions." Starting slowly, unsure how to explain what was happening to him, he pushed on. "I had a pleasant sensation about Princess Vivian this morning, but now it's changed to a fear, almost a dread. What is going on with me?" He asked because his oath required it. In the past, he would have held the emotions secretly, appearing untouched by them. Help and understanding would come from people more knowledgeable.

Afton and Clacks looked at each other before Clacks said, "Perhaps your affection for the Princess makes you overly concerned about her welfare."

That was probably the right answer, but it did nothing to assuage the anguish building in Jake.

****

Back in the Library, Jake researched his mother. Vivian was late. The Gleane was on edge, waiting, hoping, praying she was all right. Everyone recognized her stock, and the word passed about her mission. All wanted her home safe. He needed a distraction.

"Mary MacCorkle."

The familiar mist rose, and he entered his mother's vision. Her voice spoke her story.

****

I sense it is the end for me. I travel the familiar path to visit my friend, Ly Erg, and to say goodbye. Few times has he opened the conversation. Today he did.

"You are come to your last breath," Ly Erg said, sitting stoically in his tattered blood-encrusted uniform.

"Yes. The Orb says I will die. In hours. Today is goodbye, my friend."

"Friend?" His voice signaled true surprise.

"Our talks have brought us at least that," I said.

"I will remember you, for I have no other called 'friend.'"

"May I impose?"

"One thing," Ly Erg said, never raising his head.

"May I touch my friend?"

Ly Erg shuddered. "No human touch have I had, not in five hundred years. The last was my mother's on the day I went to war."

"My son is at war in Afghanistan."

Moments passed before he said quietly, "I grant your request."

Slowly, as if approaching a wounded animal, I rose and eased in front of him. He wore a blue uniform, military, torn, buttons hanging loose. His stained, blue pants had a red stripe down the sides. He looked younger than I expected, maybe seventeen. His expression was keen. I saw a savagery in his eyes. I sensed a gentle, pain-filled spirit underneath, and I reached to touch it.

"I am hideous to you," he whispered.

"No, you are my son."

I heard a constant rhythmic plop of droplets. His hands, both hands, dripped as if he plunged them into water, but there was no water. Manufactured from his skin, his hands dripped blood.

I pulled a handkerchief, dipped it in the lake, and touched his arm. Ly Erg shuddered. He dropped his head and started to pull his arm away. I kept it in a gentle grip. I kneeled, working down his arm until I reached his right hand,

and washed the blood away. White skin appeared, tinged pink by prolonged seeping blood. I cleansed the right hand and then the left. Both clean.

We sat for the last time, and I held his hands in mine.

"It won't last," he said.

"Perhaps not. Done for now." I smiled at him.

A faint smile touched his lips. "Thank you."

In less time than either of us wanted, I stood and kept my hand on his shoulder. The rough wool of his uniform felt uneven to my fingertips. "I must go."

"You have done me a great kindness. I will repay it."

I smiled, knowing I would never see it repaid.

****

Jake closed the Journal. Tears flowed. Jake couldn't tell whom his tears were for: his mother, Ly Erg, or himself. Droplets landed on the pages of the Journal. He reached to wipe them away, but they were gone, pulled into the rough pages of the old book.

CHAPTER 56

Vivian's brain came online in fits and starts. Her eyes fluttered but wouldn't open. Ears registered faint voices. Noises, a rumbling of tires, the creak of mechanical sounds, filtered into consciousness. Shifting movement sloshed her body in rhythm with the sounds. She pressed against something hard. Steel? A rumbling roared under her. As sensation increased, a throbbing echoed in the back of her head. *Where am I?*

Other body parts felt anesthetized, flaccid, as if she'd received a spinal injection. *What happened?* Her mind pictured her capture like flipping through a series of snapshots on a phone. *I was in the Registry. Grezil … the dog … running … explosion … falling … grabbed. Kidnapped?*

Bewildered surprise and shock ran down her spine. *Grezil has me!*

Think. Think. *When they took me, why didn't they kill me? Bait. Bait to trap Lothian. Oh, God, why was I so stupid? I should have gotten those articles and left.*

Escape? The Orb.

Her mind generated a picture, but unlike past images where she could command it, the Orb didn't brighten. Her mental picture didn't summon the Orb; it was only a memory. The connection she needed to break the spell that bound her was gone. Fighting the enchantment that lay on her would make it worse. She was helpless and alone.

Breathing deeper, she relaxed. The amulet pulsed against her chest. She focused on it. Pain declined. A warmth flowed into her body.

Jake.

The amulet contained power. When the right time came, she would use it to free herself and fight. Feigning unconsciousness, she listened.

"I don't care what kind of Wyzard you are. A little tap to the skull, and you go right down."

"Smart move, herding her right where we wanted her to go."

"Yeah, when she saw I tracked her, she panicked and ran, just like a rabbit into the trap."

The talk changed. "Why the forest?" a voice asked. "That place gives me the heebie-jeebies." No one responded.

The voices quieted. Time dragged. Vivian fell asleep. The vehicle jerked to a stop. The *whurrrr whump* sounded as the door slid back. Fresh, clean air flowed across the floor. Vivian gathered energy from the amulet. A tingling awoke in her body. Eyes closed, she waited for her chance. *Get ready.*

A woman spoke from the front seat: "Strong as vine. Take this line. Make it bind."

No. Vivian pushed herself to rise. Her muscles, dormant, frozen for hours, refused. An innocent-looking strap sprang around her with the speed of a snake constricting its lunch. Ankles, legs, torso, and arms were bound tight in an instant. Rough hands dragged her across the steel floor and propped her up on her feet.

A short woman—bleached-blonde hair, a buzz cut on one side of her head, and a rooster comb sticking up six inches on the other—stared up at Vivian, who towered a foot and a half over her.

"I would kill you here and let the crows pick out your eyes, but Grezil wants you whole," the dyed-blonde said, glaring up at her face.

Vivian sagged. She wasn't going to make it easy for them.

One of the hard-looking men threw her across his shoulder like a sack of potatoes. Stepping away from the carpark, he trod a thin foot path carved two feet into the ground from centuries of use. Vivian bounced against his shoulder, head down and stomach pinched against his collarbone. Before he traversed fifty feet, she made a retching sound. "I'm getting sick." On his shoulder, she saw only the ground and his backside. She had to see direction, memorize landmarks, recall details if she was ever to escape or help rescuers.

"Don't you puke on me," her bearer growled.

"Put me down. If I sit a minute, I can walk."

"And run, I wager," Simion said.

"Where would I go?"

The bearer spun around to look at the dyed-blonde woman and tall man, flipping Vivian's head left and right.

"Put her down," the spiky woman said.

Like he was off-loading a bale of hay, he dropped her. "Carrying her is like carrying eighteen stone," he complained, huffing and puffing.

Lying on the green bracken, Vivian oriented herself. The gravel carpark was a hundred feet to her right. A single blue van.

A trail cut into the undergrowth, ran up a small hill, around a bend, and out of sight to her left. Individual, scrubby, twisted Scot pine grew at random. Ahead, rowan and birch trees stood in clumps. A thin forest clung to the slopes on her right. Cataloging the areas by grid, she memorized the place.

"If you loosen my legs, I can walk," Vivian said.

The tall man looked at the blonde. She nodded.

I see who's in charge.

The blonde woman spoke, "Strongest twine. Make this line. Unbind."

The coils loosened. One of the hard-looking men unwound her legs to her waist.

"Hold the end and lead her," the blonde said. "Take no chances."

Vivian's arms remained clasped to her chest like a mummy in a sarcophagus. No one helped. She leaned to her right, struggled to her knees, and after several attempts, stood up. Her bearer pulled the end of Vivian's tether. She concentrated on the amulet and recorded every step.

Jake will come.

The trail went up, traversed a small hillock, wound up and down along a ridge, and curved left and right following the ground contours, ending on a high peak. A beautiful valley lay before them.

Painting the scene in her mind, Vivian compiled every feature from the path meandering west into the setting sun to spotty stands of Scot pine and rowan. Splitting the landscape was a small silvery stream, entering from the north and traversing the valley's center until a larger stream gathered it in. From the mountaintop, the large stream looked like a dark thread against a green canvas.

From the hilltop, two valleys stood back-to-back, looking like link sausages, fat in the middle and narrow where they joined. The stream gushed merrily through the first valley until the narrow sausage-link gap blocked it. Undeterred, it backed briefly at the narrows before it burst free and wild into the far-right side of the second valley.

Surrounding the sausage-link coves, a ring of aged mountains rose on either side. Tall crags oversaw the green undergrowth and passed stingy sun to the trees. Looking like pebbles from this distance, fallen rocks blockaded side ravines in and out of the valleys.

Beyond the narrows, the river clung to the far-right wall and skirted out of view. The space vacated by the river formed a wide-open field strewn with sleepy gray boulders that stuck their heads up in unorganized clusters.

Green heather spewed in and around everything. At the end of the second valley, a thick forest of dark and light trees fused. The forest flattened and expanded toward a further valley hidden deep in the forest. Despite the clear day, a grayish-white light dulled the vista's beauty. A quiet dread that matched the look of the place filled Vivian. How would anyone ever find her?

The kidnapper's troop moved down the trail into the first valley. A crystal clear, rock-bound stream joined and accompanied them. Keeping left, the interlopers plodded through a thick, spongy carpet of wintergreen along its bank.

Rock crags rose higher around them. Forced into a diminishing width, the stream darkened. Depth increased. Water raced. To avoid the swift current, the party clung to overhanging rock walls and walked in single file on a thin band of sand.

Without hands for balance, Vivian slipped. The rope cut her upper body when the man jerked it. She skidded on a slick rock and fell into the water. He dragged her back to the sand like he was landing a carp. Soaking wet, scraped, and cut, she struggled to her feet. A snicker rose, but without comment, the little caravan trudged on.

As the stream curved away to the right, the second valley opened into a broad plain, three-quarters of a mile long, half a mile wide. Sheer cliffs cradled three sides until a forest opened at the far end. Cracked and dislodged boulders, some as large as a car, had fallen and littered the valley edges. Scruffy twisted trees battled for a foothold against the stone.

Through prickly gorse, heather, fern, and bracken, they trekked to the far end of the valley. Rushing water sounds diminished to an echoing splash as the stream turned toward the far wall. A thick stand of birch marched into the valley's upper edge and flared out like people coming out of a ballgame. *Only a single way in or out. Ambush?*

At the far end of the valley, they halted. Vivian rested her back against a huge stone. There was no pretense, no discussion; they waited like soldiers on guard duty.

Within the hour, a whirlwind scooted down the valley. At its center, a tiny speck grew into a tiny figure. Grezil's triumphant face leered out at Vivian as she paraded out of the whirlwind.

Vivian's spine stiffened. She faced Grezil as her monarch. "A traitor, one who killed her own family, have you come to be my murderer?"

"You speak as if those were bad things. As to your death, we shall see," Grezil said smiling. She added, "I have no allegiance to you, I serve the true heir."

"The progeny of a traitor who was banished is no heir."

Grezil bristled. "Heir enough without sniveling brats on the throne." Grezil raised her hand and the strap, which had been loosened from her legs, re-bound Vivian head to toe.

Grezil raised her hands like she manipulated a marionette. "Light as a feather, rise."

Vivian struggled against the enchantment. Grezil walked to the left corner of the valley. Vivian floated behind her like a balloon on a string. Ten feet below the birch forest sat a mammoth stone, half-buried in the earth. As if she was measuring it, Grezil paused.

Is she going to smash me against it? Vivian thought as terror rose. Breathing tightened in her chest. Bracing for impact, she didn't hear Grezil's words.

"Open now, enclose her carcass. Tight to hold, limbs caress. 'Til the time the master come. Then life is done, and to death succumb."

Vivian hovered over the stone for an instant before starting down. When her feet touched the stone, it liquefied and opened to accommodate them. Her ankles passed in. Like an apple dunked in caramel, she sank into the stone.

Noooo. She's going to trap me in the stone. Vivian, screaming, fought futile helplessness as she slid deeper and deeper. As her knees, hips, and hands slipped into the stone coffin, the strap holding her became superfluous and popped away. Her terrible scream bounced across uncaring rock, pierced the forest, and echoed up the valley. Her stone crypt closed over her head.

Eyes blinded by her gray tomb, her heart beat erratically in her chest. She strained to think of something, anything. *Jake.* Hopes faded. *Hold me, Jake.*

****

In the deep birch shadows next to his lake, Ly Erg heard the scream and prepared.

"Who intrudes on my solitude?" *I sense nothing worth my time.* Human squabbles didn't arouse him. Hikers came and went. He let them pass without challenge, but these were no hikers. *A coming war?*

"Who trespasses in my valley?"

CHAPTER 57

"I have her." Grezil stood before Weir's partner desk. She smiled, knowing they were a single step away from owning the Gleane.

"Where?" Weir asked.

"Cairngorms National Park. A small cove. Her personal resting place for eternity."

"She's dead?"

"No. A heartbeat remains. When we have the brother, the coffin will hide her body forever."

"Acceptable."

****

A rough sketch of the Cairngorm cove lay on the small table in Weir's office. Atop it was a crudely drawn battle plan showing positions for attack and defense. Childlike in scope but detailed enough to know what it was. Weir examined it. "Explain."

Simion sat, not in his corner, but at the big people's table. Holding the drawing in the air, he said, "I drew a picture of the valley with good ambush sites."

Pointing to his map, he said, "Lookouts here and here, high enough that they can signal when the enemy arrives. A small group, perhaps eight, to open a skirmish and draw them into the valley. Skirmishers retreat, giving a false sense of hope and drawing them to the center of the valley where cover is limited. The lookout and four others, hidden here at the narrow entrance, block escape. We spring the trap and kill them all."

The plan fit the terrain. The execution worked. The finality was exact. Weir looked up. Everyone waited for his pronouncement.

"How many soldiers do you need?"

"Fifty inside the valley and another fifty hidden outside in this cove ready to assist."

"Simion, people rarely surprise me," Weir said. "Today you have done so. We will do as you suggest."

Simion grinned with undisguised joy. Never, not one time, had Weir congratulated him for anything he'd done. To give him command, was …

magnificent. Finally.

"Transport our people to the cove," Weir said. "Grezil, coordinate with Simion. Be my liaison."

"Of course," Grezil said. A faint, secret smile passed from his sister.

Simion glanced at Isobel's perturbation with satisfaction.

****

Vivian's sense of time evaporated while floating in a hard, crusty shell. No sight. No sound. The stone's rough pinch worked against her skin until she felt nothing. No tidbit of sensation left, her brain stultified and blunted. Thoughts despaired. *Jake will come for me. Won't he?*

Nerves tore into raw sinews until, as she breathed, she felt a small stone push against her breast. *The amulet.* Demanding her mind to function, she reconnected to it. *Recall the color, shape, facet, clasp, and chain.* As each connection was reclaimed, she quieted and propelled a single message into the stone. *Help me!*

****

Training was over for the day. The Swan was noisy.

The same odd feeling had stolen over Jake for the past few hours, like he had to do something. Something important—no, critical.

Jake returned to the Library. The feeling toddled after him like a child who was reaching for him. It nagged him. Demanding he do something. He concentrated on the Journal. A vision failed, and no specific discernment came. He had to get out of here for a while. Take a walk. Relax.

Down the tunnel behind the castle, he headed to the forest. The feeling tracked him like a ghost in moonlight. He felt haunted.

Vivian.

The thought propagated.

Help me!

Jake ran to the round door and up the stone steps. Lothian and Erceldoune were in the small gray room across from Lothian's chambers overlooking the patio.

"Something is wrong with Vivian. I know it. She's caught or trapped. In trouble. She needs us."

"How do you know?" Lothian asked.

"I feel it. It's been nagging at me for hours. A moment ago, it came together. We have to help her."

Erceldoune was on his feet. He closed his eyes and reached for Vivian. Nothing.

Lothian grabbed the Orb. "Locate Vivian."

The Orb generated a cool white mist that cascaded into purple, green, blue, and red, as if searching. It swirled to black.

"Show Vivian," Lothian ordered.

They waited.

"If she is in magical transport," Lothian said to Jake, "the Orb cannot locate her, but it can show her."

The swirl came and went black. No picture. No color. No Vivian.

"Jake, sense Vivian," Erceldoune said.

As he'd done with Clacks and Afton, he searched his mind for a defining characteristic. *Her laugh.* A natural, relaxed, rich enjoyment of life. Jake pictured her smile becoming her laugh.

A feeling of dread swallowed him. He was alone. A deep isolation engulfed him. Constriction, not tightening about him, but constraining him, confining his entire body. Ink-spot black blotted his vision like when he was lost in the tunnel.

"She's trapped, held in a container, unable to move. All is black. Restrained by a force she cannot shift."

Lothian's eyes grew wide, and his voice came in gasps. "We must go to her. Help her."

"We lost the following," Erceldoune said. "We need Afton."

"But I need to go to her—" Jake's perception of Vivian's plight frightened him.

"Find Afton now, please."

Jake hesitated. Finding Afton Thish was not the action he wanted. When he looked into Erceldoune's eyes, he knew it was the right one.

Jake sprinted for the Swan. People sensed urgency and dodged away. Jake took the Swan steps two at a time. Bursting through the doors, he called to Afton. "Erceldoune needs you now." Afton rose and ran with Jake.

As soon as they came into view, Erceldoune called down the hall, "Where is your mother?"

Afton stopped midstride, closed his eyes, and took a deep breath. When his eyes opened, he said, "At the house in Atlanta."

How did he know that?

"We search Atlanta," Erceldoune said, "before we commit to Scotland. We find Grezil, we find Vivian."

CHAPTER 58

Jake scrambled after Erceldoune, who scaled the twelve-foot wall with no problem. Entering at the northwest corner, a strange formation of thin, ruler-straight trees formed a perfect triangle, a small mound at its center. Odd formation to have in one's yard.

Erceldoune moved across the ground like a sapper clearing mines. Shifting to his right, he mumbled a counter to an enchantment. Moving to his left, he waved off weak enchantments with a flick of his wrist.

Jake stood where Erceldoune stood, waited when he waited, and realized this was an advanced course in sensing. Twenty minutes into his lesson, Jake envisioned silver wires and wispy entrapments about them like spider webs. *Is that really there?*

In answer to Jake's thought, Erceldoune whispered, "Yes, it is."

A hundred feet from the back of the house, a formal garden maze blocked them. Erceldoune passed through it as if on a Sunday stroll through the Atlanta Botanical Gardens. The house was a different problem.

Erceldoune hesitated. He meditated for a moment, then spoke in a low singsong voice. "A rune once writ may not be changed. A spell once spoke becomes estranged. Passage safe a truth to know. Expose, reveal, the path to go. Create a way, before untold. Coming out, the same unfold."

Erceldoune picked up a small limb and handed it to Jake.

"A flashlight?" Jake asked.

Erceldoune gave him a knowing grin. The long and complicated spell gave them access through unknown enchantments, if, and only if, they came out the exact way they went in. Jake glanced across the garden. Faint footsteps glowed. They ended at Jake's shoes.

"An added precaution," Erceldoune whispered to Jake. He put his hand on Jake's shoulder. "I choose to be, where no one can see."

"Are you sure this will work?" Jake asked.

"Concentrate and repeat the words as you do in the Library."

"I choose to be, where no one can see."

"Again."

Jake focused, relaxed, and spoke as he did when he summoned visions from the Journal. "I choose to be, where no one can see."

No tilt-a-whirl. No lurch. Jake felt the same.

"What does that do?" Jake asked.

"Makes you invisible. An old and simple enchantment used by faeries to visit man's world undetected."

So, that's how Clacks and Afton disappear in the forest.

"I don't feel any different," Jake said.

"Excellent."

At the back of the three-story manor house, a flagstone patio held a white wicker table and chairs. A three-foot wall enclosed it. Twelve-pane, double French doors led off it into the house. Erceldoune waved his hand. The doors drew back. An enormous dining room surfaced from the gloom.

The thin glow from Jake's wand cast streaks across a highly polished table. Sparkles glinted around the room, flitting in the cut glass candelabra, dinnerware, glassware, silverware, and an immense Chippendale china cabinet as if the room held a bevy of fireflies.

Erceldoune motioned to Jake to come near.

Can he see me? The hot breath tickled his ear.

"You said she was someplace dark, alone, and frightful," Erceldoune whispered. "I doubt it is in the main living areas. Search this floor to the right and above. I will take this floor to the left and below. Quiet. You are invisible, but they can hear you."

Am I really invisible? He's looking right at me.

"Yes, you're really invisible," Erceldoune replied to Jake's thoughts. "Now step lightly."

Jake skirted the edge of the room to the first of the in-out doors beside the sideboard. Easing it open, a large kitchen loomed. His stick glowed. The storage rooms and a walk-in freezer held nothing. Through the opposite door, he stepped back into the dining room.

A door exited to his right into an open, two-story, marquetry foyer. Moonlight twinkled through the front windows and joined his tiny light, bouncing off the crystal chandelier. Oblong light framed by the front windows slid shapes across the mosaic floor. Curving staircases wound to the second floor. Jake went right.

Quiet as a lion stalking an antelope, Jake eased the central door open. A bathroom. He flashed his light around it. Nothing. He backed out and closed the door.

As he crossed the threshold into the next room, evil beckoned Jake. Hairs stood out on his neck and arms. Jake rubbed the chill away and shivered like a dog shaking off raindrops. He forced himself to enter.

Dominating the room was a huge double-sided partner desk with a high-backed leather chair behind it. A credenza was on the right. On the left, a small table had four upholstered chairs around it. Each desk and credenza drawer eased out. Nothing of interest. On the small table, a drawing like a child's rendering lay unfolded.

Why am I drawn to that?

Hanging on one wall was a framed floor plan of the house. Next to it hung a woven tapestry depicting a group performing an eighteenth-century play, but on closer inspection, one woman passed a note to a man behind the back of her partner as they stood arm in arm.

Odd thing to have in an office. Secrets?

Jake peeked behind the tapestry. Nothing.

Jake returned to the drawing on the table. Nagged by it, he picked it up, folded it, and put it in his jacket pocket.

At his command, the improvised wand dulled to an ember. He kept to the outside of the circular stone stairs as he edged up it. *Go slow. Attic first.*

Left at the top of the stairs, Jake found narrow wooden stairs going up. With a hand against the rough stone, he ascended in silence. The wide attic floorboards complained when he stepped on them. Each step became measured, waiting on one foot, listening to ensure he attracted no interest from below before moving forward.

The attic held nothing but boxes and crates stacked in an unorganized clutter. Jake retraced his steps to the landing. Hall boards creaked. He waited, motionless. All clear. First door on the right—zilch. Other rooms contained slumbering lumps in four-poster beds. No Vivian.

Jake's confidence increased as he passed in and out of occupied rooms with impunity. The last room, at the far end of the hall, was larger than the others. He checked the closet and turned to leave. A bedside light blinded him. A man lay against the pillows, looking right at him.

"Mr. MacCorkle. May I have a word?"

Jake froze. His breath caught like he couldn't find any air. He sucked in little quiet gasps and blew them out his mouth in a controlled whisper.

A heavy man with sparse salt and pepper hair rose in the bed. His tone was casual, like they were two friends meeting for lunch. He looked right at Jake as if he could see him—or maybe sense him. "I know why you are in my house at this hour. I have watched you, my boy. I think it is time for you to consider your future. A real future. I know you miss your family. I welcome you into ours. I have certain modest abilities. I can help you regain lost moments, let you see what life was like with your people, help you feel the security that your parents offered. Let me show you."

The man moved his hands. A scene formed. *It's the same as the Journal.*

A playground. His mother stood next to a picnic table laying out paper plates and fried chicken. Jake, about six years old, was in a swing pushing its limits. "Higher, Daddy," Jake yelled. His father laughed and smiled at his mother.

The scene shifted. Jake, about fourteen, played catch with his dad while his mother sat on a blanket, watching and smiling. Warm sensations rose into his chest. *I want this.*

"Your family," the heavy man said. "I can give you that power and more. With me, you have control and can never be hurt." The man's announcer voice enhanced the scene. "Forgive me, Jake; I haven't told you my name. I'm Augustus Weir—"

Jake winced. *I need to shut up. He's playing me.* A picture of the man playing a flute before a cobra flashed through Jake's mind. But reuniting with his lost family tempted him, and before he thought, he asked a question. "What about the Daione Sìthe?"

Weir shifted his head slightly to track the voice. "Your friends won't suffer. They will live in the Gleane under my care."

An odd thought came to Jake. Weir wanted to rule the Gleane, make the People his subjects, but why was he interested in Jake? This thought clashed headlong into the belief he could have his family. "What about the Princess?" Again, he spoke. Again, Weir shifted, tracking him.

"She is under my protection. I can release her whenever I want. You will never find her on your own. You are a reasonable man. You can have everything you want—power, your family around you, and protection for the Daione Sìthe. Join me. Save them all."

The bargain gnawed at Jake. He could save Vivian. Save the People. But at what price? What was Weir really offering?

What do I know? Sense him.

Jake directed his energy at Weir. Wave after wave of nausea attacked Jake. His legs buckled. The picture transformed. The People of Peace worked, slaving to enrich Weir. Lothian's body swung from a tree. Vivian's decayed corpse lay frozen in a crypt. Jake gagged.

Weir hadn't noticed the shift. He prattled on, pitching his flawed tale. "My friend, I have the gift of second sight. I see the future. I'll show it to you now."

Another vision rose. A group with Jake entered a valley. They stepped around a stream and passed through a narrow gap. A second valley opened. Green-gray bracken carpeted its floor. Evergreen trees battled through cracks in stone slag. At the upper end, silver birch trees marched into the valley as if year after year they stole a little more real estate. Huge stone walls towered around the sides.

A sudden explosion blew people into the air. A tall man standing in the open fired darts. Jake dove behind the rocks. Darts flew. Chaos overtook confusion.

One person's head gaped open as his blood gushed onto the ground. He was dying. A single glance into dull eyes told Jake another was dead. The attack intensified. The tall man fled. Jake surrendered. Isobel stepped behind him. He felt the dagger at his throat. Screaming with delight, she whipped it across his neck. Blood gushed. His clothes were drenched. He lay gasping until he bled out. *It's a vision. Breathe. Breathe.* The battlefield scenario faded.

"Does the witch Isobel work for you?"

"Not anymore." Weir said it like it was a firing, like he decided she should be elsewhere.

"But she did?"

"Yes, but she often acted on impulse without my sanction. Her ways are not my ways. I am not responsible for what she does on her own whim. That's why we parted."

Jake regained his wits. Weir was tracking his voice. *A lie. Move, fool.* He kept quiet.

With quiet restraint, Jake took a silent sidestep toward the door. Another. Weir's focus remained on the last spot where he last spoke.

"Mr. MacCorkle?"

He can't see me. Staying quiet, he took a step closer to the door.

"Your silence betrays your decision. Pity. You play at being a Wyzard. It is time you learn what real magic does. A lesson you will never forget. There will be no rescue. I will leave the Princess in the stone until her body rots."

She's not here.

Quicker than lightning, a dart shattered the closet door to Jake's right. Jake flinched. Weir aimed at the sound Jake made.

Sheets and blankets spun in the air, sounding like the whirr of ten thousand bats leaving their cave on a night flight as they grabbed Weir. Twisting into knots, they wound around him like the coils of a huge cloth anaconda. Bound and gagged by his own bedclothes, he thudded to the floor.

An invisible hand grabbed Jake's sleeve. Erceldoune's voice spoke next to his ear: "Time to go."

Erceldoune's unseen hand guided him into the hall. Weir offered up a muffled cry. Doors flung back. Two figures rushed into the hall. Jake recognized both: Simion and Isobel. He started for them. A vice-like grip tightened on his arm and backed him against the stair rail. The pair passed within inches of them.

Isobel froze at the door. "I sense … MacCorkle." The pair passed to Wier's aide.

Jake and Erceldoune hustled down the stairs with urgent quiet.

"MacCorkle is here!" Weir shouted. "Kill him!"

Erceldoune's grip on Jake's arm never wavered. Reaching the bottom step, he guided Jake past the foyer, through the dining room, and out the French doors. The glowing footsteps brightened.

A howl echoed behind them. Erceldoune guided Jake along the footsteps.

Another howl, closer this time.

Running and clawing sounds rent the earth fifty feet back. Grunts and growls hurtled toward them. Jake ran for the wall. Erceldoune diverted him to the triangle of trees and steered him onto the mound. Erceldoune wrapped a long arm around Jake. Snarls came from twenty feet away. Out of the dark, a black shadow streaked toward them. The trees twinkled. Tilt-a-whirl.

The beast leaped.

CHAPTER 59

Jake and Erceldoune materialized in the Ministry Hall. The gray stone walls were dim and silent. Its activity long finished for the day, the flag's outline lay in shadows.

Erceldoune's arm remained wrapped around Jake's shoulder like a father side-hugging his son. "Illuminate," Erceldoune said.

Light sprang into the hall. Jake's adrenaline pumped. Exhilarated by their near-miss success, a slow relief washed through Jake's body. *We made it.*

"Are you hurt?" Erceldoune asked.

Jake patted his body. "I'm good. That dog went right for my throat." The danger made him feel alive.

Erceldoune refocused him. "Are you, as I am, convinced Princess Vivian is not held in Atlanta?"

"Yes, I didn't—" *He'll think I'm stupid. Say it anyway.* "I didn't sense her there."

"Neither did I."

Erceldoune's answer surprised Jake.

"Come. Lothian waits in his chambers."

Crossing the foyer to the curved stone steps, Erceldoune said, "I didn't hear the whole conversation, but I gather Weir offered you a faerie gift."

"A what?"

"A seductive, unearned perk designed to entice. It turns to dust after it serves its purpose."

"What purpose?"

"A diversion, a manipulation used to buy the person off, steal their power, and kill time until the offeror gets what he or she wants from them."

"Weir offered my family."

"An evil temptation he could never deliver."

****

Weir ushered Isobel, Simion, and Grezil to the tall, upholstered chairs around the small table in his office. Their unannounced guests were gone.

Weir was vexed. "I expected MacCorkle," Weir said, "not the other. Who was he?"

"Erceldoune. I sensed his cunning." Isobel folded and refolded her hands.

Weir turned to Simion. "You cut the line very close."

"I got caught up in the chase."

Weir knew Simion tried to kill MacCorkle, considering their history. No matter. It didn't change anything.

"Prepare as if they're not fools," Weir said.

"Leaving the map on your desk where they would find it was a nice touch," Grezil said. "How long before they know the place?"

"A day at most," Weir said.

"How did they find the house?" Isobel asked.

"My dear sister's son visited here to get instructions. Once he turned, he told them everything."

"You knew they would come?" Isobel asked.

"Of course," Grezil said. "They must have hope. They must believe a successful rescue of their beloved Princess is possible. Otherwise, the Prince would not come."

"What if they don't figure out where she is?" Isobel asked.

"They will," Weir said. "Prepare our mercenaries. Twenty-four-hour watch. Put your plan in place, Simion."

Simion nodded and left to prepare.

"I'm so close to the crown, I can feel it on my head." Weir smiled.

CHAPTER 60

Lothian, Clacks, and Erceldoune sat in Lothian's chambers. Jake stood by the fireplace and studied each face. A deep awareness came to him unbidden, a knowledge of each person, unavailable to him before his training.

He witnessed a taut rubber band of emotion stretched near the breaking point across Lothian's face, hidden by a thin formality. Love hidden under fear. He showed a brave face, but he seemed unsure if Vivian, the last of his family, was lost to him forever. Jake knew Lothian was torn between going after his sister and serving his country.

Clacks's face was grim, ready for a dirty job. Steady, solid, dependable, and reliable, he was a soul eager to help. He had honed skills. He was ready to handle this job. Jake had seen that look before, in Afghanistan.

Erceldoune remained calm, steady, displaying relentless energy. He was an uncompromising judge of right and wrong, unbending under pressure, and unbendable to another's will. He chose his own way, supported any other who rightfully requested his help, and never wavered once committed. As Jake studied him, an image of gears in a watch mechanism came to him.

How do I know all this? I'm sensing it from them. The information flows in my mind. Jake surveyed each persona. *What do I know?* The ever-present statement generated more knowledge than he believed possible.

"Show us Weir's depiction of our future," Erceldoune said to Jake as the Orb appeared in his hand.

Jake stepped forward and placed his right hand on it. The stream, the valley, and the lost battle projected on the wall to their left. Lothian's chamber grew silent as each of them watched his proposed death.

"A convenient vision—for him," Erceldoune said. "He predicts our future, but future changes with decisions made in the present."

Jake unfolded and smoothed the crude map.

"It looks like a child's drawing," Clacks said.

"It's a depiction of Weir's fantasy." To Jake, it seemed obvious.

"It could be anywhere," Clacks said.

"Can Afton find it?" Jake asked. "He found the house."

"He can locate his mother, so if she is with Vivian, perhaps. In this case, there is another way, but it may be dangerous."

Erceldoune paused, thinking. Everyone waited on him to speak again.

"Jake, I sent your amulet to Princess Vivian," Erceldoune said. "It was sentimental, and I thought it a nice gesture. And it added a layer of protection for her. But now, it may be pivotal to her survival. Before we go further, I want to draw an obvious conclusion. Finding this information, the map, Weir's fantasy, as Jake puts it, and our close escape seems to me, very convenient. What if the events were orchestrated?"

"We were set up?" Jake asked.

"Highly likely. Before we launch a mission to save her, we need proof Princess Vivian is alive."

Lothian and Clacks agreed. Jake protested: "We can't waste time. We must—"

"Jake. With the Orb, there is a way. Since you created the amulet, you can engage it. With assistance from the Orb, you may join her and experience her imprisonment as she does."

Dread permeated Jake. The memory of the sorrowful, wracking pain, the desolate imprisonment, that had made him ache for her last time. *Can I stand it? I have to, for her.*

Jake closed his eyes and pictured her smile become her laugh. As if his arms were three thousand miles long, his mind reached to hold her. A convulsion rocked him. His body froze upright, arms across his chest like a mummy laid in a sarcophagus, legs jammed together, head locked forward, and eyes open, staring into blackness. His inflexible body rose and floated six inches off the floor. Senses became deprived, no light, no tactile sensation, nothing. He existed in an abysmal, unseeing helplessness. His body should have pitched forward onto the floor. It did not. He floated erect as if encased in an invisible jacket of … something. Claustrophobic panic raced through his body. *Get out! Have to get out!* The thought was strong and demanding, but his muscles, frozen and inert, couldn't respond.

The amulet.

In a catatonic physical state, Jake's mind traveled beyond his body. Dispassionate observation balanced intense participation. He connected to the amulet. Through it, he touched Vivian. His breathing synchronized with hers, growing shallow and faint.

Jake felt Erceldoune gently remove his right hand and place it on the Orb. In isolated darkness, the amulet brightened. Panic eased. Fear diminished. Erceldoune took Jake's left hand and placed it on the crude map. The map gelled with the amulet. Both conjoined with the Orb.

What do I know?

A dot of light appeared at the edge of Jake's vision. It expanded. Like a comet, it flew at him. When it flashed in his vision, the jolt was excruciating. Jake knew if he fought it, he would lose her. He entered it. *What do I know?*

Vivian's mind joined his in the light. A flood of mental images ran headlong into each other. A dart. Old building like a library. Steel floor. Moving. In a vehicle. Bound. Walking a path. Vistas. Grezil. Stone chamber. A forest, left. A valley, right. Stone escarpments. Scrubby trees. Rock-strewn stream. Deeply rutted trail.

Each image melded to the next. They ended at a gravel lot containing a single blue van. Jake traveled beside her each step. Forward and backward, backward and forward, he crisscrossed the route. Every detail committed to memory. Hope built. Love toughened. Fear receded.

I am with you, Vivian.

Jake awoke. Every detail knitted into his memory. Clacks grabbed him before he hit the floor.

CHAPTER 61

Faerie mercenaries were a tough breed. They had no Clan, no allegiance. Fifty hard men and women from different parts of the world arrived in the gravel lot and made the trek into the valley.

Simion staged another fifty outside the valley, ready at a moment's notice. The cost didn't matter. The plan—his plan—had to work. But was it enough? MacCorkle had entered Weir's house like it wasn't enchanted. Thoughts rattled in Simion's brain as he set out the troops in the valley. It had been hilarious to see Weir wrestling in those sheets, but who could do that to Weir? MacCorkle? Or someone with him? They were not afraid of Weir. Why not?

At the far end, he put eight warriors under Isobel's command: "Attack when you see them enter the valley. Draw them into the middle. Kill everyone they send."

He turned to Grezil. "Take command of ten warriors near the narrow stream entrance. Close the trap and smash them from behind."

Grezil refused. "I prefer to roam free and be where I am needed."

Simion protested. "You must. Worst case, we drive them into the stream, pin them against the far crags, and slaughter them."

But Grezil ignored him.

He placed troops down the side of the valley across from the stream. A massive broken rock touched the northern stream bank and blocked any escape beyond it.

The two entrances were the narrows at the stream and the birch forest. Unless they flew in, every avenue was blocked by sheer cliffs and heaps of broken rocks and slag.

Nervous energy ticked-tocked in Simion's chest. He paced, changed into a dog, and checked the positions for the tenth time. Grezil was of no help, but he hoped he could count on Isobel unless she, too, would defy his orders.

****

Isobel ordered eight men to follow her into the forest. She glanced at the stone where Vivian rested. Isobel had little use for Weir's sister, but hiding Vivian in that stone was brilliant. Simple Simion's plan on the other hand was flawed. A battle was coming, and Jake MacCorkle would be there. She alone would kill MacCorkle and the Prince. And if Grezil or Simion had a nasty accident in the process, so be it.

Small birch trees marched down the slope into the valley. Behind them, larger cousins swayed back and forth as the wind played in the branches. Isobel's troops followed her through the forest. At the valley's end, a small, silent cove held an oddly positioned log near a dark azure lake. Erceldoune wouldn't walk into a trap. *He'll come this way.*

Setting her troops equidistance between the lake and the valley, Isobel dispersed them in a rough horseshoe shape as she took the apex position. Reaching up, she stroked her neck where Jake had grabbed it. Revenge sounded sweet. First the meddler, Erceldoune, dies. Next, she'd crush MacCorkle.

****

Grezil refused to serve in Simion's militia. Along the stream, below the forest, was her best vantage point. *They won't prance in here to be killed.*

To her right, the birch forest was quiet. *Isobel's gone. Setting her own trap?* She glanced up. Simion struggled to climb the southern crag. *He wants to see the whole battlefield, but he'll be so far away he won't be able to command. Typical.*

A question came from Weir to Grezil: "Prepared?"

"Yes, but Simion wrestles with pygmies," Grezil replied.

"I expected as much. Take command."

CHAPTER 62

An argument raged in Lothian's chamber. None of it mattered to Jake. The sensation of Vivian in the dark place was not a latent frustration anymore but a burning desire to act, to move, to attack, to annihilate anyone who stood between him and her. Now, this moment. Talk did nothing. He opened his mouth to speak but Lothian, his brow creased and voice smothered in stress, cut him off.

"I must go to Vivian." Lothian's voice sounded strained.

"I agree," Clacks said. "The kidnappers expect Prince Lothian. If he does not go, we have no leverage."

"My Prince, you cannot," Erceldoune said. "Ask your Bard."

"Ask me? What? I can't—" Jake, prepared to fight, wasn't prepared to act as anyone's counselor.

"Bard?" Lothian asked in surprise, like he'd forgotten he had one. He pounced on Jake, eager for a different answer. "What do you advise?"

The full gravity of the question bored into Jake. Prior to the question, he'd stayed clear of the discussion, wanting it to be over, to get on with the mission. He couldn't tell a Prince what to do. *Can I?* He weighed his answer. Breathing deeply, he opened his heart. *What do I know?* Words flowed.

"Your Highness, your People need you. No one in this room deprives you of an opportunity to rescue your sister. If the situation demanded it, you must go. It does not. Able men stand ready to represent you on this mission. We are your emissaries. We love your sister as you do and will never rest until Princess Vivian is returned safe to the Gleane. I advise this: send your best people. Trust them to succeed. Give them your blessing. Let them carry your battle to our enemies."

"Well spoken," Clacks said.

Everyone awaited Lothian. He appeared deep in thought.

"I withdraw on one condition. I choose the people to go. I give my decision within the hour."

"As you consider," Clacks said, "include one solution. Weir expects you to lead the rescue."

Erceldoune placed his hand on Clacks's shoulder. "I think we can work around that. Send for Afton Thish."

Afton arrived at the Prince's chambers, panting from the run. A grim group greeted him. He bowed to his Prince. "I thank you for the honor to join the rescue party."

"How did you know?" Lothian asked.

"It is the talk of the Gleane. Everyone wants to help. Men at arms stand ready for a word from you."

"How many?"

"Hundreds. More every hour. Everyone in the area has come into town hoping to serve."

Lothian looked at Erceldoune. "The People love their Princess. They will not tolerate her peril."

"Raise an army?" Lothian asked to the room.

Clacks pointed at Jake. "Ask your Bard."

Me again? Jake readied himself.

Lothian looked at Jake. "I seek council."

Jake was thrilled to be asked, to be respected, by his Prince. Old feelings reached for him. *Failed my men. Failed Vivian. Stop it.* Jake held his hand up and beckoned the Orb. It flew to him.

"Address your People. Reassure them. Allow them to contribute. Raise the army. Do not commit it. A small force fights with a passion the enemy lacks." Jake handed the Orb to Lothian.

"Counselor. I will do as you advise," Lothian said. "I do not need an hour to consider. My army is in this room. Prepare."

****

Erceldoune was confident in Lothian's decision, but as the others left the room, Erceldoune motioned for Afton and Lothian to join him before the fireplace.

"Clacks makes a critical point," Erceldoune said. "Weir wants both monarchs dead. That is his revenge for the banishment of his ancestor."

"How am I to lead the expedition and remain in the Gleane?" Lothian asked.

"There is an ancient spell, little known today. It renders a willing person into an exact replica—not a stock, but a perfect replica, identical in every way, in both voice and action. I have used it successfully on several occasions. But it carries a danger. When the enchantment is removed, it can disfigure the enchanted person." Erceldoune looked at Afton.

"Me?" Afton said. He stepped back a pace as if the thought repulsed him.

"If you agree, I will perform the enchantment making you a perfect replica of Prince Lothian. Prince Lothian remains as monarch while you go to battle in his stead, but this must remain a closely held secret among us."

Afton's brow knitted. Some internal struggle played out as his shoulders pushed up like a weight bore down on them. His breathing became short and labored. He shifted from foot to foot as if he wanted to run, but he stuck to the spot, measuring the request.

"Why not a stock?" Afton asked, not dodging the weight but offering options.

"A stock is too dull and dimwitted; it would be discovered within an hour," Erceldoune said. "With the Prince gone, who would direct the People after they discovered both monarchs at risk?"

In slow, direct speech Afton said, "Your Highness, I wish to serve. I do not hesitate out of fear for myself, but respect. For me, this service is a great honor, and I receive it as such. With all my heart, I choose to serve my Lord in any manner I can. I accept."

"When can we do it?" Lothian asked.

"Now. Are you ready?" Erceldoune asked.

Both Lothian and Afton nodded. Erceldoune stepped between them, turned each to face the other, put his hand on each man's shoulder, and spoke an enchantment. "A look, a look, for all to see. One who owns it, gives it free. One who takes it, on him be."

A mist formed between them. It swirled to the left and back to the right, grew until it consumed them, and dissipated. Standing next to the fireplace was a perfect replica of Lothian, right down to the laces on his boots.

Surprised by his mirror image, Lothian asked. "Afton?"

"Yes."

"It's a perfect disguise," Lothian said, the surprise still in his voice. "Afton, prepare for the journey. I wish to discuss one more point with Erceldoune."

When they were alone, Lothian said, "What if Afton stays here, and I leave to rescue my sister?" Excitement and hope rose in his voice.

"There is only one condition under which I would consider it," Erceldoune said.

"What is the condition?"

"In truth, we have asked the son of a murderer and spy to join our expedition. Do you mistrust Afton Thish's loyalty to you or consider him a danger to the rescue effort?"

Lothian recoiled. Neither the idea of Afton's past nor any aspect that he might threaten the mission had crossed his mind. *Is Afton a danger?* He pictured and assessed his sense of Afton's being. Nothing disturbed him. He answered honestly, "I see no danger in him. He will give his entire being to rescue my sister."

"My Prince, two monarchs rule the Gleane," Erceldoune said. "One is in grave danger. One is needed by the People. Clacks's earlier problem is solved in that you may appear to go and yet remain. It seems you answer your own question."

Lothian touched Erceldoune's sleeve. "Take the Orb. I want every advantage. Vivian cannot be lost to me." Lothian's voice cracked.

Erceldoune nodded. He held out his right hand. The Orb sprang to him like a returning yo-yo. A soft knock came at the door.

"Enter," Lothian said.

Afton entered as Lothian's perfect replica. He wore a forest green shirt, brown pants, and leather boots.

Lothian handed him his crown. "Wear this until you leave," he said, "it will complete the illusion."

Another knock came. Lothian disappeared. Lothian's replica and Erceldoune remained. Jake and Clacks entered.

Erceldoune spoke, "After further discussion, it is decided that the Prince will accompany us and Afton will remain." He pushed on eliminating any questions. "Jake, visualize Vivian's arrival point, the gravel lot."

Jake nodded.

"Since we have the Orb, we will use it to travel. Touch the Orb with your right hand," Erceldoune said. "Together."

The four stood together—Afton as Lothian's replica, Erceldoune, Clacks, and Jake. Four right hands landed atop each other as a white cocoon formed.

CHAPTER 63

The entire operation hung on Jake directing the Orb to the right location. Jake closed his eyes and pictured the gravel lot where the blue van was parked. His eyes jerked open. This was nothing he'd experienced before.

After a slow start, the room spun faster and faster. Centrifugal force crushed Jake against the white wall until he felt glued in place. The room vanished. Adjusting to the odd physical change, his mind wavered. *The gravel lot. Concentrate. The gravel lot.*

Following Jake's on and off vision, the Orb struck an approximate path toward the lot. The image shifted to a road, to a path, to a streambed. After each approximation, each change, he grabbed, released, and re-raised "gravel lot." *What if it drops us too close?*

Spinning slowed … and stopped. Three people floated to the ground like professional parachutists, but the fourth hit the soil with the grace of an elephant ballerina.

Jake dusted his butt.

The landing zone was a two-rut dirt road. The gravel lot was one hundred and fifty feet farther up. Yellowish-orange dirt showed recent tracks both of vehicle and animal, but the road was little used.

A thick ground cover of spongy bracken and ferns crawled from the forest and rested along the sides of the ruts, waiting for its chance to overtake them. Scraggy evergreen trees grew everywhere. Rocks stuck through the undergrowth at varying heights from a few inches to taller than Jake's six foot two. Erceldoune tucked the Orb into his robe.

Clacks patted Jake's back. "Not bad for your first navigation."

"I don't sense anyone watching this far out," Erceldoune said, "but lookouts will be posted. They will know we are here before we see them."

The four figures left the two-rut lane and entered the trees. A small opening beside a large boulder offered cover. Jake staggered slightly until the tilt-a-whirl feeling cleared.

"I considered our situation," Erceldoune said. "We are a small, highly mobile, committed team entertaining a superior force."

Like the Rangers. The comparison inspired Jake.

"Why not double our forces?" Erceldoune asked with a twinkle.

"What are you talking about?" Jake asked.

Clacks offered. "I'll lead them."

What are they talking about? His mind focused on Vivian. Irritation goaded him to get into action. Attention flagged until he heard his name.

"I propose Jake go with you. Lothian and I will move west and come up the valley from the other end."

Lothian and Erceldoune spoke almost in unison.

"Bifurcate, duplicate, Lothian."

"Bifurcate, duplicate, Erceldoune." Each seemed to go out of focus, shudder, and split into a duplicate.

Jake took a step back. Reading about an enchantment was one thing; watching a friend split in half reminded him how little he knew. *Stocks?*

The dull look without real comprehension, the eager smile without appreciation, confirmed it. Duplicates correct in nearly every detail stood before him awaiting instructions.

"This is Clackmannan. Do exactly as he says," Erceldoune told his stock. Lothian repeated the same specific instruction to his stock.

"Stand and wait," Clacks said. The stocks stood and waited.

"We will take the Orb," Erceldoune said to Clacks, "fly west, and enter the forest above the valley. Walking, it will take you and Jake an hour to reach the second valley from the gravel lot. We will be in position by the time you cross the stream."

The stocks added a diversion. Jake stepped forward, kneeled and grabbed a stick. Drawing the valleys on the ground, he said, "The objective is to locate Vivian and get everyone out safely. What if, when Clacks and I enter the valley, we create stocks of ourselves and send our stocks with the others? The map showed their plan to trap us in the center of the valley. If they trap the stocks, we can slip around to you, find Vivian, and get out before they know we are here."

"Ideal," Erceldoune said. "With one addition: become invisible as you enter the valley."

"Brilliant." Clacks smiled and smacked Jake's shoulder. He's acting like this is a training exercise in the forest. Jake was confident until the last suggestion. He'd never learned or practiced how to become invisible. Could he do it?

"I have one task before we go," Erceldoune said. "Jake, hold the Orb for me, please."

Although frustrated by the delay, Jake took the Orb. Erceldoune took the stick Jake used as a marker and ranged into the forest. He picked up another stick, discarded it, examined a different stick, and tossed it. When he found one to his liking, he started the search again.

With two sticks of the same approximate length and thickness, he held them together in his left hand. Erceldoune jerked a two-foot piece of vine out of the bracken. The vine became rope. In tight coils with coarse knots, the sticks were bound together. With the ends in either hand, he gently set the bundle four inches over the Orb in Jake's hand. It suspended like a magnetic toy.

"Grow together, ossify. Fetch the power, amplify. Strength the hand, increase the eye. Wield the wand like samurai."

Erceldoune winked at Jake. "I added the samurai part. Nice touch, don't you think?"

"I have no idea what you're doing. We don't have time for this." Jake's frustration gnawed at him.

The sticks glowed and spun like wood in a high-speed lathe. The vine squeezed and bit into the bark. The bark yielded, popped up, and flaked away. Bare wood, white and misting from the heat, fused lengthwise. The glow increased. Light penetrated and squeezed the sticks. The vine cut and inlaid the wood. Three separate pieces coalesced into a single crooked stick eighteen inches long.

Retrieving it from the Orb, Erceldoune lifted it and waved it through the air. Each movement left a faint vapor trail. He flipped it right and then left. He scribed circles, squares, and a triangle. He wrote his name in the air. "Good balance for an improvised wand. You never know when a good stick may be useful." He tucked the finished joinery into Jake's belt.

"What is this?" Jake asked. "We have to get to the valley and you're making toys?"

"We will meet in one hour," Erceldoune said, ignoring Jake. Erceldoune and Lothian, who had said nothing since they arrived, touched the Orb and vanished.

"What is this stick about?" Jake pulled it out.

"Hawthorne and rowan," Clacks said. "Two magical woods, bonded. Each enhances the magical potential of the other. Erceldoune designed a wand to magnify your magic."

Jake flicked the wand up and down. A thin afterimage emanated from the tip. Turning it in his hand, a particular knot fitted into his right hand like a glove. Holding it lightly, like an orchestra conductor, he played with the curvy stick. *It likes me. Is that a weird thought?*

"How do I use it?" Jake asked Clacks as they turned for the parking lot.

"A wand protects and serves its owner. It senses what you intend and produces it. Some wands adapt within moments to its Wyzard. Others require years of patient work."

Wyzard? "How do I know if it will work?"

"You won't until you use it."

They started up the rutted road, Jake laughing at Clacks as he instructed the stocks. "Stand. Go first. Go second. Look left and right as you walk."

"It's weird to see Erceldoune nodding his head with a stupid smile on his face."

"Yeah, stocks are a hoot."

They reached the gravel lot. Around it, rolling hills flowed into rocky escarpments, crags, streams, lakes, and boulder-dotted valleys. The blue van was the only sign of civilization. Jake shaded his eyes to peek into the van's interior. Nothing.

"Stand ready," Clacks called to the stocks who were moving across to the trail without them. Both halted and looked left and right. Catching up, Clacks ordered them to walk the trail.

The quartet trudged toward the valley.

CHAPTER 64

Simion's spy saw the four leave the gravel lot. The message came: "Four." The message passed in the ranks. Like fireflies shutting off at daybreak, mercenaries became invisible. Grezil remained visible. She pulled into the shadows of several boulders along the streambed. Simion reveled from his perch atop the southern crag. Everything was ready and flawless. *Perfect! I did it.*

In dog form, he danced along the ridge. This day would be his day. Excitement flowed over him in waves. *I have to pee.* Without transforming, he raised his leg on the nearest rock. Then he made for the valley and padded among his troops.

Rumors raged like wildfire and traveled faster than a chameleon snapped up a bug: "I heard one of the four is a dangerous Wyzard," "I heard he owns a dragon," "I heard this is the front line of a huge army."

Simion shifted shape. "If you don't shut your mouths, I'll kill you myself!"

The troops slunk lower into position. No one spoke. The valley was quiet again.

"Professionals, my ass. Spread out. A single dart would kill you all."

Simion knew his criticism stung them. They moved apart, and Simion could sense their sullen, angry looks firing at his back.

Why only four? Who are they? Simion wondered, but his excitement about an easy victory squelched his curiosity.

****

Jake followed the two stocks as Clacks led the little group down the trail. He looked at the wand in his right hand, doubting it was of much value. With his limited magical knowledge, it might not work.

Where the ridge stuck out and the path dropped down to the valley, Clacks halted. He formed a prism. Little information came from it. A flash of a single green shirt showed.

"All are hidden or invisible," Clacks said to Jake. He ordered the stocks to look through the prism. He pointed to the rocks.

"When I say to go, run to this rock. Count to one hundred. Run to this rock. Count to one hundred. Run to this rock. Wait there. Look left and right

192

at each stop."

The dull faces looked, smiled, nodded, looked from left to right. *I'm not sure they get it.*

"Remember, our stocks go with the others."

Jake swallowed hard. "I don't know that enchantment."

"Use the wand."

How?

"Touch it to your chest when you say the words."

I have no idea if it will work. If it doesn't, I'm the one left visible.

"If need be, I will help."

"I will tell our stocks to do exactly as the others," Clacks said. "As we enter the valley, you go left, and I'll go right. Meet Erceldoune and Lothian at the forest. Find Princess Vivian. Touch the Orb and go home."

"Sounds right to me. I know she's near the far end of the valley close to the forest, on the left. But—"

"What is it, Jake?"

"I've lost sense of Vivian," Jake said as dread sought him.

Offering a broad grin, Clacks said, "It will return." The smile eased Jake's worry—some.

The yellowish-gray trail curved down. Halfway to the valley it met the stream tumbling along its right side. The grade was less severe. The noisy, rock-strewn stream sang a bubbling song. Despite the risk they courted in the valley, the water sounds soothed Jake. A small tributary joined it, another, and a third. The stream's width grew. Its water changed its tune to a raucous, raging, action-packed beat. The streambed deepened. Rocks submarined below the surface.

The valley entrance married where two stone-lined hills touched. The opening's width was the stream's flow plus an extra ten feet of sandy beach on the left side. The water on the right side slammed against a rock wall and deigned to topple it in a frothy display of power. Beyond the opening and the brief glimpses Vivian had given Jake, the valley was a mystery.

Jake's combat senses were on high alert. *When are they going to hit us?* He fingered the wand under his robe.

At the small strip of sand with the rock overhang, Clacks halted. "Ready? Use your wand."

"How?"

"Repeat what I say and touch it to your chest when you say the enchantment: 'Bifurcate, duplicate, Clackmannan.'"

Jake pulled his wand and repeated, "Bifurcate, duplicate, MacCorkle."

When the wand touched his chest, a weird, squishy, gelatin sensation fluttered through his body. His duplicate appeared in front of him like Jake was looking in a mirror.

"Follow behind these two and do exactly as they do," Clacks said. Jake repeated the instruction to his stock, and both responded with dull acknowledgement.

Clacks waved the stocks forward. "Go!"

"I want to be, where no one can see," Jake and Clacks whispered in virtual unison. Jake tapped his chest and disappeared. Four stocks filed past Jake to their doom. Invisible, Clacks and Jake knelt under the stone overhang. *Did the switch take too long?*

CHAPTER 65

As Lothian's perfect replica, Afton knelt next to Erceldoune. They watched for movement below. Nothing.

The Orb transported them to a steep hill overlooking a small shimmering lake. Scot pines grew in abundance. Thin scrubby groundcover peeked from centuries of dropped pine needles. Skidding down the incline, the sturdy trees made excellent brake stops.

On flat land, trees thinned. Ferns and bracken grew. A stream babbled around rocks. It crossed their path as it flowed downhill toward the lake below. Wandering its stony banks, they watched for a decent fording place.

Without forewarning, a strange young man, dressed in a faded, unkempt army uniform ran from the cover of the trees. His hands were red. He held one up in a sign that they should stop. Afton raised his hands to attack.

Erceldoune rested his hands on Afton's and gently lowered them. "Look down," he said to Afton. "Look at your shoes. Don't face him. For god's sake, keep your eyes off him." Erceldoune dropped his face toward the ground.

Afton followed suit. It was hard to do, like someone telling you not to look when they see a movie star in a restaurant. "Who is it?"

Before Erceldoune could answer, the young man questioned them. "Who intrudes on my solitude?" The voice was strong but held a resigned quality like someone who had done a job for a long time and was tired of it.

Erceldoune kept his eyes on the ground when he spoke. "Two humble travelers seeking friends in the next valley. Please forgive our intrusion."

"I sense battle." The young voice conveyed a hint of edgy anticipation.

"We fear it," Erceldoune said.

"You fight. Why?"

"To fight is not our desire. Our friend, Princess Vivian has been stolen. We seek to recover her."

"Who seeks her? I sense a power from you. A worthy adversary?"

"Not I. We are humble faeries. Clackmannan, Lothian, Erceldoune, and a human, MacCorkle. All of the Daione Sìthe. Our lost comrade is Princess Vivian, Prince Lothian's sister."

"MacCorkle? Kin to Mary?" The voice changed from resigned anticipation to recognition.

"His mother."

"Pass."

Heads down as if in a permanent bow, Afton and Erceldoune crossed the creek and moved into the forest.

"Ly Erg," Erceldoune said before Afton asked.

"My God. I didn't know. I thought he was a myth." Afton shuddered as if to shake off the feel of Ly Erg.

"What was that about? He seems to have known Jake?"

"He knows something we don't. Perhaps, Jake, John, or Mary offended him. If so, we need to find Vivian and leave before he finds Jake."

"What was on his hands? It looked like—"

"Blood."

CHAPTER 66

Kneeling under the overhang, Jake closed his eyes. He reached for Vivian. *I am here.* Feedback muffled like a bad cellphone connection. No exact location came, no specific target, but he sensed her at the far end of the valley. The place she was held was pitch dark even though it was light outside. *A cave?*

The stocks performed as ordered. They ran to the first set of stones and crouched, looking left and right. Jake and Clacks slipped in behind them. No sound. An eerie calm blanketed the valley.

Jake went to the left, along an array of large and small fallen stones loosened from the crags above. No contact. He skirted one-third of the valley before he saw why.

Hidden from view on the backside of the rocks away from the narrows entrance were shimmering images like a mirage formed by the sun on a hot day, not people per se, but a silver afterimage of them. Dozens of them. Waiting and watching the stocks as they moved to the second set of stones. *How can I see that? Why didn't they see me?*

The stocks acted as instructed without realizing a superior force waited for the right moment to annihilate them. An odd sense of loss struck Jake. He shook if off. He needed to get to Vivian before the ambushers realized the deception.

Keeping his footfall as silent as possible, Jake ran toward the end of the valley.

****

Clacks went right along the streambank. No soldiers. Moving from rock to rock, he sensed no one. Get to the birch forest, find Princess Vivian and—

Grezil knelt behind a waist-high stone next to a white birch, tracking the four stocks. Clacks slid out of her line of sight behind a small outcrop. From his angle, she was exposed. A single dart would … No, keep quiet. When the stocks are attacked, I'll move. Princess Vivian comes first. Clacks crept toward the next stone.

A dart exploded and rolled him over. Surprised but unhurt, he scrambled behind the stone. *She senses me.* The hit was close but not direct. She doesn't know exactly where I am.

With one eye, he peeked around the stone. Walking onto the battlefield, dart spinning on her palm, right toward his stone, came Grezil. Clacks formed a dart and aimed it at her head.

****

An explosion came from his right. Jake dove flat on his belly and shrank his body into the smallest target he could. As his adrenaline lessened, muffled voices reached him.

"Should we fire? I have the tall gray-beard sighted."

"Orders. We wait for the forest group to attack."

With the speed of a mime, Jake crawled to the stone and raised to one knee on the opposite side of the speaker's stone.

"What's that?"

"What?"

"A Wyzard, nearby. I sense him. Is anybody missing from the four?"

"No."

Two men and a woman eased over the rock and seemed to look right at Jake. No reaction. Jake stood as still as a snake sunning. While they could not see him, he saw their shimmering outlines. *Fire? No. Vivian first.*

"Maybe we're supposed to fire on our own. I see the targets. Shouldn't we kill 'em?"

The three dropped out of sight behind the rock. Inch by inch like he was in a minefield, Jake passed their hiding place. Across the valley, Grezil walked out of cover.

Clacks is in trouble.

Jake shifted his path right. Unsure of the wand's effect, he flipped his wrist in Grezil's direction. Nothing. Again. Nothing. He reached for a stone to make a dart. The wand's tip whizzed, and a lightning bolt struck a stout tree limb two feet over her head. Partially severed, the limb swung down and twisted into Grezil's face. Swatted by the limb like a giant hand, she reeled and fell. *Holy crap. How do I aim it?*

The trio behind the rock fired. Others followed. Within minutes, a massive barrage hurtled toward the stocks hidden behind three large rocks in the center of the valley.

Flat on her back, Grezil struggled to get the limb off her. Jake sprinted into the forest with the sounds of Clacks running nearby.

CHAPTER 67

Tall, white-barked trees grew thick in the birch forest. Black marks like half-opened, frowning mouths pocked the bark where limbs once lived. Through it, Afton found walking in a straight line impossible.

Afton and Erceldoune crossed back and forth following the path of least resistance. From time to time, they wandered as much as fifteen feet apart before weaving back together. Thick fronds and bracken eliminated any sound of footfalls. Despite the chaotic tree placement, the pair made good time toward the valley.

"What do you think we will find?" Afton asked from ten feet away.

Erceldoune halted and motioned him close. "Remember," Erceldoune whispered, "there are more fae here than we see. Keep quiet and be ready."

Afton saw nothing but stooped and gathered several stones for darts.

A shrill voice spoke from the wood, "Erceldoune, sneaking about the forest like a thief, what bottom-dwelling slug have you become?"

Afton froze.

Isobel stepped out from a cluster of white-silver trees with frowning mouths. "Not all bad. You brought my prize."

A wave of nausea hit Afton's stomach. It was the razor-cut blonde-from-a-bottle he saw at Weir's house. Pulling his shoulders back, he stood a little taller and played the part of Prince Lothian.

"Greetings, Isobel," Erceldoune said. "A rumor bandied about is an untrained human bested you. Slipping, my dear?"

Isobel ignored Erceldoune's jab. "Well, Prince Lothian, have you come for your sister? I offer a trade. The Princess for the Orb?" Lothian remained silent.

"You do. Do you? Does your master know you're out here in the woods bargaining with his prize?" Erceldoune said.

"What he knows will not matter to you in ten minutes. I change my offer. Your lives for the Orb."

"Your addled, pea brain deceives you," Erceldoune said, his voice carrying an odd amusement. "We didn't come here to trade. What to do?"

Afton balanced on his toes. Darts ready. He waited. Out of the corner of his eye, a branch twitched as if something pulled it down for a better aim. *Did I imagine that?* The branch shifted in an odd way again.

"What will it be, Prince Lothian?" Isobel forced her attention away from Erceldoune.

Afton acted. A dart rocketed at the branch. A hidden target felt the sting of his answer.

A scream pierced the forest followed by a moan from the spot. Silence.

Erceldoune dropped his hands and turned his palms away from Isobel. A gust of wind swished his robe. With open palms, he caught wind behind his back. His hands moved in small circles like mixing batter in a bowl until a wind's force lay captured.

Afton dove behind a stone.

Three silvery silhouettes half-hidden in the trees sent darts at Erceldoune. Three separate whirlwinds answered. Wind and dart met. Darts tangled, spun, and dropped to the ground, wasted. The winds passed on unaffected. Three hidden targets were grabbed by a howling force and dangled above the ground, twisting head over heels.

"Damn you!" invisible voices screamed and cursed.

Darts flew from hidden sources and rained down on Erceldoune. He waved his hands. Tree branches closed in front to shield him. Darts struck the branches and fell, spent, to the ground. Through the branches, dart after dart left his hand.

An enemy circled to attack Erceldoune's rear. Lying on his back, Afton fired. His dart hit the target square in the chest, lifting him off the ground, and smacking him into a tree—dead.

Isobel's darts stalked Afton as dart after dart slammed his hiding place. Huddling low against the base of the stone, dirt and stone chips flew over his body and clothes. Peeking around the stone for a target, another whizzed by his ear. To keep her off him, he sent a torrent of darts in her direction. Unbothered, she flicked them away with a turn of her wrist. Nothing he sent reached her.

Erceldoune reached inside his robe and withdrew a dime-sized piece of steel. "Evil come, evil go. Back to she, who made it so." The metal glowed white hot and spun on his palm. Standing sideways like he was hitting a tennis backhand, he flicked his wrist. The steel missile left his palm like a lightning bolt.

"You send a simple dart?" Isobel turned to Erceldoune and mocked. She raised her hand to ward it off. No dart. An object returned to its owner shredded her hand and burrowed deep into her brain. Isobel fell dead.

CHAPTER 68

Screams filtered through the forest. Jake pulled his wand. He dodged trees left and right chasing the sound. Cries ceased. Jake picked up his pace. *Am I too late?*

A crash on his right. Shifting behind a break in two trees, he kneeled, readied his wand, and waited.

A silvery outline slipped back and forth through the trees headed right at him. Jake raised his wand.

"Jake?" Clacks's voice called to him. Jake dropped his wand and realized he was holding his breath.

"I'm here," Jake said. Neither spoke as they moved forward. A white robe outlined against the black and white of the birch trees made Erceldoune look like a shimmering apparition. Isobel lay against a tree. A tiny hole in her forehead showed entry of a killing object. A single trickle of blood ran between her eyes, across her nose, and down her left cheek.

Staring at her corpse, Jake felt … nothing. The fear of her when she paralyzed him at the house, the anger that consumed him when she took his mother and father from him, was gone. A casualty of war, a byproduct of violence, begun by someone else, finished by the final dart.

"What happened?" Jake asked.

Afton got to his feet, still shaky from the firefight. "She tried to make her own deal for the Orb."

"Who killed her?"

"It was weird—nothing touched her until Erceldoune took something out of his robe and sent a dart … beyond her magic."

Jake turned to Erceldoune. "What was it?"

"When your mother died, the tip of the dagger that killed her remained. I removed it and waited for an opportunity to return it to its owner. An evil enchanted object returns two-fold to its creator. No time for talk. Jake, locate Vivian."

"I think Vivian's dying." A tear choked in his voice.

"Jake, focus," Clacks said. "How many hostiles did you see?"

"I saw forty hidden on my side. What about you?"

"Only Grezil."

"Probably twenty more you didn't see," Erceldoune added.

"What do we do?"

"Start a war." Erceldoune turned to Jake. "What do you recommend, Lieutenant?"

"Spread out," Jake ordered, as if command was natural for him. "Keep twenty feet between us and walk in a straight line until we meet resistance." No one questioned him. The determined line of four moved to the edge of the birch forest and into the upper valley without resistance. As he knelt behind a meager cover, Jake's mind reached for Vivian.

The amulet felt nearby. "She's close." Jake said to himself, as he closed his eyes and let his senses guide him. When his eyes opened, he was staring at three short stones standing in a group one hundred feet to his right. A single multi-ton boulder towered behind them. Something about the massive stone drew him. Using whatever thin cover was available, he crept toward the it. Within twenty feet, his honed senses tingled, and he knew. "Oh my god, she's trapped inside the stone." Frantic, he kneeled and crawled to it. Staring up at the monolith, a helpless sense of foreboding raced through his body. Any help for Vivian was beyond his skill.

From forty feet to his left, as if he read Jake's mind, Jake saw Erceldoune, robe hitched up to his knees, coming at a run.

Jake pointed. "The stone. She's trapped inside. Get her out. Please get her out." From somewhere far away, he heard a voice begging Erceldoune to help.

Erceldoune's exposed run drew attention. A dart struck within ten feet. Dirt spit over them. Jake dove behind Vivian's stone. Erceldoune stood in the open and returned fire. Incoming explosions rained like a firework display. A dart hit Vivian's stone. Shards and dust flew into Jake's face. He low-crawled to his right, away from Vivian, found a crevice, and reached for his wand. Gone. Gathering stones, he fired frantically, hoping to draw fire away from Vivian.

Erceldoune remained protecting the stone and returning a barrage toward the attackers. A powerful dart hit the stone. A chunk the size of a hubcap flew up and knocked Erceldoune to the ground.

"Are you alright?" Jake yelled. No response. *Is he dead?*

Clacks skidded into Jake's sanctuary, firing darts like a machine gun.

"Help Lothian. He's pinned down at the edge of the forest," Clacks said. Before Jake could respond, Clacks leaped up and ran straight into the valley, taking the battle to the attackers.

Incoming fire slackened.

Jake swooped and grabbed pebbles for darts as he ran to Lothian's aide. A pain like a switch stung the backside of his hand. The stones dropped. Reaching for another handful, the sting came again. Glancing at his hand, the wand hovered next to it, slapping him to get his attention.

My wand comes like the Orb.

Increasing his speed, Jake opened his hand, and the wand flew to him.

CHAPTER 69

Afton was alone in the forest on the far left above the streambed. Darts strafed trees to his right and left, forcing him into the center of the valley. An isolated outcrop of stubby rocks offered meager cover. Six mercenaries advanced up the valley peppering him with darts. Pinned down, he tried to squeeze his body to the size of a postage stamp as he fired back.

Afton sensed her before he saw her. *Mother?* Grezil smacked down an errant dart like swatting a fly. She had seen the Prince and was coming to kill him.

"He's mine," she called to the attackers down the valley. Firing ceased. Clacks streaked down the valley below Afton, unaware of Afton's doom. No help was coming for him. Jake and Erceldoune were fighting behind him. Like the standoff in a spaghetti western, Afton stood alone to face his mother, knowing he was no match for her.

"You are my prize," Grezil said.

Should I call out and tell her who I am? No, I agreed to this role. I must play it out to the end. Afton stood and looked at Grezil.

Facing the moment of his death, Afton felt an odd calm. Even pride. His debt to his Prince and Princess would be paid with his life. In silent resolution, Afton dropped his hands and waited on the blow.

Grezil took her time. A stone dart spun on her palm, aimed at his heart. With glee, she released it as a grotesque grin twisted onto her face.

Jake sprinted across the valley. Darts flew near his legs and zinged by his face. He dove in front of Afton, wand across his chest. Grezil's dart flew true. A split second before it struck her son, Jake's wand deflected it straight back to her.

Grezil tried to dodge. A mediocre athlete, accustomed to state dinners, her attempt was inadequate. Her returned dart spun her into the air and dropped her into the stream. Airborne, Jake sailed passed Afton and crashed headfirst into a hidden stone. He lay still.

****

Simion peeked from a crevice between two thick slabs of stone. He witnessed Grezil's attempt to fly come to a bad end when she crashed into the stony streambed. *She's dead.* What little courage he'd mustered when he was commanding vanished. Anxiety crept over him, knowing there would be no excuses. *It's not my fault. Where is Isobel? She ruined everything.* He knew what Weir was capable of if he failed. *He would butcher me and hang—*

Simion dithered.

He backed further into his cubby like a canine hit by a truck, licking his fatal wounds.

****

Afton thought for a moment to check his mother, see if she was alive, but he had to get Jake to safety. He grabbed Jake's arms. In short, choppy back steps, he dragged him across the bracken. The nearest refuge was three tall stones forming an irregular triangle near the heart of the valley. He pulled Jake there and lay him down so he would be a smaller target.

He scanned the area. Darts whizzed past, not meant for them. Their source was a white-robed figure lying prone near a tall stone at the end of the valley. *Erceldoune?* Bracken waved as silky silhouettes crisscrossed the valley.

More are coming.

CHAPTER 70

An explosion followed by a shockwave shook Vivian's stone. A large section near her face broke away. Sensations—wind, warmth, light—touched her cheek. Head locked in a guillotine restraint, she wanted to turn to it, but frozen forward, she could not.

A tiny glint of light followed the shockwave. Sensing the outside, her mind raced. *How do I get out?*

Shapeshifting to a butterfly failed. Without hands and weakened by her confinement, powers lagged. Evil had lain hold of her and taken its toll. The stone held her fast. *The amulet? Start smaller.*

Willing tiny stones to move, she shifted a pebble below her eye. It loosened and rolled down her cheek.

Battle sounds raged. Explosions sounded. She wanted to hurry. *No. No. Slow down.* Breathing slowed. She must connect to the amulet. *To Jake. Meld with Jake.* Battle sounds faded. A connection formed. She saw Jake lying on the valley floor. Urgency overwhelmed calm. *Go to him. No. Focus. Focus.*

Conjuring a picture of the hug in the kitchen, under the misty eyes of her nanny, she guided her thoughts and coupled her emotions to his image, his look when he saw her, his crooked grin, his awkward surprise, his warmth. All grew in her mind's eye. She felt Jake's love. In her mind, she commanded, *Stone touching my left cheek, feel the wind, see the light. Remove the stone that blocks my flight.*

A small patch of loose stone shook and dropped away from her cheek. *I did it. I did it.* Calming her excitement, she focused again. A small stone popped against her skin, cracked, and fell away. Small bit by tiny flake, the stone prison pardoned her.

****

Jake woke in a protected alcove formed by three stones as tall as a man. A percussion band marched in his throbbing head. Blood stuck to his hair and face. Sticking up in the bracken, his wand lay fifteen feet away. He raised his hand, and it flew to him.

Rising slowly, easing to a knee, a woozy nauseous feeling flooded his stomach. Sweeping the area, Grezil lay in a heap in the stream bed, water rushing against and over her body as if she were a log placed there to block it. No one else was around. Lothian was gone. At least he survived. That's more than I can say for Grezil. Shaky, Jake stood. A flash came from his right. Without thinking, he ducked. The wand reacted, and a dart headed for him dissipated three feet away. Searching for its sender, he saw Simion duck into a rock outcrop. The wand fired, but Simion was well out of harm's way long before the dart got to him. *The wand anticipated me.* Woozy, Jake let him go as he looked across at Vivian's stone. *I need to go to her.*

Midway in the valley, a dozen silvery silhouettes fired darts into a small indention surrounded by smaller stones. Someone, Clacks or Lothian or both, was pinned down fifty feet below him. Jake's first steps were wobbly as he ran. Flicking his wand at attackers, it fired a series of near-miss shots and one direct hit, striking with the force of a rocket grenade. Bodies scattered, became visible, and fell to the ground, broken. Without leadership, attackers scrambled away like rats when the light comes on. Clacks stood and watched the retreating fae.

Clacks grinned at Jake. "Not the first time a human turned the tide of a battle."

CHAPTER 71

A chunk of stone broke from Vivian's mouth. Spitting small stone particles, she jutted her chin against the cracked stone. It broke away. Speaking the enchantment aloud, stones popped, cracked, broke, and fell more quickly.

Working the muscles of her face felt good. An itch on her cheek pushed her to work faster. Larger pieces bounced on the spongy turf and rolled away. Arms uncrossed, she reached them out of the stone casket like a child reaching for its mother. With her chest freed, she took her first deep breath in days. Restrained muscles ached.

Having her hands free strengthened her ability to remove stone. Her torso and legs came free. With agonizing patience, she eased her entire body out of her tomb. Bits of rock clung to her clothes and auburn braid. She dropped to her knees, fell forward, and lay exhausted. The grassy, rock-strewn, bracken mattress caressed her.

A voice she knew, but never expected, addressed her from behind her crypt. "I sense Vivian. Are you free?"

Free! Erceldoune?

Not trusting her legs, Vivian pushed herself up on her elbows and dragged her nearly spent body toward him. Weak as a newborn, she rested against her gravestone.

"I am free. You're hurt," she said.

An ugly gash ran from Erceldoune's forehead to the middle of his left cheek and across his left eye as if a prehistoric stone knife had slashed his face. Blood covered his face and neck. Stanched with his sleeve, it soaked into the fibers of his white robe giving it an odd variegated whitish-pink pattern. Blood ran down and pooled at the neck of the robe creating a deep red ringed collar.

"Where is the Orb?" Vivian asked.

"I have it," Erceldoune said.

"Use it on your wound."

"We haven't time. We must help the others. Are you able to walk?"

"I don't know. Are you?" Vivian rubbed her legs and stretched her feet.

"Walk, yes, but I am blind. Take me to a central point in the valley. I sense the enemy. I can fight from there. We need shelter."

The shock of Erceldoune being blind numbed her. Holding the tall stone, Vivian tested her legs. They were weak but workable. "Ready," Vivian said.

"Lead me." Erceldoune put his hand on Vivian's shoulder.

In tandem, along a wobbly line, they reached three central stones where the sacrificial stocks evaporated. Weakened by her imprisonment and exertion, Vivian fluttered to the ground like a wounded bird.

"When you are recovered, collect Afton, Jake, and Clacks and bring them here."

Afton? Vivian's thought didn't take root. "Shouldn't I stay with you?"

"I'm blind, not helpless."

****

Erceldoune set to work. The three stones formed an odd-shaped isosceles triangle with a central alcove eight feet around. Worn and chipped, they resembled the stones at the Gleane, but older and wiser. In the center, Erceldoune took the Orb from his robe and raised it in his right hand. "Hidden here, 'neath golden glow. No one breach it, nothing reach it. Retain all power, 'til 'er we go."

A golden light emanated from the Orb. Out and down, it spread until it contained the three stones in a protective dome. Erceldoune released the Orb. Floating in place, the golden curtain pulsed like a strobe.

"That should do it," Erceldoune said. The golden dome was tall enough that a person could stand in it. He leaned against one of the stones and knelt before he sat on the ground. A cooling mist wrapped around his head. But could it restore sight?

CHAPTER 72

Simion shivered, not from cold, but fear. His mercenaries were losing. Grezil was surely dead. Isobel was missing or maybe dead too. His addled brain, unused to leadership, even a leadership of folly, forgot Plan B. *Weir will—*

A kernel popped in his overtaxed mind. Simion transformed and hotfooted as fast as four legs could carry him for the narrows. Crossing the sandy patch, he saw them: fifty mercenaries marched for the valley. *How did they know? Who told them to come?* Leading the army into the valley was Weir. He shook. Simion slinked back into the valley and snuggled into the bosom of two tall stones to hide.

****

Cold mountain water washed around Grezil as her head bobbed in the shifting current. In a slow progression, her body roused, her arms flopped, and she rolled face first into the cold shallow water. A mouthful of water roused her in a fit of coughing and spitting. Body aches entered consciousness. Nothing was broken. *That idiot MacCorkle. He couldn't fire a killing dart if he had to.*

Rage overtook her senses and roared for revenge. Checking her body parts, everything worked. Bruises were beginning to spread across her injured flesh. "I'll kill that …," Grezil muttered.

Sopping wet, she lifted herself from the streambed, crawled to the bank, and struggled to the rock from which she had surveyed the valley earlier. Staring across the top of the valley, she located the stone where the Princess was imprisoned. The front gaped open like a tooth with a massive cavity. *So, she's out. That will make it easier.*

Across the valley, chaos ruled. Darts flew like fireworks shot from roman candles. No real target. Clusters of fighters acted undirected. Simion was gone. *That dog will be hairless when I finish with him.*

She sent a message to Weir: "Both Princess and Prince are here. No focused attack. Our troops are in disarray. Without leadership, all is lost."

An answer came at once. "I am moving into the valley with mercenaries as we speak. Take charge."

Grezil limped down the stream, collecting soldiers.

CHAPTER 73

Jake and Clacks drove six more fae from the rocky sidelines along the right side. Dead and dying mercenaries littered the field. Silvery outlines scrambled away, all the fight gone from them, toward the narrow entrance to get out the valley.

"Where is the Princess?" Clacks said.

"Trapped in a stone," Jake said.

"Do you know where?"

"Yes, Erceldoune is with her."

"I have this in hand. Go to her. The quicker she is free, the quicker we leave." Clacks grinned.

Jake hesitated. *He means it.*

Clacks nodded. "Go," he said.

Jake sprinted toward Vivian's stone prison.

****

Like a ninja, Clacks moved down the valley, bypassing here, attacking there. He was near the narrows when several fae surrendered. *I don't need prisoners.*

When he didn't kill them, they vanished. Across the valley, as if they'd been summoned, mercenaries ran toward the streambed. They were massing.

Resistance was minimal on his side. Clacks turned and trotted up the valley to join Jake. A dart struck from behind him. And another, and another. A barrage hit around him. He dove behind a cluster of short stones. Darts were on him whenever he twitched. He picked his next sanctuary. Peeking over his refuge, fear gripped him. Streaming into the valley, walking in the water, jumping stone to stone, were fresh mercenaries. Twenty were in, but more, many more, followed. Clacks had to warn the others.

A handful of pebbles spun on his hand. He sent a scattered and unaimed barrage at the narrows. The mercenaries dove for cover. Bolting from his hiding place, for a moment, he ran free. Then, rocks and dirt stung his legs and hands as he zigzagged up the valley. To his right, mercenaries formed around Grezil at the streambed. The barrage on him heightened. Large explosions shattered around him. No matter his direction, he drew fire.

212

Clacks scampered into a small crater guarded by a stone outcrop. The attack intensified. Each twitch brought more darts.

Lying still, gasping short breaths, he risked a quick look. *They're coming.*

****

Afton fought his way down the middle of the valley. Resistance was light. Fighters withdrew when he approached. Tripping over a half-hidden stone, he caught himself on his hands and glanced toward the streambed; several figures massed. *Mother!* She's alive.

Scrambling to his feet, he cut left, away from her and toward the three stones where he had left Jake. A faint golden glow rose over the stones. *Erceldoune. Safety.*

A dart exploded. Chunks of rock smacked his right arm and hip. The force twisted and skidded him across the ground. Struggling to rise, his right leg didn't work. He reached for stones to make darts, but his right arm hung useless.

The shrill voice of his mother mocked him: "No one meddles this time. You die, Prince." *Right here, right now, my mother is going to kill me.*

Nothing for it. Nowhere to hide. No way to fight. Run or die. Afton braced against a protruding stone and forced himself up on his left side. His right hip was mangled, but he could keep balance. *Move.* Trudging in a shuffling pace, disabled arm hanging limp, sensing the evil coming, Afton pushed himself toward the glowing dome that seemed forever away.

CHAPTER 74

Sitting in the shelter of the Orb's dome, Vivian's strength grew.

"I am ready," she said. Still shaky, she couldn't sit quietly while others were in danger.

"Head down the valley," Erceldoune said. She helped him to his feet, and he placed his hand on her shoulder.

Walking at a steady pace, her guard up, they proceeded. No one was about. The dead or dying were littered in odd, grotesque shapes. One leaned against a stone as if he were sleeping.

Forty yards below the dome sanctuary, Lothian shuffled toward them. His head was down, his right arm dangled helpless at his side, left arm reaching across to support it. He ambled along like a condemned man headed to the gallows, feet moving in short half steps.

"Lothian!" Vivian cried and increased her pace. She wanted to run to him, but Erceldoune gripped her shoulder. "It's Lothian. Let me go!"

"Careful. He is tracked. Locate his trackers."

****

Weir ducked under the outcrop at the narrows and entered the valley as if he were a conquering Caesar. "Make a line, sweep the valley, and kill everyone you find in it."

A ragged line of thirty mercenaries formed.

"What about the one we have pinned over there?" a rough-looking man asked as he came running up to the reinforcements.

"No hurry. Keep his head down. We'll scoop him up on the way. No one escapes."

The line lurched forward, searching every crevice.

****

Grezil placed a killing stone on her palm and aimed it at a dejected Lothian tottering along over a gray-green bracken sea, like a dinghy that floats in and out on the tide. She wouldn't miss him from there. She didn't want to kill him; she wanted to pulverize him, separate his limbs, and leave raw meat lying in the dust.

"There's movement," a man called to Grezil.

"It must be the Princess. One cannot rest if the other is in danger." Grezil's body thrilled at its core. "Hold fire!"

She flew a message to Weir: "Brother. Come at once. I have both."

****

"Prepare for your crown." Grezil's message thrilled Weir. He didn't want to miss the climax. From the middle of his line, he ran toward the streambed. Unused to physical exertion, his breath gave out. Wheezing, he shortcut the end of his line and staggered on ahead of it.

Like miniatures, Grezil and her band appeared in the distance, intent on something in the field outside his view. Hands on his knees, he took a quick breather, and hurried on.

The entire scene opened to him. He slowed, caught in its perfection. The Prince slowly traversed the distance to the Princess, the Princess waited with a tall man in a white robe, and Grezil watched them come together. Hellfire would rain and rip their bodies apart. It was too delicious.

A sense of the tall man reached Weir: Erceldoune, the trespasser. *He won't impede me anymore. Let Grezil have her victory. I'm almost a king.*

Near a large outcrop with an unimpeded view, Weir kneeled, waiting like a king at his coronation, accepting a crown.

****

Vivian's stone was deserted. Jake skirted the top of the field, slipping from stone outcrop to tree to hillock. No resistance. No fighters on this end of the valley. Where the stream rushed over dark stones, he skidded into a crevice. *Grezil's gone.*

Jake sensed it. Deep in the valley a horrible evil built. It made his skin crawl like he'd walked into a massive spider web. Closer, toward the interior of the valley, a malicious power was waiting, holding. Cautiously raising his head over the rock in front of him, he chanced a look.

Near the middle of the valley, a golden dome pulsed. *The Orb. It must be.* Staying low, Jake moved to it.

Enclosing the three stones where he'd awoken thirty minutes ago, the Orb pulsed. Jake pushed the dome's skin. It yielded as if it was made of thick plastic, but he could not penetrate it. *Empty. Where are they?*

The entire valley was quiet. Too quiet. Slipping around the dome, he stood for a better look. As if someone threw a bucket of ice water on him, his breath caught in his chest.

Down the center of the valley, moving in stumbling steps, Vivian led Erceldoune. To the left below them, a group of mercenaries watched. *Grezil.* Up the valley came a limping Lothian. *A trap!*

The group by the stream was mesmerized by the coming destruction and never looked his way. *Run to them? No. Flank them. Hurry.*

Jake slipped left. In a rapid military low-crawl, he gained a post thirty feet away from Grezil. Darts aimed; they didn't fire. Why? *They are waiting for a* clear shot at Vivian and Erceldoune.

Jake raised his wand. In a dim recess of his mind, he sensed some threat from the edge of the forest. Swiveling to look, a blue clad figure stood in the open and watched from the forest.

****

Vivian struggled to pull away from Erceldoune's grip and run to Lothian, but he strengthened his hold on her shoulders. While his eyes were weakened, his grip was not. An agony beyond the feeling of being lowered into the stone prison gripped her. "He's hurt and alone. I must—"

"Tell me where they are," Erceldoune said. "I sense evil to the left. How many? Where?"

Erceldoune's quiet voice pulled her back from her fears, calmed her, and returned her focus.

"Direct my aim," Erceldoune said.

"On the left a small band, standing together," Vivian said. "We are moving into their line of sight in six more paces."

"Exact location on the clock."

"Ten o'clock from where we face."

"And Afton? Is he outside the target?"

"Afton?"

"Don't let your eyes fool you."

"Lothian is at one o'clock."

"Go to him when I tell you."

Vivian trembled. Anger replaced fear. She would save her brother.

Erceldoune pulled her to a stop and shifted around in front of her. His robe glowed with the sheen of the sun. There was not a spot of blood on it. In a booming voice, Erceldoune spoke: "A look, a look, for all to see. One who has it, returned it be. One who shows it, him be free."

The enchantment echoed down the valley. A whisp of mist appeared, grew, and traversed the gap to Lothian. In seconds it reached him. It swirled at his feet to the left, grew thicker, covered his legs and torso, and swirled around his head until his body disappeared in it. The mist whirled the opposite direction, churned back down his body, and dissipated.

Wearing Lothian's stained and torn clothes, hobbling up the valley, was Afton Thish.

CHAPTER 75

Clacks's small hiding place was unsustainable. They were coming, and they knew where he was. *Got to move.*

At a low crawl, he struggled to traverse over stone and bracken that cut into his forearms and knees. His clothes ripped as he looked for a place where he could defend himself. Keeping the three stones in sight, he crossed a slight rise.

"He's moving!" a shout came.

Darts hit around him. Explosions threw rocks that tore at his body and face. As if zeroing in on a target range, darts tracked him, closer and closer. Trapped in the only tenuous hiding place available, facing an ever-closer barrage, Clacks saw no other option. He jumped up and ran. Within five feet, a dart from the left struck his back and blew his legs out from under him. He collapsed in a heap.

****

Simion's dart hit its mark—blowing apart the faerie's body, shattering his legs, and crumbling him to the ground. A fatal blow. Satisfied, Simion pulled back into his stone shelter.

****

Jake thrust his wand at Grezil's head. A gawking faerie, entranced by Afton's transformation, stepped into the line of fire. The strike killed him and knocked Grezil down underneath his body. Grezil was up in an instant.

"Traitor!" Grezil screamed after her son and scrambled to prepare darts to kill him. Before she could fire, Jake's wand spoke. He moved, changed positions, and drew their fire, giving the others an opening. Grezil's men rained darts on his location, but Jake kept up an ongoing firefight.

"Go!" Erceldoune's voice was only for Vivian, but Jake sensed the quiet order. His body responded with her's. Whipping around, her fear drove him, his adrenaline surged with hers, and his muscles contracted as she sprinted for Afton. Darts flew from her hand. His wand matched her attack. The crossfire from Vivian and Jake drove the attackers for cover. Reaching Afton, she swung him to her side. Using her body as his crutch, she half-carried him toward the dome.

217

****

Erceldoune's hands moved at light-speed. Into the air they thrust, waved air into swales, and captured the vibrating wind. Casting his hands toward the ground, swinging them up, he dashed the wind back and forth in a single speedy motion. As if gathering it to his chest, he harvested the wind. The entire movement was accomplished in an instant.

Making a deep turn to his right, he twisted to the front and cast the wind to ten o'clock. Power surged. Wind raced forward like a speeding freight train. At the sound, every being in the valley froze. Turning as directed, the wind stripped every shred of vegetation, stick, and loose stone from its path as it cut a swath thirty feet across and carried its bounty of weaponized nature right at Grezil and her band of mercenaries. Straw, sticks, plants, pebbles, and rocks pummeled them.

The wind picked up speed and lifted bodies into the air, flipped them end over end, bouncing them along the ground. Helpless, uncontrolled forms became airborne across the stream and dashed against unyielding stone. Speckled gradients of red interspersed with pulp spread across fifty feet. For minutes, blood ran down crevices and into the stream, ceasing when the pulped bodies were drained. Flattened carcasses reposed, unrecognizable, among the stone.

****

Ahead of Jake, Vivian negotiated the distance to the dome, Afton under one arm and Erceldoune's robe clutched in her hand. The dome opened for Erceldoune as if it recognized him. Jake converged with them at the entrance and staggered in. The dome closed.

"What was that?" Jake asked.

"A killing wind," Erceldoune answered. His voice was distant and flat as if the effort had robbed him of some life force.

Vivian helped Afton to sit against a large stone. Jake reached for her. "Vivian, I—"

Vivian threw her arms around him.

"I'm so sorry," he said into her neck. He drew her closer, holding her gently, but with all his might as if he wanted to meld with her into one person.

"Quiet. Later." She nuzzled against him.

Fresh white mists formed around Afton's injured arm, chest, and hip. Then it encircled Erceldoune's eyes and Jake's head.

"Where's Clackmannan?" Erceldoune asked.

"The last time I saw him he was on the left side near the narrows," Jake said.

"He may be injured," Erceldoune said. "Find him, Jake."

Jake closed his eyes and pictured Clack's smile. *I've got you.*

CHAPTER 76

As the killing wind abated, all movement in the valley ceased. Key witness to the carnage, Weir stood immobile. He was far enough away to be physically untouched but near enough to be emotionally terrified by what he'd seen.

Walking to the cleared swath of dirt dug by the wind, he faced the stream bank strewn with carnage. Trying to pick out his sister was like working a jigsaw puzzle with all red pieces.

Alone, Weir paced up and back. Shock and agitation heaved in his chest. Breathing was difficult. His skin crawled, itching to change what he saw. The horror called him. As if he had no control over his eyes, they darted to the scene and away like a man staring at a terrible wreck. Emotions were a kettle on boil. Rage simmered, bubbled, and exploded.

A half mile behind him, his line clung to the ground or scrambled for cover. Some shirked back toward the narrows or sprinted away.

All was quiet.

Traitors will pay.

One was still pinned down. *Where? On the left side. Is he still there?*

Weir ran straight across the valley.

****

"I'm coming with you," Vivian said to Jake.

"No." The thought of her in danger terrified him. "I just got you back."

"I'm coming." Her voice was forceful.

Erceldoune wheeled on her. "Don't risk everything we worked for."

"I am the only other person here who can fight. If Jake has to carry Clacks, he's helpless."

"No time to argue. Do as you wish." Erceldoune was short with her. Vivian passed the amulet to Jake.

"For luck," she said.

Jake slipped it into his pocket.

Erceldoune reached his hands toward them. His hair stood wild about his ears; his beard tucked into his robe. Jake and Vivian each grasped one of his hands, and they passed together through the back of the dome.

"Dark clouds ring. Lighting sing. Thick fog bring." Erceldoune raised his hands like an orchestra conductor. Black storm clouds gathered. Wind rose. Air crackled. A fog stole out of the forest. Every crack and crevice seeped thin wisps that spun together into a tapestry of thickening mist. Murkiness grew. Visibility diminished.

Erceldoune clapped. Lighting struck the southern crag and rebounded off the rocks sending chunks flying.

"Muster Clackmannan."

Jake and Vivian ran toward cover and down the valley.

****

Erceldoune whipped around toward the upper end of the valley. "Quick, Afton, be my eyes."

Afton struggled to rise. He groaned from the pain.

Erceldoune reached a hand to him. "What do you see at the end of the valley?"

Through the fog, a short figure in a blue uniform marched into the valley.

"Ly Erg." Afton reached for a stone to steady his balance. He stepped away from Erceldoune.

"What are you doing?" Erceldoune asked.

"I must get to Jake. I have to help."

"Your wounds prevent it."

"Ly Erg came out of the forest and followed Jake and Vivian."

"I will contact Vivian. She can relay it to Jake through the amulet. As long as no one challenges him, he will leave them be."

"No," Afton said. "The amulet is here. I see it at your feet." Erceldoune bent down, felt, and rose with it in his hand.

CHAPTER 77

Fog filled the valley. Jake and Vivian paused at a rock outcrop.

"I can see nothing," Vivian said.

"Stay here," Jake said. "I know where Clacks is. I'll get him and meet you here."

Fog grew thicker. Jake sensed Clacks. Tripping over torn and chewed divots of gray-green bracken scattered in haphazard patterns, Jake came to a small indention. In it, Clacks lay still.

****

Pockets of white fog leeched from the rocks on the sides of the valley. Vivian kept Jake's outline in sight until the soupy whiteness disoriented her.

A message came: "Amulet dropped. Ly Erg following."

Horror gripped her. Ly Erg. Jake wouldn't know who or what Ly Erg was.

Blindly rushing after Jake, she hovered like a guardian angel, darts at the ready, searching for danger, searching for Jake. A noise came from behind her. She turned to track it, a killing dart spinning on her hand.

****

Jake felt Clacks' neck. His own heart beat like a cannon. No pulse.

Clacks' body was shredded. One leg mangled. Cuts and gashes covered him. Grabbing one arm, Jake pulled him into a fireman's carry and rose. He concentrated on the memory of Vivian's laugh and hustled toward her.

Within five steps, a person materialized on his right. Not Vivian. He hustled left, hoping for Vivian's help. Another person loomed in front of him. A tuft of bracken grabbed his boot and he fell face first to the ground. Clacks landed on top of him, pinning him down. Fear rattled in Jake's stomach as if he was a kid afraid to look under his bed.

Another body landed on top of him.

"Lay still," Vivian said. "No matter what happens do not look at him." Jake felt another person kneel next him, but he did not look up. The stench of blood and rotting flesh assaulted his senses. He gagged. A wet hand touched the top of his head.

"Your mother did me a great kindness. She was my friend. I return her kindness today," he spoke and was gone.

****

Weir sensed MacCorkle, but the fog was stifling and closed before he reached his target.

I'm going to end this.

He waved his hands. "Fog is near. Fog be clear. Obliterate. Dissipate." He spit the enchantment out like it was a curse.

The fog did not lift completely, but it swirled away leaving a ten-foot circle of clear space around him. He tried again. No change. Fifteen hard men and women looked to him for orders.

"Sweep around and close the circle," he ordered. Weir took the lead and picked up the pace. His troops followed at a trot.

The circle moved with him until the front edge illuminated the place where he expected MacCorkle to be. Standing, where he sensed MacCorkle, was a young man in a tattered blue uniform with his right hand raised. Something was wrong.

"Who are you?" Weir demanded.

The uniformed boy turned and raised his hand again. Blood dripped from it and ran down his uniform sleeve. Weir knew.

"Kill him," he ordered and backed into the fog.

****

Vivian helped Jake raise Clacks over his shoulder. Staggering up the valley, Jake focused on Afton.

A scream shrieked through the fog. And another. Another. Jake shuddered. Time and again new sounds came. Grunts, shouts, orders rose and fell like someone playing a very serious game of capture the flag in the fog.

The dome glowed ahead.

CHAPTER 78

The dome opened as they arrived. Erceldoune touched Clacks's chest. "Thank God, he lives," Erceldoune said. "Prepare to leave. I will take Afton and Clacks with me directly to the castle. Jake, can you manage?"

"I'm good." Vivian stepped beside him, held his arm, leaned into him, and he was better.

"I will take the severely injured with the Orb. Follow immediately," Erceldoune raised his hand. The Orb leaped into it. The dome vanished.

Afton held out the amulet to Vivian. She clasped it to her heart and returned a smile. Afton slid next to Clacks and put his arm around him. A white cocoon engulfed them. Erceldoune placed his hand with the Orb into the healing cocoon. A bandage formed over his eyes. The trio disappeared.

Vivian spoke the words: "A wind to travel. A wing to ride. O'er the distance make great stride. Bring us home where we abide."

A wind swirled from nowhere. It caught the fog and built a white funnel that folded around them and gathered speed. Like being inside the eye of a tornado, the wind did not touch them.

As they left the earth, Jake held Vivian in a firm, gentle embrace. Adrenaline slackened. Jake grinned. Vivian smiled—the same smile that let him find her in the darkness of the stone.

Moving west, yard by yard, mile by mile, speed increased. The valley blinked away. Scotland passed under them. Time eked along before earthy smells of dirt, trees, and vegetation shifted to salty ocean smells. Across to the ocean, they sped. Green water splashed about the tail of their conveyance as it pushed them across it. Ocean receded. They were over land, over water, and land again. Speed decreased. The whirlwind slowed. Not flashing past at an unrecognizable speed, landmarks became visible. Towns blipped by. Cities passed under them. Jake saw none of it, only Vivian. Mountains showed in the distance. Jake's gaze was on Vivian, and he didn't see anything but her.

****

A runner dashed up the hall to Prince Lothian's chambers. "Your Highness, they arrive!"

"Where?" Lothian asked. "Are they well?"

"All are wounded. Erceldoune transported them to the hospital."

Prince Lothian ran. During their absence, his nervous energy disallowed idleness. Every able woman and man drilled for war, transforming the Gleane into an efficient military unit. Those unable to fight gathered herb, made bandages, and prayed for Vivian's and her rescuers' safe return. The Ministry Hall became a hospital awaiting casualties. He raced down the foyer steps to the hospital.

"Where is my sister?" Lothian asked as he entered.

"Yes, we are quite well. Thank you for inquiring after us. A few nicks and scratches." Erceldoune smiled up in his direction from a bed against the far wall. A thick patch of white mist swathed his eyes.

"Forgive me. I—"

"Your sister, for some unfathomable reason, chose to travel with your Bard. They should arrive within the hour."

"How are you?"

"Well as can be expected. Neither Afton nor Clacks are awake. Afton will heal, but I grieve for Clackmannan. He has a chance—a slim one. Jake is wounded. But Princess Vivian is unharmed from her ordeal, physically."

"Where will they arrive?"

"At the gate would be my thought. Perhaps, a reception?"

Lothian's agitation refused to let him be still, but he was not a rude man. "Tell me about your wounds."

Erceldoune ignored him. "Your Highness, I believe you are remiss not to greet your sister at the gate. You may want to mention the courtship rituals of our Clan."

Courtship?

Lothian saw his opening. He bowed to Erceldoune who did not witness it and rushed out.

Lothian planned a small greeting party, a few Ministers, the nanny, a few friends. He sent a runner to order a cake from the baker. The baker told the butcher, who told the saddle maker, who told the proprietor of the Swan, and on it went. Of course, the nanny had to share with a few close cousins.

When Lothian sent word to prepare a feast, the heavy-set, round-faced woman hung her apron on its hook, something she never did during the day, grabbed her hat, and was out the door without another word, except to all the people she met on her way through the town.

All her workers hesitated for an innocent moment before following her down the tunnel behind the castle. The town emptied. People streamed into the forest toward the gate. Shops closed. Houses were left open.

As the message passed throughout the Gleane, people came to help, to participate, to be present, but not to miss offering support to the Prince and Vivian. With a will, the throng moved through the woods toward the gate.

A tear formed in the Prince's eye. The outpouring of love was greater than he imagined. A joy rose in him he hadn't felt since before their parents disappeared. The respect and reverence the Daione Sìthe offered was unparalleled. He laughed. Tension broke for him and the people around him. In the forest and around the gate, people climbed trees to get a better view. He raised his hands to quiet the throng.

"When she comes, everybody hide."

A roar went up from the crowd at the humor. All could be invisible, none wished to be. The atmosphere turned into a celebration.

****

Trees whipped left and right, caught in the swirl. Along the road to the gate, the whirlwind dissipated. Vivian stepped out of the cloud as if she were stepping out of a limo onto the red carpet. Jake ran forward, lost his balance, skipped once, twice, and fell face first, rolling into a ditch.

Vivian laughed, not a titter, but the same laugh that had stolen Jake's heart years ago. The sound of it was a treasure. For the first time, he let himself love her completely. He dusted his rear end and smiled sheepishly. She opened her arms, and he walked into them.

With Jake nestled against her, she whispered, "I've waited so long for you."

Jake walked up the rutted road with her hand clasped in his. He studied her profile without letting her know he watched. Her auburn hair in its perpetual braid was tucked around her neck. She walked as if she flowed a few inches above the ground while he seemed to trip on every pebble. *She is so beautiful.*

She caught him looking and smiled—a different smile, a kinder, gentler smile, not humorous, but rising from her heart. A gift to him, a statement that he would be with her, always. She took his hand and held it close to her heart.

Arms entwined, hand in hand, they strolled to the gate. Behind it stood Prince Lothian and a few thousand of his closest friends.

CHAPTER 79

Tears stung Jake's eyes. The chair pulled inches from Clacks's bed was as close as he could get to trying to help his friend, trying to give him strength, praying …

"I'm here," Jake said. Visiting long hours, he was a fixture as the Orb worked its magic, healing others, even himself, but months later, Clacks lay swathed in a white cocoon, physically broken and unconscious. Looking at his friend's inert form, Jake teared again. What was the use? He wasn't going to make it. Reaching for Clacks's hand, he grasped it.

"Any change?" Erceldoune asked from the door.

"No." Jake's answer was all he could muster. Nothing bad to say; nothing good.

As he had every day since they returned, Erceldoune checked on Clacks. His healed eye seeking, searching, but not twinkling. The other eye was a gouged socket with a thin red roadmap scar running from his left temple across the bridge of his nose, ending at the middle of his cheek. He adopted a white patch, which added a bit of dignity to the scar.

While Erceldoune didn't seem to care about the physical deformity to his face, the emotional change was dramatic. The inevitable twinkle was hidden. On occasion it bounced out, but mostly his emotion remained dormant, unused, replaced by a critical edge that kept everyone at arm's length. Not quite biting sarcasm but a close cousin.

Jake asked Lothian about him. "Why has he changed?"

Lothian sat back and grimaced. "Killing wind is a deadly enchantment used with devasting effect."

"I saw it." The memory made his stomach lurch.

Lothian continued. "Performing dark magic produces profound emotional consequences, cutting into a person and crippling a piece of the soul. As time passes, opportunities arise to mend and weave healing into one's life, but Erceldoune has not taken that route. Not quite bitter, he remains distant and obtuse."

"But he visits Clacks every day."

"The visits may be an attempt to heal, but based on his behavior, I believe the time he spends with Clacks steels him against healing, keeping his wound open."

Jake stood, released Clacks's hand, and laid it on the bed.

For the past few months, training was different. Erceldoune was distant. Clacks was incapacitated. Lothian had asked Afton to become his mentor. Jake headed for the Swan.

The door swung back. Jake nodded to people as he passed to Afton's table.

"Hello, there," Afton said. "Any improvement?"

"No." There was nothing more to say. Despite the crippling blow Afton took on the battlefield, his recovery was the quickest and most complete. When he healed to a point where he could work, he stepped into a leadership role within the Clan. Quiet and unassuming, unfettered by past actions, neither his family's or his own, the People knew his role in the rescue and revered him for it.

Afton's scars reached beyond the battlefield. At the instant Erceldoune withdrew the enchantment that paired him to Lothian, a lightning bolt traveled from the tip of his head, down behind his ear, across his back, and exited his heel. When the scorched skin healed, a two-inch permanent scar remained. On his head, a thin swatch of white hair showed. While clothes covered most of his burn, the exposed remainder offered a glimpse of a hero: a childish man transformed into a leader, forged in the fires of magic, and withholding nothing from his people. The swath of white hair was an outward reminder of the pain Afton endured for his Clan, Prince, and Princess.

Afton's friendship was a revelation to Jake. Never had Jake allowed himself to love others. He loved Afton as a brother. He loved the Daione Sìthe. Feelings he had secretly wished for but denied himself now flourished.

After her imprisonment, Vivian changed. At first, relief at being home dominated. Later, a subtle shift came. Independence waned. She clung to Jake, not as an adult able to cling and let go, but as a child, driven by an obsessive need to stay close and unspoken fear of loss.

Dim places were tolerated briefly. Unlit halls were bypassed. A strong nightlight became a requirement where she slept. For months, she woke with a start in the night and reached for Jake, clinging to him until her fright subsided.

In an illogical attempt to protect herself, she made a compulsive review of protective enchantment and defensive magic. She practiced fighting enchantments until they were as natural as breathing. A ritual emerged to ensure the security of her rooms.

In fits and starts, over the past months, she began to talk to Jake about her imprisonment and how it affected her. Talks lasted for hours until she was ready to quit. Jake listened without interrupting, offering no comment, only support.

A new person, Mirith, came to Clacks's bedside every day. On one visit, she and Vivian crossed paths and began to talk. From that day forward, Vivian showed a renewed interest in life, a budding happiness, and an ability to connect that had appeared to have been broken by her experience.

****

For the past year, Jake was part of the Clan, his Clan. A family he'd wanted all his life.

New friends and his new life as Bard-in-training was a profound joy. New experiences and fresh learning events came daily. The Journal instructed him, and Afton honed instruction into practical experience.

The love between he and Vivian blossomed when he released fear and opened his heart to her.

Six months ago, he'd told her his fear that he would let her down. "I love you, but I will let you down, the way I let my men down."

"What?"

"I failed my men. I deserted them after I was wounded."

Vivian's mouth opened to speak. She sat back before she said anything. "What makes you think that?"

"I have dreams where I wake, see your face, but I can't remember what happened. I know you weren't there. I tried to find it in the Journal, but nothing shows up after I go to Afghanistan."

Vivian stared at him with a look of astonishment. "That's not what happened."

"How would you know what happened?"

"Because I **was** there." The words didn't register. *What did she say?* He recalled them word by word.

"You were there?"

"Your father asked us to terminate the following. But I didn't. I watched you every day. I was so proud of you. On the day you were wounded, I was watching through the Orb. When you were hurt, I was so scared. I sent the Orb to protect you until I could get there. When I arrived, you were recovered. I wanted to bring you home, but you refused. You fought me. You got up and went to your men, gathered them, and led them to escape. Why you don't remember is beyond me, but you did nothing wrong."

"How can I believe you?"

"Look me up in the Journal. I stayed, hoping you would change your mind. I saw it all."

****

December 24 at 11:58 a.m., Jake stood alone in the small cave where a year ago he spent his first frightening night in the Gleane. The opening was there. The tunnel waited. His yellow robe was a gift. He wore a hand-crafted leather hat cocked at a rakish angle. His leather belt sported a silver buckle a rodeo cowboy would envy. The Orb hovered on his left hand, a mist floating off it. Like he had a chill, his body shook with excitement.

At precisely noon, he entered the tunnel. The Orb lit a path as he took the thousand steps to the lower edge of a quiet town. Shops were shuttered. People lined the streets in reverent attention. As Jake passed by, they bowed, fell in behind, and followed him to the castle. A multitude opened a corridor for him alone to climb the steps.

Standing on the patio before the huge doors were Erceldoune, Prince Lothian, and Princess Vivian. Erceldoune's long beard was tucked into his silver belt. His robe glowed a pristine white, matching the white patch covering his left eye. Today, his right eye twinkled with double the mischief.

Prince Lothian wore purple tights, a white silk shirt, and an embroidered vest of gold and silver threads. An elegant silver crown was visible on his brown, curly hair. A thick gold chain hung to the middle of his chest. Linked squares of gold displayed ancient runes written in the High Language.

Vivian radiated in a pale-blue dress of lightest velvet that flowed off her shoulders like shimmering water. Rubies, emeralds, and pearls studded her belt and matching necklace. Auburn hair hung free, brushed straight, no braid, loops of silver wire woven in and around it, making her, if possible, more breathtakingly beautiful.

To the left were members of the Ministerial Council adorned in black robes of office. To the right were members of the Wyzard's Council. Each robe depicting the wearer's rank by its color.

Lothian spoke: "This is a day of great joy … and sadness. We celebrate the courage, fidelity, friendship, and resilience of the Daione Sìthe, while we are ever mindful of our fallen and wounded friends."

The crowd responded with subdued applause.

Lothian continued, smiling at Jake. "I present Jake MacCorkle, Son of John, and heir to the Bardship of the Daione Sìthe, to the Ministerial Council, The Wyzard Council, and the Daione Sìthe."

Jake bowed and stepped to Vivian's right. She gave his hand a quick squeeze behind the folds of her dress.

The Prince turned and, offering his arm to Vivian, led her through the opening doors. Jake matched with Erceldoune. Two by two, the Ministers and Wyzards matched and entered. The People followed. Turning right, Lothian lead the assemblage into the ballroom. The Orb flowed mist across the floor. Lothian and Vivian appeared to be walking on clouds.

The ballroom ceiling was robin-egg blue and cloudless. Walls shimmered with the effect of the northern lights, and delicious smells permeated the air.

Lothian, Vivian, Erceldoune, and Jake ascended the dais and sat behind a long central table. Ministers peeled to the left. Wyzards peeled right. All remained standing until the Prince and Princess sat.

When everyone was seated, Lothian raised his hands. All noise ceased.

"I have several further introductions and announcements to the Clan. I present to the Wyzard Council its newest member, Clackmannan, Wyzard Extraordinaire." The joyful tone within the hall grew somber. Clacks injuries were grave. He received treatment outside the Gleane. No one knew when or if he would return.

Erceldoune stood.

"I certify Clackmannan has completed all tasks and represents the finest degree of expertise in the Wyzardry Arts. I certify he aspires to and has achieved the basic rank of Wyzard Extraordinaire."

Everyone in the hall stood and bowed to an empty chair set in the front right corner, the traditional spot for newly certified Wyzards. The crowd stood in hushed reverie.

After a moment, Lothian spoke, "I present to the Ministerial Council its newest member, Afton Thish."

Afton rose, walked to the dais, and stood before his Prince. Once a carefree Adonis, Afton bore life's burdens stoically, and his People loved him for it. The crowd waited in silent anticipation.

Afton bowed. Lothian placed a gold chain of office around his neck. Afton did smile. His confidence returned, not as it had been before, brash and self-centered, but as a calm mature servant to others. Afton moved to the Minister's side and took one of two open chairs.

The Clan broke into strong, exuberant applause.

As it died down, Lothian said, "I present Mirith, appointed Chief of the Ministers."

A short, quick, raven-haired woman came forward. Her green eyes flashed. She bowed to her Prince and Princess, acknowledged Erceldoune and Jake, received her chain and turned toward the empty chair on the Wyzard's side. Bending formally at the waist, she tried to retain composure, but Jake saw her mouth twitch and a thin tear form in her eye as she bowed to Clacks empty chair.

"There is one other appointment," Lothian said, but he sat down.

Vivian gave Jake a smile and grasped his hand under the table.

Afton rose, climbed the dais, and stood before Jake. "Please rise."

What's going on?

"As Mentor, I certify Jake MacCorkle has achieved an understanding of basic enchantment," Afton said. "As Bard, he asks to train to become Wyzard. Who accepts this initiate to become a Wyzard?"

The entire Wyzard Council boomed: "We do."

"Who accepts him as Apprentice?" The Wyzard's Council asked in one voice.

"I do," Afton said. The warmth and sincerity of the two words brought a tear to Jake's eye.

From his robe, Afton pulled a bronze wand, took it in both hands, bowed, and offered it to Jake. Everyone in the room smiled. Jake returned the bow and accepted the wand with both hands. As it entered his hands, he knew. The wand was bronze, but it was the same one he used in the valley. The comfort returned. Fitting into his hand, the wand knew him.

Afton bowed and returned to his seat.

Prince Lothian rose. "Jake MacCorkle, stand before me."

Jake did so.

"Do you agree to faithfully execute the role of Bard to the Daione Sìthe?"

"I do."

"Present your wand." Lothian held out his hand. With the wand in his left hand, Lothian waved his right hand across and handed it back. Along the curve, where it fit his hand, were a laurel wreath, paper, and quill symbols.

A cheer exploded. "Hail, Bard Jake!"

A flush of pride exploded like fireworks in Jake's chest. Ballroom lights dimmed and music broke the spell. Vivian rose and came to him. People began to dance. Servers brought mead. Lights flashed in concert with the music.

Jake leaned his head close to her neck as if he were going to speak a secret into her ear. His lips touched her neck lightly, not in a timid way, but confident and with glowing affection. Vivian turned swiftly and sought his eyes. When their eyes met, they swayed together as if melded, standing side by side, no longer two people, but one.